PENGUIN BOOKS

HEAT WAVE

1996.

Penelope Lively grew up in Egypt but settled in England after the war and took a degree in history at St Anne's College, Oxford. She is a Fellow of the Royal Society of Literature and a member of PEN and the Society of Authors. She is married to Professor Jack Lively, has a daughter, a son and four grandchildren, and lives in Oxfordshire and London.

Penelope Lively is the author of many prize-winning novels and short-story collections for both adults and children. She has twice been shortlisted for the Booker Prize; once in 1977 for her first novel, *The Road to Lichfield*, and again in 1984 for *According to Mark*. She later won the Booker Prize for her highly acclaimed novel *Moon Tiger* in 1987. Her other novels include *Passing On*, shortlisted for the 1989 *Sunday Express* Book of the Year Award, *City of the Mind*, *Cleopatra's Sister* and *Heat Wave*. Many of her books, including *Going Back*, which first appeared as a children's book, and *Oleander, Jacaranda*, an autobiographical memoir of her childhood days in Egypt, are published by Penguin.

Penelope Lively has also written radio and television scripts and has acted as presenter for a BBC Radio 4 programme on children's literature. She is a popular writer for children and has won both the Carnegie Medal and the Whitbread Award.

TITLES BY PENELOPE LIVELY IN PENGUIN

Fiction

The Road to Lichfield
Treasures of Time
Judgement Day
Next to Nature, Art
Perfect Happiness
According to Mark
Pack of Cards: Collected Short Stories 1978–1986
Moon Tiger
Passing On
City of the Mind
Cleopatra's Sister
Heat Wave

Autobiography

Oleander, Jacaranda

PENELOPE LIVELY

Heat Wave

PENGUIN BOOKS

PENGUIN BOOKS

Published by the Penguin Group
Penguin Books Ltd, 27 Wrights Lane, London W8 5TZ, England
Penguin Books USA Inc., 375 Hudson Street, New York, New York 10014, USA
Penguin Books Australia Ltd, Ringwood, Victoria, Australia
Penguin Books Canada Ltd, 10 Alcorn Avenue, Toronto, Ontario, Canada M4V 3B2
Penguin Books (NZ) Ltd, 182–190 Wairau Road, Auckland 10, New Zealand

Penguin Books Ltd, Registered Offices: Harmondsworth, Middlesex, England

First published by Viking 1996
Published in Penguin Books 1997
1 3 5 7 9 10 8 6 4 2

Copyright © Penelope Lively, 1996
All rights reserved

The moral right of the author has been asserted

Printed in England by Clays Ltd, St Ives plc

Chapter One

It is an afternoon in early May. Pauline is looking out of the window of her study at World's End. She looks not at the rich green of the field sweeping up to the cool blue of the sky, but at Teresa, who stands outside the cottages with Luke astride her hip, staring up the track towards the road. Pauline sees Teresa with double vision. She sees her daughter, who is holding her own son and waiting for the arrival of her husband. But she sees also an archetypal figure: a girl with a baby, a woman with a child. There is a whole freight of reference there, thinks Pauline. The girl, the child, the sweep of the cornfield, the long furrowed lines of the rough track reaching away to elsewhere. Seen through one lens, Teresa is a Hardy heroine – betrayed no doubt, a figure of tragedy. Seen through another, she is a lyrical image of youth and regeneration. And for Pauline there shimmers also a whole sequence of intimate references, other versions of Teresa which hitch them both to other days and different places. It is a day in May at World's End, but it is also the extent of two lives – three lives, if Luke's fifteen months are to be considered.

In fact, Teresa is standing where she is for good reason. She has already spotted the glint of the sun on the windscreen of Maurice's car as it turned off the main road, and now indeed here comes the car, creeping in the distance like some sleek dark beast amid the rippling green. And Luke too has seen it. His whole body registers attention and anticipation. He twists his head. He points with all four fingers. 'Da!' he says. 'Da!' Here comes my father, he is announcing.

Pauline hears him, through the open window. She too notes the car. She watches its approach, she sees it pull off the track on to the area alongside the cottages that serves as a parking space. Maurice gets out. He kisses Teresa and they go together into the cottage, into their half of the pair of cottages which is World's End. Pauline turns from the window and looks down again at her desk. She picks up her pencil and makes a note on the manuscript in front of her.

World's End is itself something of an archetype, and as such is unreliable. It is a grey stone building set on a hillside somewhere in the middle of England. The stone is weathered, the hill behind reaches up to a crown of trees which are a delicate tracery against the sky. Adroitly photographed, it could be used as an advertisement by car manufacturers (you need one to get there), the bread industry (there grows the good healthy wheat) or those who operate the tourist trade (come with us and you too will see such scenes). The building appears to be locked still into the early nineteenth century – a terrace of three two-storey cottages with attic dormer windows, constructed of stone dug from a quarry a few miles away and roofed with stone slate also of local provenance. There it sits, tucked snug into the fields. It could have simply grown of its own accord, you feel – made from the very bones of this land. It is an emanation of a time and a place.

The truth is that World's End is suspended in this landscape like a space capsule, with its machinery quietly humming – its computers, its phones, its faxes. Its microwaves, its freezers, its televisions and videos. World's End in fact is nicely disguised, like one of those turfed-over bunkers kitted out as command posts in the event of nuclear attack.

The building has been gutted. Three dwellings are now two, with nothing left of the original construction but windows, fireplaces, a few oak beams and a staircase. The front door of the left-hand, larger cottage – now used by Teresa and Maurice – opens straight into a big open-plan kitchen. Behind that a new extension provides the sitting-room which overlooks the garden common to both cottages. A cleverly constructed space-saving staircase twists up out of one corner of the kitchen to the bedroom and bathroom floor above. The attic is Maurice's study.

The smaller cottage – Pauline's – is rather different. Kitchen and sitting-room are paired at each side of a tiny hallway, from which the original staircase rises to the upper floor. It is a disconcertingly precipitate staircase, much too steep and with narrow treads. Pauline has had hand rails put at either side, but even so visitors have to be warned. She wishes occasionally that the staircase had been ripped out when the building was done over, but at the time it seemed appealing and in some way integral to the cottage, and now she cannot be bothered with any further upheaval.

The whole place is of course radiant with electricity and central heating. It ticks and tocks with timing mechanisms and remote-control devices. Green digits blink from display panels. Telephones are poised for action. Computers and faxes stand waiting in Pauline's study and in Maurice's. Both of them can tap into a global communication network, both can conjure up the information resources of distant libraries. World's End is a wolf in sheep's clothing – it is no more rooted in a time and a place than is the flight deck of a 747.

A curious name for a row of cottages – World's End. When Pauline bought the place ten years ago she was puzzled by the term but found no explanation until Maurice pointed out that such names were often given to farm labourers' dwellings sited out in the fields in the last century – new constructions away from village centres and labelled accordingly, places that seemed remote, or – ironically – idyllic. World's

End. Botany Bay. Tasmania. Utopia Cottages. Paradise Row. He threw out the observation casually, offhand, standing down there on the track the first time he came there, before he married Teresa – as though it were the sort of thing everyone knew.

Pauline, sitting now at her desk, making another quick note on someone else's manuscript, looks again out on to the track and sees the shadow of that Maurice, back then, making that observation. He slides her the self-deprecating glance he often uses when giving information, and she is at once interested and faintly irritated. Teresa flickers there also for a moment too, standing to one side while Pauline and Maurice talk about the cottages, her eyes on Maurice, far gone in love, snared, committed, lost.

Teresa is still in love with Maurice, three years on. This is plain for all to see. For Pauline especially to see. She saw it just now, saw it as Teresa stood watching for Maurice's car, saw it in her stance, in the movements of her head, in the way her hand frets up and down the fence. And seeing this, she knew quite precisely what Teresa felt. Pauline could take her place for an instant – becoming not Teresa but herself on another day, in another decade, waiting thus for a man.

And here he comes – not driving a car up a dirt track but walking quickly through the crowds at Victoria station. She sees him coming from a long way off and does not go forward to meet him but stays where she is because these are the best moments of all – the thrilling jolt of recognition as she identifies him, an up-rush of being as though all the senses were intensified. She will spin it out, this exquisite anticipation. And then he is yards away, is smiling, waving. And then he is holding her. She can feel him, smell him. Harry. There is nothing else like this, she knows – nothing in the world.

And as the moment comes gushing back to her today at World's End, it is the sensation that is sharpest, clearer by far than anything she sees – the station concourse, Harry's face. Harry himself is reduced to a prompt – the trigger for recovered emotion.

Pauline reads another page of the manuscript she is editing. She makes a spelling correction, draws tactful attention to the repetition of a word. Then she shunts the manuscript to one side of her desk, yawns, stretches, and sits for a few moments looking out at the end of this May afternoon. It has become warm, all of a sudden, after a chill grey spring. Summer is a distinct possibility. She has opened the window while she is working, almost for the first time. The window next door must be open also: she can hear Luke-noises – a sequence of wordless urgencies – and Teresa's responses. She can hear Maurice – an indecipherable murmur. Maurice must be on the phone. Maurice is frequently on the phone.

World's End is around a hundred and seventy years old. Pauline is fifty-five. Teresa is twenty-nine. Maurice is forty-four.

Pauline's purchase of the cottages had been made possible by her inheritance of her parents' house when her mother died two years after her father. She was still working as a full-time editor at a London publishing firm. Teresa was at art college. Maurice was unknown to either of them and therefore off-stage to all intents and purposes. In fact Maurice was busy establishing an early reputation as the maverick young author of books on quirky aspects of history that flattered the reader by being simultaneously scholarly and inviting. A sparky account of the tobacco industry, a contentious book on the marketing of the stately home business. Right now, Maurice is working on a history of tourism – a hefty project which will discuss the ways in which the natural and the manmade environments have been exploited in the interests of commerce. He is in frequent communication with an influential film producer. There is serious talk of a TV series as a tie-in with the book. These discussions have had an inevitable effect on the enthusiasm of Maurice's publisher for the work in hand. Maurice has stepped from the position of an interesting author of eccentric books to a potentially valuable asset.

It is because of this book that Maurice and Teresa are at World's End this spring. Before their marriage, Pauline used to let out the larger of the two cottages while keeping the smaller one for her own use. When Teresa married Maurice, Pauline gave her the larger cottage as a weekend retreat. This year, Maurice has announced that they will spend the whole summer down here so that he can apply himself undisturbed to the book, of which the first draft is complete. He will of course have to make occasional forays to London to check references, and his editor, James Saltash, will be coming down to World's End sometimes at weekends to go through the manuscript with Maurice. World's End will become an editorial powerhouse this summer.

Pauline gave up her job five years ago. She now works from home as a freelance copy-editor, in demand because she is widely known and highly competent. She takes on as much or as little work as she wishes, and spends her time rescuing authors from semantic outrages and the carelessness of creative zest. She plods through novels checking that the heroine's eyes have not turned from blue to grey half-way along, that spring has not suddenly given way to winter, that Sunday does not follow Monday. She queries awkward sentence constructions and tactfully indicates that the colon and the semicolon are not interchangeable. The manuscripts on which she works are peppered with her succinct and neutral comments – questioning the sense of a tortuous passage, drawing attention to a cliché. The author will of course go his or her own sweet way in any case. Many will accept some or all of Pauline's amendments, with a varying degree of resistance.

The intransigent few will fight to the last comma for the principle of authorial infallibility. Pauline rather enjoys these exchanges – the trading of dictionary references and literary precedent, and of course so far as she is concerned if they so wish they can go down with all solecisms blazing. It's no skin off her nose. She has done her stuff, and enjoyed the doing of it, working away through long quiet days at her desk in front of the window, lifting her eyes now and then to note the changing light on the field as the sun swings up and over, getting up from her chair to take down a reference book or make a cup of coffee.

Pauline knows this field intimately – its range of mood and colour, its seasonal changes. It is growing wheat – winter wheat which at this May moment is a rich green pelt. It is a large field and will yield sixty tons of wheat in a reasonable harvest. So the emerald quilt which ripples silver in the wind represents around £5,000. Pauline has established these facts from Chaundy, the farmer from whom she bought World's End. Chaundy is not an overly friendly man and their relationship is one of guarded acquaintance, no more, but from time to time they meet on the track and a desultory conversation takes place. On one of these occasions Pauline solicited this information about the field.

'Thinking of taking up farming?' said Chaundy, sardonic.

'Certainly not. But I look out at that field all the time – I thought I'd like to know more about it.'

Chaundy was not interested in Pauline's interest. He answered her queries grudgingly, in a throwaway manner. Acreage. Yield. He is not interested in Pauline, come to that. She is simply someone with whom he once did business and who is now a neighbour, but in a peripheral way, since she is not of his community. He is not obliged to deal with her from day to day. She does not work for him, or sell him fertilizer, or buy his grain, or share his concerns. She does not inhabit his world, except in a literal sense.

Chaundy is a big farmer, as they go. He has land here, and also over in the next valley. He runs a caravan site ten miles away, and a pick-it-yourself fruit farm on the other side of the hill, complete with farm shop and restaurant. He also has a large range of broiler chicken houses. Chaundy probably does not get his hands dirty very much, these days. Mostly he drives from one to another of his concerns in a newish but battered Peugeot, issuing terse instructions. Quite a lot of people work for Chaundy, most of them for rather small amounts of money.

Up at the top left-hand corner of the field, where its neighbour begins, there is a triangle of glaring yellow which tips away over the crown of the hill. Oilseed rape. Pauline is not entirely sure where she stands, *vis-à-vis* oilseed rape. Aesthetic opinion is sharply divided over this issue. There are those who find it cheerful – a nice splash of colour. The purists – who are the most vociferous – deplore it as a discordant and jarring note amid the subtle tones of the English landscape. The stuff is decried as an intrusive blight from across the Channel (EC agricultural policy has made rape a profitable cash crop) and it has therefore achieved sinister political overtones, as well as being a nasty colour. Pauline, looking over at that citron flag on the hillside, has mixed feelings. Sometimes it does indeed strike a note of gaiety – she thinks of the warm south, of fields of sunflowers. At others it appears as an aggressive shout against the skyline. But in any case it will pass. By June it will be extinguished, in line with the ephemeral qualities of this landscape.

Thus, World's End, on this May afternoon which shades off now into evening, as Pauline tidies her desk, leaves her study and goes down that odd precipitate staircase to see what she has got in the fridge for supper. And thus also

Pauline, Teresa, Maurice. Mother, daughter, son-in-law and husband. Neighbours, relatives, poised for this agreeable summer of industry and companionship.

Chapter Two

It is ten o'clock on the following morning. Pauline, Teresa, Maurice and Luke are gathered together in the open-plan kitchen of Teresa's cottage.

Teresa is talking to Luke – the murmuring pigeon-talk of a mother to a baby – inconsequential chatter to an adult ear, a luminous revelation to the baby. '*There* we are . . .' says Teresa. 'Trousers on now. One leg . . . Other leg . . . *Red* trousers today. *There* we go.' And Luke perceives that the sounds he hears are mysteriously linked to the things he sees. 'Da,' he says. 'Da.' Or perhaps ba, or doh. His sounds are not yet hitched to anything – to objects nor yet to vowels or consonants. They are simply sounds. The radio talks about an election in Italy, breaks off for a burst of music, talks now of slaughter in Rwanda. Pauline is reading a letter. She looks across at Teresa and says: 'Jane has this flat in Venice for September. Maybe I'll go there for a week.' 'Oh, right . . .' says Teresa. 'D'you want some banana, Luke? Mmmn . . . nana?' Maurice is on the phone: 'So we'll see you both this weekend. Excellent. Oh . . . and could you bring a copy of Defoe's *Tour through the Whole Island of Great Britain*, James, if you can lay hands on one? Thanks.'

There is a blizzard of words in this room – Luke is bombarded with them, they stream through his head like particles through matter. He is battered by sensation – the white noise of language, the brilliance of the visible world. For him the room and the day blaze with novelty and revelation. The kettle whose shining surface dances with the reflection of blue flowers in a vase; the chair whose feet shriek against the floor as his father rises. Knowing nothing, he is astonished by everything. He exists on a different plane from Teresa, from Pauline, from Maurice – seeing what they cannot see, hearing what they cannot hear. Of the four of them, it is Luke who is in a state of shimmering perception. He sits there on Teresa's lap, a visitor from a world of lost capacities. 'Da,' he says. And Teresa beams, uncomprehending. 'He's got that rash again,' she says to Pauline.

Maurice is standing now at the window, holding a cup of coffee. He turns, lowering his cup. 'We might go somewhere on Sunday, if this weather holds. James and Carol are coming for the weekend. James wants to go over Chapter Six again.'

'I'll do a big shop in Hadbury this morning,' says Teresa. 'Maybe we'll have a leg of lamb.'

Pauline stows her letter in her pocket. 'Carol?' she says.

Maurice has picked up the newspaper now, is scanning the front page, abstracted.

'She lives with James,' Teresa tells her mother. 'Carol . . . oh, what is her other name, Maurice? Anyway . . . will they come on Friday or Saturday?'

'Saturday morning,' says Maurice. He puts down the paper, finishes his coffee, moves towards the door. 'So . . . back to the grindstone.' He looks over at Pauline. He smiles – a propitiating, lop-sided, characteristic smile. 'How's your grindstone at the moment, Pauline? Anything interesting?'

'Not specially,' says Pauline. There is the faintest edge to her voice, a tiny hardness. Perhaps it is because she has opened another letter and is picking at a staple in the corner of some papers, always an irritating process.

Maurice leaves the room. He goes upstairs. Both women hear the door of his study close. Pauline succeeds in detaching that staple and glances through a torrent of justifications from an author which he, in his fervour, had stapled together out of sequence. She continues to see Maurice's face superimposed above the text, like the Cheshire Cat, and thinks about faces – those presences in the mind. A face is an image, as insubstantial as a way of moving or the inflexion of a voice. A face cannot be translated into words – or only up to a point.

Maurice's face is triangular. The forehead is broad and the eyes set wide apart, the nose is thin and quite pronounced. The planes of his cheeks slope sharply inwards to a pointed chin. His hair springs upwards, thick and wavy and light brown. Words . . . which give a notion of what Maurice looks like, which might form the basis of an Identikit portrait, but which are a feeble reflection of the particularity of features – that quality which means that those who know him well can conjure up Maurice's face at will, which means that Luke could pick it out from a dozen others and say, 'Da!'

Luke's face is an assemblage of references. Pauline sees Maurice there, in the spacing of his eyes. She sees Teresa's nose and a suggestion of her high curved eyebrows. She sees also something of herself – a quality of expression that she catches in the mirror and has caught also as Luke turns his head and stares up at her. She sees also a flicker of her mother and a shimmer of her father and once she has caught an echo of an aunt she barely knew but whose distinctive features look out from a photo in a family album. It is as though Luke is in the process of trying out this feature and then that until eventually he arrives at some acceptable synthesis.

Teresa's face is oval, pale-skinned, dark-eyed. She has thick eyebrows and a high forehead from which her dark hair is pulled back and held by a band at the nape of her neck. When Pauline looks at her she sees all this, and sees also her serious, faintly anxious expression. But she sees something else as well, perceptible only to her, which is that eerie echo of self that a parent sees in a child. Teresa and Pauline are not alike – Pauline's features are broader, flatter, her mouth is larger, her eyes are greenish, her hair a coppery brown streaked now with grey. Nevertheless, that echo is there, that mirror-glimpse of self – elusive, indefinable, but inescapable. There she is, thinks Pauline – Teresa. And there somehow am I too, she does not think but simply sees. And there also, inescapably, is Harry.

'More coffee?' says Teresa.

'Mmn . . . Thanks.'

Teresa, Pauline and Luke are alone in the kitchen. Everything is subtly different, as though the wind has shifted direction. There is a change of key as the two women speak. Certain resonances are lost, others have arrived. Only Luke, busy with his own concerns, remains constant.

'You may as well leave Luke with me while you do the shopping,' says Pauline.

Teresa demurs. 'You're working.'

'I can stop working and catch up tonight. My time is my own these days.'

'OK then,' says Teresa. 'Thanks. Anything I can get you?'

'Bread, I could do with. Some fruit. I'll have a think.'

There is silence, invaded only by Luke's comings and goings around the room, his commentaries, his exclamations.

'Nescafé,' says Pauline. 'And plain yoghurt. Otherwise I'm fine.'

'Right.' Teresa is making a list. She breaks off and stares at the table. She chews her lip. Perhaps she is thinking about groceries. Perhaps not.

Pauline looks at Teresa. 'Where are they at, on this book? Maurice and James thing?'

'Saltash. They're sort of at the beginning of the second draft, I think.'

'Maurice seems to need a lot of editorial input.'

'Maurice says James is very constructive. James has been talking to this film guy too and they've got to be sure Maurice gets the book right if the TV programme is really going to come off.'

'Ah.'

'Luke could have scrambled egg for his lunch,' continues Teresa. 'If I'm late back.'

'What about Maurice? Do I provide him with scrambled egg too?'

'Maurice won't mind waiting,' says Teresa.

A mundane enough exchange. Useful, though – an arrangement has been made, information has been given and received. There are echoes and reverberations, there is a shimmer on the bland surface. Ordinary words are loaded, there are echoes of other events, other exchanges, of different manifestations of Pauline, of Teresa. A cycle of inescapable involvement is manifested in each inflexion of their voices. They are talking not just of shopping lists and lunch, but of a shared history.

And Pauline, seeing Teresa chewing her lip as she stares mutely at the kitchen table, sees her dissolve for an instant into another Teresa, staring at a different kitchen table in another house – to look up suddenly and say, 'I'm not going out with Don tonight.'

'Huh!' says Pauline. 'Standing him up, are you?'

Teresa looks awkward now. 'Not exactly. Just . . . well, it's all gone a bit stale, so I said maybe it's better if we don't go out together tonight.'

'It's called standing a person up,' Pauline advises. 'If you're just sitting there fancy free could you do me a favour and stir that. I have twenty people coming here in three hours' time.'

Teresa, now, is mortified. She has gone pink in the face. She is a kind girl, that is the problem.

'He'll get over it,' says Pauline. 'It'll be water down the drain by the end of next week.'

'Thanks,' says Teresa, mildly offended.

'Because he's young and healthy. And now here you are footloose on New Year's Eve. What are you going to do?'

'I'm coming to your party,' says Teresa.

'Oh, you are, are you? All the more reason to get stuck in here, in that case. That has to be spread on those, and we're going to make some sort of punch.'

'Who's coming?' enquires Teresa.

One echo among many – extinguished already by the onward rush of things as Teresa gathers up her purse, her car keys, her shopping bag, as Luke howls briefly in protest, as Pauline sweeps him up and out into the garden to distract him from the departure of his mother.

The garden at World's End is a rectangle jutting out into a field. It is the amalgamation of the three long thin strips which were the gardens of the original cottages – the sparse gesture which allowed each labouring family its own small plot on which to grow a few vegetables. And flowers – cottage garden flowers whose descendants tenaciously reappear year after year. At the end of the garden is an orchard of ancient apple trees, way past their prime, which deliver a crop of scabby fruit. These also are presumably relics of the former inhabitants of the place, cherished assets back then which are united now into a neglected place of lush grass which no one ever gets around to cutting.

The surrounding field is planted not with wheat but with young cabbages, rank upon rank of bluish-grey plants which merge into a swathe of delicate colour. This is a smaller field, bounded by a hedgerow. Beyond the hedge the hill rises, another acreage of green wheat. But this field is not the same uninterrupted green sweep as that overlooked by Pauline's study. Here, the line is broken half-way up the hill by a fence, beyond which a further discordant note is struck – a rim of autumnal gold. This field appears to be a waste of dead grass, now in May when everything else is in vibrant growth. Its colour, though, is the more disturbing because it is not the fawn of winter decay but an unnatural harsh yellow, the raw shade of a verge that has been treated with weedkiller. And that is precisely the case. This field is set-aside. It is a product of the policy whereby the government pays farmers not to farm. Chaundy collects several hundred pounds in return for not growing anything in that field this year. Its random growth has been sprayed so that it can subsequently be ploughed up. The landscape is scarred with similar fields, provocative blotches amid the orderly line-up of wheat, barley, brussels sprouts, leeks, sheep, cows and of course battery chickens, caravan sites and pick-it-yourself fruit farms. A nice irony, thinks Pauline – this land which has ground down generations of labourers is now too productive for its own good. It has outstripped the economic climate and must be laid waste with weedkiller.

Pauline sometimes thinks of the people who have lived at World's End before her. The real inhabitants – those who lived here seriously, because they had to. She sees stunted people with skins ripened by dirt and weather. Most of these people would have been old at fifty-five – at her age – keeling over, heading for their hole in the turf, worked quite literally into the ground. They would have looked rather differently upon the silver gleam of winter sunshine on ploughlands, upon the billowing gold of an August cornfield. All very fine for us, thinks Pauline – playing at Marie Antoinette, soothing the troubled soul with contemplation of nature. Time was, this place was for real.

Luke is heading for the long grass of the orchard, wet still with dew, in which he will get soaked. It is almost as tall as he is. Pursuing him, Pauline sees it for an instant through his eyes – an inviting wonderland of sensual possibilities, a cyberspace of light and shade, of things that wave and twitch and bob. She picks him up, redirects him towards the house, and sees Maurice coming out of the french windows towards them.

Maurice has a mug of coffee in his hand. Maurice is fuelled by coffee throughout the day. 'Hi, you two,' he says. 'Where's Teresa?'

'Gone shopping. You have guests for the weekend. Remember? Food has to be bought.'

Maurice smiles – the lop-sided Maurice smile. It is a smile that seems designed to side-step difficulties, such as any implications of what Pauline has just said. He looks down at Luke, who is clutching his knees, asking to be picked up. He pats his head. Maurice has not offered to look after Luke while Teresa goes shopping because it would not have occurred to him. Indeed, it seems that he had not taken on board the proposed shopping expedition. 'How do you spell *gesellschaft*?' he inquires.

Pauline tells him. 'I thought this book was about the British tourist trade?'

'It is indeed. But I need to demonstrate a bit of cultural eclecticism, don't I?' He lifts the mug to his lips and looks at Pauline over the top of it with that winning and attentive look that is central to Maurice's charm. Those on the receiving end feel flattered, and enhanced.

But Pauline, who is familiar with the look, remains impervious. She sees Maurice peering at her above a blue-and-white china mug in the garden at World's End, and that Maurice gives way to another Maurice, leaning up against the mantelpiece of her flat in London, lifting a wine glass to his lips and staring over it into the crowded room. 'So that's the daughter,' he says. Red wine with the light shining through it, and Maurice's eyes, intent.

Maurice gives in to Luke's urgent noises and picks him up. He holds him awkwardly. Maurice is not adroit, physically, which is unexpected in a man of swift and elusive mental processes. He drops things and knocks things over. He is a bad driver. He is hopeless at tasks like putting on an electric plug or changing a tyre. Some of this clumsiness is attributable to a minor limp, the result of an accident in childhood. He lurches slightly, under certain circumstances. But that does not account for the hamhandedness, in evidence now as he shifts Luke from one arm to the other. And of course fatherhood has come late to Maurice. He is old at forty-four to be the father of an infant. Harder to pick up new skills, when you have tipped forty.

Maurice is terrified of age. He is incredulous that age is stalking him, that the ageing process applies to him also, that he is not somehow exempt. Pauline has seen the sudden onset of panic, has noted the way in which he makes sure to surround himself with younger people, the way that he keeps up a frenetic pace, is always on the move, is always shooting off in pursuit of some new interest, some new acquaintance. And of course men thus affected frequently turn to women much younger than themselves.

Pauline has known Maurice for six years. She knew him in a desultory way for three years before he married Teresa. His books were published by an imprint of the publishing conglomerate for which she worked. She met him at a sales conference and struck up a mild acquaintance. She met him again at a party and experienced Maurice in conversational overdrive. Maurice is a beguiling conversationalist – flattering and stimulating. He phoned her to check on the title of a book she had mentioned. The acquaintance firmed up. Maurice would cross the room to talk to Pauline if he caught sight of her at social gatherings. They had a drink together once or twice. Pauline invited Maurice to a New Year's Eve party.

Those of Maurice's circle who knew him well enough to be aware of the usual sequence of events were astonished to learn that he was going to marry Teresa. A period of cohabitation was the normal thing. Why marry her? they wondered. A delightful girl, to be sure. But marriage? Maurice – marrying?

Pauline was of his circle, in that sense.

'Why?' she said to Teresa, clenched in disbelief and dismay. 'Why get *married*?'

'I'm in love with him,' said Teresa, incandescent with happiness.

'Think about it for a bit,' wailed Pauline.

'You can't think when you're in love,' said Teresa, reasonably enough.

There is nothing inherently dangerous about marrying a man fifteen years older than yourself. If you fall deeply in love, and find to your delight and amazement that your love is apparently returned, then if marriage is proposed that seems a natural step.

Luke is wriggling now, aware perhaps of Maurice's uncertain grip. Maurice puts him down and he potters off to investigate a clump of grass. He picks something up and puts it in his mouth. Pauline intervenes, extracts a twig from Luke's pink maw. Maurice looks on benignly. Maurice loves Luke – in his way. But it has to be said that what Maurice feels for Luke bears little resemblance to what Pauline feels for Teresa, or to what Teresa feels for Luke. Luke is something that has happened to Maurice along the way. Maurice is pleased enough that Luke happened. He finds Luke engaging. He would be much concerned if Luke were seriously ill, or hurt. If Luke died Maurice would be deeply shaken. But on the Richter scale of parental commitment Maurice only gets up to about three points.

Fortunate Maurice, one may think.

'Have you ever been to Bradley Castle?' says Maurice.

'Certainly not,' Pauline replies. Bradley Castle is a sixteenth-century pile some ten miles away which has been reinvented as a theme park. It offers the Robin Hood Experience, along with jousting matches, falconry displays and medieval banquets on Saturday nights.

'I thought we might all go there this weekend.'

Pauline raises her eyebrows. 'I can think of better ways to entertain your visitors.'

'I'm getting too detached,' says Maurice. 'I need to get my sights on a few real tourists.'

'Ah. I see. The book.' This expedition, Pauline perceives, is not to do with amusing Maurice's guests but is in the service of a preoccupation of Maurice's.

Maurice's egotism is not overly apparent. He is not conspicuously self-absorbed. He does not talk all that much about himself or his concerns. Indeed, he probes other people about theirs. He will interrogate, with that aloof, amused expression: 'Why do you think that?' 'What made you do that?' Maurice's egotism is the more subtle version – that of implacable purpose. Only when you know Maurice well – when you have had occasion to observe his habits over time – only then do you see that he practises a system of relentless manipulation. All those in his orbit do what Maurice requires that they should do, to the greater convenience of Maurice. It is a brilliant operation.

'Count me out,' says Pauline.

Maurice considers her. He looks at her quizzically. 'We need you, Pauline,' he says. 'And you might enjoy it – who can tell?'

'I'll see. When the time comes.'

Maurice grins. 'What a sternly independent woman you are. Have you always been like that?'

His question is not a casual one. He is interested. And Pauline is not going to reply, because the answer would be revealing, and she does not care to reveal herself to Maurice. Instead, she turns to Luke. She shows him how to blow the down from a dandelion clock. Maurice watches for a few moments. He finishes his coffee and goes back into the house.

If asked, Pauline would say that she was happy, generally speaking. As it is, few people would have the temerity to ask. Pauline is seen as self-sufficient, confident, and possessed of a nice balance between good self-esteem and a healthy regard for others. She is the sort of woman who would have a therapist running for cover. Or so it seems.

She is indeed independent. But the independence is hard won, which is why she prefers not to answer Maurice's question. She is a woman who has lived alone since her daughter grew up and left. Well, not always entirely alone. There have been men now and then, a couple of whom have had, for a while, quasi-resident status. But she has been alone in principle, leading the flexible, slightly opportunistic life of the unattached. She has the habits of those who are solitary, whether by choice or by circumstance – changing plans to indulge the mood of the moment, making and breaking contingency arrangements. She is practised in social duplicity. It is often a good life, occasionally a bad one. A life rich in carefully nurtured minor satisfactions, in the easy gratification of self-indulgences. An unfettered life, a life without the grating irritation of presences that are too present, a life in which anything might happen and in which it sometimes did. A life also in which a day could suddenly become a treacherous void, in which spectres come swarming round the bed in the small hours.

Unlike Maurice, Pauline is not outraged by the fact that she is getting older. When she considers the matter – when she remembers that she is fifty-five – she is amazed rather than offended. Amazed to be here, thus, at this point, having negotiated so much. The long continuous present of childhood and the helter-skelter of youth and then the ferocious onward rush of events. Here she is – now, today – and it is not too bad, though perhaps in some areas it is not too good either. There are brown blotches on her hands, her teeth look like giving out before the rest of her, and the libido is no longer what it was, which is perhaps just as well. But the world still shines for her, expectation is as rich.

Luke has lost interest in the dandelion clocks. He has found his ball. He throws it, pursues it, falls over, picks himself up again, throws the ball once more – a burgeoning skill. Pauline, watching him, thinks that there is also this phenomenon which is Luke-time, a process of accelerated change whereby Luke seems as though he is not hitched to the ordinary passage of the calendar year but is set on some hectic course of his own which has spawned a dizzying sequence of Lukes – the sloe-eyed baby with waving starfish hands has become the pneumatic crawler and is now this tottering figure weaving in pursuit of a slippery plastic globe. Luke is on a fast-track which is not synchronized with Pauline's days, nor indeed with those of his parents.

It has clouded over. The weather is playing false once more, capricious as ever – the bright morning giving way to looming skies. A grey pall has come tilting up from behind the hill, intensifying the green of fields and trees and hedges. The landscape is vivid. And the first drops of rain begin to fall.

Pauline carries Luke inside.

Chapter Three

Pauline remembers the first time she saw Teresa with Luke. She walks down the hospital ward between a double rank of legs – legs ranged carelessly on beds, sticking out below nighties and dressing-gowns. Brown legs, black legs, pale pink legs. An acreage of female flesh, casually exposed, legs and thighs and whole breasts into which are tucked the furry heads of babies. No one is modest or prudish here, there is a frank acceptance of what is going on. This is all about bodies – the bodies of women. And the place is awash with people. Nurses hurrying up and down, acolytes around each bed – the husbands and the friends and the parents, the brothers and sisters. There are flowers and the occasional bottle of champagne. There is eating and drinking. This is not so much a hospital ward as a municipal park on a Bank Holiday afternoon.

Fine, thinks Pauline, fine. She makes her way down the alley of sprawling legs, past the families and the eddying toddlers and the partners. 'Visiting hours from 3 to 6', said the notice in the lift. 'Partners may visit at all times.' So what happened to husbands? thinks Pauline. Obsolete. Defunct. So be it.

She sees Teresa now. Teresa is alone. She is alone with Luke. Pauline approaches, and then stands for a moment, unseen by Teresa. She sees that Teresa is in every sense alone, away in a bubble of content. The intensity of experience. She is holding Luke in front of her, cradling him so that his face looks into hers. She is seeing nothing but Luke. And Luke presumably sees nothing but her – his first and crucial revelation of the world.

She knows now, thinks Pauline. Yesterday she didn't know. Today she knows it all.

She steps up to the bed. 'Hi!' she says. 'So here he is.'

They admire Luke. They assess him, inch by inch – eyes, nose, mouth, hair, fingers, toes. They revel in him.

'How was it?' asks Pauline.

'Ghastly,' says Teresa. 'Frightful. And terrific. Both at once. You know.'

'Yup,' says Pauline briskly. 'I know.'

She knows all right. That is the one thing that remains with you, for ever.

She is grabbed in a vice of pain. She is clenched by a great fist of pain which wrings her till she yells and then releases her. It will come again. And again. She asks the time. Three o'clock. The small hours of this night which is going on for ever.

She is alone with the midwife in the cramped bedroom of the flat. Harry is in the next room. From time to time he peers round the door, looking worried. The midwife reassures him and shoos him away. The midwife is a year older than Pauline – a fact established earlier when this sort of chat was still possible. Now, it is not. Pauline can see in the midwife's face that things are not going right. The midwife has phoned for the doctor. For Pauline, fear and pain are compounded into one hideous roaring black event.

She tells the midwife, 'I don't want to die.'

'You're going to be fine,' says the midwife, not quite confidently enough.

What happens next is compacted – both then and now – into a sequence of impression and sensation. Men carrying her on a stretcher. The howling of the ambulance siren. This is for me, she thinks. This is happening to me, not to someone else. She stares up at a white ceiling from which is suspended a harsh white light under a green shade. There are faces looking down at her – dispassionate, assessing faces. People hurry to and fro. Feet tap on a linoleum floor.

She is washed up on this high table, staring still at the ceiling. The people have gone. She can see the trolley thing in which they have put the baby. She sees its face, and the quiff of its hair. It? Her. She tries to think of this baby, this child, her child, but she is too weak to think. Something is awry. She is so weak that she is floating. She can see the room – the white ceiling, the green-shaded light, the baby in a trolley, the back view of a nurse doing something at a sink, but she can neither think nor speak. She knows that this is not right, that she must tell the nurse what is happening, but she can neither speak nor move. She lies there, floating.

And then the nurse turns, and comes across, and looks down at her. And there are feet tap-tapping again, and more people, more faces looking down, and voices that boom, that come from far away.

When Pauline conjures all this up today she is awed. This is herself, but a self so far removed that there is nothing left but these echoes. Echoes of such raw intensity that they are always there, ringing down the years, hitching her to this eerie stranger. Shadows in the mind, far away and deep within.

The foetus had got stuck. A deep transverse arrest. The midwife could no longer cope. The home delivery that was the standard procedure back then was now not advisable. Hence the ambulance, the hospital doctor brought bustling from his tea break, the scurrying nurses. The forceps. And Pauline – that shadow Pauline – went into shock and had to have a blood transfusion. No great crisis, in the scale of things, and both mother and child came out of it unscathed.

But the bald narrative and the technical explanation seem quite unrelated to those messages from the person who was there. It was like this, says the shadow Pauline, the echo Pauline – the steel-hard pain, the tapping feet, that green lampshade.

And Harry, who comes and stands looking down at her. 'Hello,' he says. He takes her hand. She stares at him. She has nothing to say to him. It is as though she has been on some tremendous journey, has travelled so far and for so long that she no longer speaks his language.

Now, today, this May morning at World's End, Pauline receives a letter from Harry. This sometimes happens. Once a year or so. She stands beside the post van on the track outside the cottages and takes the letters from the postman, who sits with engine running and tells her the weather forecast, a speciality of his. Pauline hears that it is going to be a bit dodgy today, Friday, but will clear up for the weekend. She sorts the letters – those for Maurice and Teresa, those for her – and sees the California postmark on the airmail envelope, which means Harry. She shoves her own letters in her pocket and takes the rest next door, where Teresa and Maurice are having breakfast. She relays the weather forecast.

'Excellent,' says Maurice. 'All set for Bradley Castle, then?'

'You don't have to, Mum,' says Teresa.

'Of course she has to,' says Maurice. 'We need her company, and she'll enjoy it.'

'You're a bully, Maurice,' says Pauline. 'And I'll do as I think fit, when the time comes.'

'Of course,' says Maurice, heading for the stairs. 'Quite right too. But at least join us for dinner on Saturday. We'll all be fed up with each other by then.'

It is the custom, at World's End, for the two households to remain separate, up to a point. There is of course a great deal of coming and going between the cottages, but Pauline spends her evenings alone. There has been tacit agreement that proximity will be successful only with a firm acknowledgement of privacy. But an informal agreement has arrived that everyone should eat together on Saturday evenings. Sometimes Pauline has a cooking spree, sometimes it is she who is the guest.

'OK,' says Pauline. 'Thank you kindly.'

Maurice is now half-way up the stairs. 'Do you think you could bring me up a coffee in about an hour or so, Teresa?' Teresa nods. He disappears.

Maurice never uses endearments. Darling. Sweetie. This, Pauline tells herself, means nothing. Nothing whatsoever. She thinks of Harry, from whose mouth endearments showered. My love, my sweet, my pet.

'We've been up since five,' Teresa explains. 'Luke wakes with the dawn chorus. Now he's out cold, of course. I'd forgotten the country is so noisy – it's ages since I was here at this time of year.'

'It was worse when Chaundy had lambing ewes in the big field,' says Pauline. 'He gave them up some time back. The bottom fell out of the lamb market, I suppose.'

'Maurice says he'll have to go home to Camden for some peace and quiet. He doesn't really mean it.'

'Given his present trade Maurice should know perfectly well that the cult of rural bliss is a myth,' says Pauline.

Tacitly, she concedes that Maurice has a point, if not several. In spring the spasmodic gunfire of crop-scarers wakes Pauline at dawn and keeps her nicely alert while she is working. May and June are relatively peaceful, except for the clamour of birds in the full vigour of reproduction. But come high summer and the real fun begins. The roar of agricultural machinery pervades the landscape – the rhythmic thrash of hay-making, mammoth combines pulverizing a field of wheat, the attendant tractors grinding to and fro. Admittedly the place is no longer ablaze into the bargain – straw-burning is now outlawed so it is possible to breathe fresh air in August and September. But the tranquillity of rural life is an urban legend. And it is of course ludicrous to expect tranquillity. Agriculture is an industry. Industry generates noise and pollution. If you inhabit an industrial area – and by choice at that – you must accept the consequences.

Teresa yawns. 'Maybe I'll have a nap till Luke wakes up.'

'You do that.' Pauline is already heading for the door, her mind now on her own plans for the day. Phone calls to be made. That manuscript.

Back in her study, she drops the letters on her desk and leaves them lying there, because she had already seen that there is nothing that requires her urgent attention. She looks out at the field and immediately Teresa's face is imposed upon the green – yawning, a healthy pink cavern fringed with neat white teeth. Teresa has good teeth, because Pauline took a strong line about diet, way back. Thinking of this, she sees another Teresa, with cropped hair and a ragged fringe, gap-toothed – and further Teresas yet, a procession of them. There is not one Teresa, but a metamorphosis, a succession of which she is always vaguely aware. And when she dreams of Teresa, it is always of a child that she dreams. Teresa is once again four, or six, or nine – and Pauline is unsurprised. Dreaming, she accepts without question this reincarnation, and is carried along by the dream's narrative of anxiety, or protection, or annoyance. The next day, it is for a moment unsettling to find again the adult and alien Teresa, who is at the same time deeply familiar and in some profound way quite unknown. She is the person Pauline knows best and knows least – and the depth of this unknowing is because of the intensity of the knowing.

Pauline becomes aware once more of the real world

beyond the window. A light wind ruffles the field – shadows course across the young wheat. The whole place is an exercise in colour, as it races into growth. The trees are green flames and the hedges billow brilliantly across the landscape. The old hedgerow at the bottom of the garden has a palette that runs from cream through lemon yellow and all the greens to apricot, russet and a vivid crimson. Each burst of new leaf adds some subtle difference to the range. For a couple of weeks the whole world glows.

Spring came late this year. It was winter still in April, the landscape clenched with cold. Slowly, reluctantly, a green mist spread over the hedges, a frosting of blackthorn appeared. And then at the end of the month the temperature rocketed. It occurs to Pauline that already she can no longer remember exactly what that stripped wintry landscape looked like. She cannot summon it up in the head as she can summon up the metamorphoses of Teresa. This suggests that the physical world is more insubstantial than a person. And in no way is that the case, thinks Pauline. She thinks of the deceptive tenacious life of World's End, and of its vanished and extinguished occupants.

She reaches now for that pile of letters, and abandons them yet again as the phone rings.

'It's me,' says Hugh. 'Am I interrupting?'

'Go right ahead and interrupt. I'm procrastinating as it is.'

'Aren't you getting sick of it down there yet?'

'It's spring,' says Pauline. 'Cuckoos. Flowers. All that.'

'We've got it here too. I went past Green Park this morning in a bus and it was looking very pretty. When are you coming to London?'

'Soon, I dare say. I ought to check out the flat at some point. Don't tell me you're missing me.'

'Of course I'm missing you,' says Hugh crossly. 'You've never skived off down there for the whole summer before.'

'I'm getting through no end of work. Come down for a day or two.'

'Mmn. Well . . . maybe.'

'Hugh,' she says. 'You are the original townsman, you really are. You panic as soon as you haven't got a pavement underfoot. So . . . what's been happening?'

Hugh Follett is an antiquarian bookseller. He is a large shambling man with a thatch of pepper-and-salt hair, a round amiable pink face and thick glasses that always need a good cleaning. Pauline is probably more fond of him than of anyone she knows.

Hugh has a shop and a business. He also has a home in Henley, where lives his wife Elaine. Elaine has got something terrible wrong with her, some affliction of the mind which has crippled her and laid waste her life. Her illness has no name. She is unable to cope with social situations, or to receive visitors. She cannot travel. She seldom leaves the house, where she exists holed up in this cocoon of neurosis. If anyone comes there to see Hugh – and mostly they do not – she retreats to her bedroom until they are gone. She does not answer the phone. If Hugh is out, the answering machine is on.

When and how all this came about Pauline does not know. Occasionally she speculates about Elaine, wondering what fearful trauma has driven the poor woman into this state of wilful isolation. Surely it cannot be anything Hugh has done? Genial, decent, tolerant Hugh. And Hugh is silent on the subject of Elaine. An absolute, implacable and perhaps eloquent silence. Suffice it that he has stayed with her, that he never complains, that he will see it out. He goes home most nights. If he is away from home he checks in, leaving a message on that stonewall answering machine. Once in a while Elaine will call back, as Pauline has had occasion to note, and there is a brief exchange about some practical matter: the boiler is giving trouble, someone has been trying to reach Hugh.

For a while, way back, Pauline and Hugh were lovers. There was even a tremulous and now hazy period when things hovered on the brink of becoming more serious yet, when Hugh's contained and stolid endurance of his marriage was perhaps in doubt. And then that time passed. Both stepped back from something that was probably never a sensible consideration – and eventually they weren't going to bed together any more either. It had always been a homely, companionable form of sex – rather like married sex, Pauline supposed, or at least what she imagined much married sex to be like. Hugh, she realized, was somewhat take it or leave it where sex was concerned. And so, tacitly, they decided to leave it, without a shred of ill feeling on either side, and settled to a mutually satisfactory friendship with overtones of something else. People who know them both probably assume a carnal relationship. In a fit of compunction Pauline had once asked Hugh what Elaine would feel if she knew of Hugh's visits to Pauline in London and (more rarely) at World's End. Hugh's face had emptied of expression. 'Elaine wouldn't be remotely interested,' he replied. Pauline found this remark unutterably bleak.

But he has a life – a work life and a leisure life. His work life is focused upon one of those deeply specialist and exclusive establishments, off-putting to the ordinary book browser by reason of its minimalist window display (two or three choice volumes) and hushed interior (carpets, glass-fronted bookcases). Hugh's work life centres upon the shop (that seems too mundane a word), though he is not often there, leaving it for the most part in the charge of Margery, who has been his assistant for many years – a brisk woman as adept at freezing out inappropriate stray customers as she is at recognizing and cosseting Hugh's long-term clients. A cup of coffee for them, and a copy of the new catalogue – and a quick phone call to Hugh from behind the scenes if he is at home or in his club.

They come from all over, the clients. Collectors, dealers. American, German, Japanese. And Hugh moves around too, disappearing hither and thither for unspecified periods of time on book-related business. He does not expand upon these trips. He simply vanishes, and returns. Pauline will learn in due course that he has been in Los Angeles, or has popped over to Frankfurt for a couple of days. She has dropped him off at Heathrow once or twice – a figure in a shabby raincoat carrying a large battered briefcase. Not at all the international businessman. In the briefcase there are sometimes books. Hugh will dip in and pull out a first edition Joyce, or a Nonesuch Shakespeare. Once, he unfurled from a sheet of *The Times* a tiny volume of eighteenth-century erotica, with delicate little pictures of couples in improbable postures. Not really his field, he explained sheepishly, but it happened to come his way and he knew just where to unload it. Pauline remarked on the fine binding and the charmingly engraved frontispiece. 'Oh yes,' said Hugh. 'Your porn merchant has always liked a nice-looking book.'

Pauline would be distinctly miffed if she found that Hugh was sleeping with someone else. An irrational and possessive attitude, she would be the first to admit. Probably he is not. She knows the pattern of his life – the lunches at his club, the journeyings around the country to view executors' sales or visit clients, the afternoons pottering with catalogues and correspondence in his office behind the shop. Of course, he could be getting up to anything on those sudden sorties across the Atlantic or the Channel. And in the last resort she has no claim on him, none whatsoever. Nor he on her. Each is fond of the other, but fonder yet of an entrenched independence.

'I had to nip over to Paris last week,' says Hugh. 'I had some extraordinarily good nosh. I've found a new place.' He proceeds to detail two lunches and a dinner. Pauline listens with indulgence. She has never been able to share Hugh's obsession with good food. Sometimes she sees it as comfort eating, a desperate compensation for the things that have gone wrong in his life. Or it may just be that Hugh responds to elegant cooking in the same way that he responds to a well-made book. And he is not boring when he talks about food – he brings to the subject all the infectious intensity of an obsession. She enjoys sharing a classy meal with Hugh while recognizing that her level of appreciation is woefully short of his, and that he knows this.

'And I went to the Russian icon exhibition,' he continues. 'Superb. You'd love it.'

'I'm sure I would. Lucky you. Down here we have nothing but rural fayres and car-boot sales. I am threatened with a summer of stately home visiting – Maurice is doing home-work for his tourist book.'

'Come up to town for the weekend. I can see if I could get tickets for the ENO *Parsifal*.'

'Mmn . . . Maybe a bit later on. I'm nicely acclimatized here at the moment.'

'Well, my dear,' says Hugh. 'If you insist on this course of self-immolation there's nothing I can do. Eventually I shall be forced to come down and take you out for a decent meal, if nothing else.'

Pauline laughs. She hears Margery's voice in the back-ground, with some discreet request. Hugh must be in the office behind the shop. 'I'll have to go,' he says. They chat for a few moments longer, and then she puts the phone down.

Hugh would have made someone a good father. But Hugh and Elaine are childless. Pauline has sometimes seen a com-plicated expression on Hugh's face when children are talked about. He likes the young – he has always taken a benign interest in Teresa.

He would have made Teresa a good father, no doubt.

For some years after Teresa became effectively fatherless she would say to Pauline from time to time, 'Dad is going to come back really, isn't he?'

'No,' Pauline would say. 'He isn't, I'm afraid.' And the child's expectant face would wither in disappointment and disbelief.

Teresa has long since come to terms with her father's defection, but she remains fatally endowed with expectations for the best. Being herself without malevolence, deviousness or duplicity she expects others to behave as she would and is perplexed rather than enlightened when they do not. She has never become attuned to the treachery of circumstance. When the rocks loom she does not recognize them.

Teresa has always allowed things to happen to her. As a child, she seemed to move about in a trance. In adolescence, she was like a sleepwalker, drifting from one day into another. Pauline, exasperated, would try to chivvy her into a more aggressive state. Teresa's peers, by contrast, seemed all to seize life by the scruff of the neck, jockeying for position with university entrance authorities, besieging employment agencies. Teresa said she would like to go to art school.

'Then do something about it,' exhorted Pauline. 'Fill in entrance forms. Get competitive. They're not going to send a chauffeured car for you, you know.'

Teresa looked pained.

But she is not spineless. Nor is she lumpen, lazy or unmotivated. The problem is this misplaced belief that everything will turn out all right. Teresa had a talent for design and construction, which blossomed from an absorption with paints and paper in infancy into an ability to make bizarre constructions out of improbable materials. When she was a child the house was always full of gaudy sculptures created from domestic litter – brilliant esoteric birds, architectural fantasies. At school, she spent most of her time in the art room, in a contented trance. This was the sort of thing she was going to do in life – so what was the problem?

Teresa did go to art school, forced to match up her own ambitions with the requirements of the system. If you are going to earn your living doing what you want to do and what you enjoy doing, then you have to discover how to sell your abilities. Teresa battled with entrance forms and interviews, fetched up at a London art college, and emerged with distinctly marketable skills. By the time she met Maurice she was happily established as a freelance designer, equally prepared to set up a window display in a high-class emporium or to supply artefacts for a theatre design department.

Teresa's career is pretty well in abeyance right now, on account of Luke. She does not seem unduly disturbed about this – yet. And perhaps, thinks Pauline, there will be another child. Perhaps.

When Teresa told Pauline that she was going to marry Maurice she said, with absolute sincerity, 'I didn't know you *could* be so happy' – and Pauline had been overcome with dismay. Not just because of Maurice (you don't know him *all* that well, she told herself. He could turn out quite differently. And the fifteen years are neither here nor there) but because Teresa meant what she said. She spoke as though she had been granted an extra sense. And Pauline could see nothing but an awful vulnerability. The blazing expectation in Teresa's face made her seem like a child again – a child up against the treachery of circumstance.

Down below, a door bangs. Maurice has come out of the cottage. Pauline watches him head for his car, get in, start the engine, back up and out on to the track. He drives off, rather too fast. Where is he going? The morning's work does not prosper, presumably. And Maurice is forever restless. He will take off, suddenly, without saying why or whither. I never know where he is, says Teresa placidly.

Right now, Pauline guesses, he is probably heading for the village to get an extra newspaper, or to satisfy some other need. She dismisses Maurice, and turns at last to her mail: the electricity bill, her bank statement, payment for an editorial job, two charity appeals and that airmail envelope with the California postmark.

Chapter Four

The postman's weather bulletin is accurate, as usual. There are cloudless skies on Saturday. It is a blue and green May morning, there is a crisp and sparkling landscape. Pauline, coming outside after breakfast, decides to set to and do something about her front garden – the small area in front of the cottage at each side of the path to the door. She is a desultory gardener, spurred into activity by spring and apathetic for the rest of the year. As a result of this the two beds are a confusion of overgrown plants – leggy lavender, a rose in need of pruning, a potentilla half-smothered by goosegrass, and a rich growth of couch grass swarming up through everything. Pauline inspects this and experiences the familiar seasonal burst of resolution. She fetches her gardening implements and gets going with the sun on her back and the wind in her hair, a businesslike figure in cord trousers and a baggy sweater.

Thus it is that Pauline is hard at work when a car comes shining down the track towards World's End. She has forgotten the expected arrival of Maurice's weekend guests. Of course, she thinks – them. And here is Teresa, coming out with Luke to wave and greet. Maurice has not yet seen or heard, presumably, up in his study.

'This'll be James and Carol,' says Teresa. 'You've been busy. I must do something about our bit, too. Unless . . .'

Teresa too is a perfunctory gardener.

'All right,' says Pauline. 'If I don't run out of steam.

You've hardly got anything there worth keeping anyway. If I dig it over you could put in some annuals.'

The car has pulled up. Its occupants get out.

'Whew!' says James Saltash. '"Fairly isolated", Maurice said. He didn't mention the half-mile drive across a cornfield.'

He is in his mid-thirties, tall and gangling, with black hair that flops over one eye. His companion barely reaches his shoulder. She has straight gold hair with a fringe cropped like a child's. A trim figure nicely displayed by a tight black top tucked into a long green skirt. Thonged sandals, bare legs – an outfit a little too summery for the day, which looks warmer than it is. The town-dweller's mistake, thinks Pauline idly, observing. She would like to get back to what she is doing, but it might look rude to do this immediately.

'Not half a *mile*,' says Teresa, smiling reproachfully. 'But it is a bit bumpy, I'm afraid. Anyway, you've found us . . .'

'Gorgeous place,' states Carol. She has surveyed her sur-roundings. She beams at Teresa, and now at Maurice, who has emerged from the cottage.

'Hi, James. Hi, Carol,' says Maurice. 'This is Pauline, Teresa's mother.'

'Hello,' says Carol. The beam loses its intensity. She is not interested in someone's mother, it would seem.

'And Luke.'

Carol dabs a finger at Luke's cheek. She is not much inter-ested in babies either, by the look of it.

'Have you got a plaster handy?' says James. 'Carol went for a pee in some primitive loo at a garage we stopped at and gashed her leg on a rusty pipe.'

Carol lifts her skirt to show a slick of dried blood across her calf. 'I'm being incredibly brave,' she says.

'I've got antiseptic and things in the kitchen,' says Teresa. 'Come in. Mum – could you hold Luke for a minute?'

They all go inside. Teresa pulls a chair out from the table, and Carol sits. Teresa hunts in the kitchen drawer. 'Here we are. Plaster. Savlon. Better wash it first.' She produces a bowl of water and cotton wool.

Carol is the centre of attention. Even Luke is marginalized, gazing warily at these invading strangers. Carol props her leg on another chair, while James, on his knees, wipes the wound. Carol protests, laughing. *'Ouch!* James, you're being absolutely brutal. Ow!'

Maurice steps forward. He squats down. 'James, if I may say so you're making the most awful hash of this. Here . . .'

And thus it is Maurice who bathes Carol's cut, and applies the antiseptic and the plaster. He does the job with surprising efficiency, given his usual ineptness. James hangs over Carol, talking worriedly now of tetanus jabs.

'James, don't mother me,' says Carol, laughing across at Teresa.

Maurice completes the task. He lays his hand for an instant on Carol's knee, without looking at her, and says lightly, as though calming a child, 'There, all better now.' He turns to James. 'Did you by any chance remember to bring a copy of Defoe?'

'Sure did,' says James. 'Plus one or two other things I thought might come in handy. I'll bring our stuff in from the car, shall I?'

The men go outside. Carol starts to tell Teresa about this extraordinary procession of antique cars they passed on the motorway, breaks off to call to James to bring her sweater off the back seat, please, resumes her account of the cars . . . dozens of them, is there some sort of rally going on somewhere, would it be fun to go? Teresa is wearing the stiff expression that means that she is not quite at her ease. How well does she know this Carol? Pauline wonders. Luke is agitating to be put down. Pauline sees her opportunity to escape,

39

releases Luke, raises an eyebrow at Teresa and moves towards the door.

'Oh ...' says Teresa, breaking into Carol's flow. 'See you tonight, then. My mother's coming over for supper.'

Carol glimmers briefly at Pauline. 'Oh ... right.'

Pauline returns to her gardening. James Saltash takes a break from hefting possessions out of the car and comes over to say that he remembers they met once at ... where, now? The London Book Fair, could it have been? And Pauline too vaguely remembers some passing introduction over a drink. She and James chat for a few moments, and Pauline glimpses the personality that accompanies the awkward stooping frame and the unruly black hair – a rather disarming combination of diffidence and enthusiasm, like a dog uncertain of its reception. A nice guy, thinks Pauline, but not Maurice's type really, I'd have thought. Does he have the measure of Maurice, I wonder, or is he just an acolyte? Maurice does rather go in for acolytes. And what about this young woman? Her with the Dora Carrington hairstyle?

James disappears into the cottage. Pauline applies herself to the bedraggled rose, which is a thicket of dead wood. She forgets the visitors as she snips and tweaks, thinking of Harry, which is unusual, she hardly ever thinks directly of Harry. But of course there was that letter. She has not yet got around to mentioning to Teresa that there was a letter from her father.

When Pauline thinks of Harry it is always the Harry of then, not now. The Harry of today – unthinkable and un-reachable – is on another plane of existence, and Pauline is not much interested. Somewhere out there on the west coast of the United States Harry is walking and talking, wowing his California students with his laid-back British style, driving some sleek automobile up the driveway of his sprawling white house, getting into bed at night with his wife Nadia who is thirty-nine and teaches Creative Writing. Pauline cannot conceive of this Harry, nor does she wish to. He does not concern her. Teresa has visited Harry in California – has stepped off into that other plane of existence, has stayed in the sprawling white house and later released to Pauline tactful anodyne nuggets of information: the vibrant flowers that grow in Californian gardens, the ubiquitous swimming pools, Harry's flowered Bermuda shorts. She treads carefully. Pauline is aware of Teresa's anxious eyes, trying to assess the effect of what she is saying. She does not want Pauline to be upset. Reminded of what happened. Made jealous.

And Pauline is more moved by Teresa's anxiety than by any potent whiff of Harry. She would like to be able to say – don't worry, it isn't anything to do with me, all this. Him, now. Her, who is neither here nor there so far as I'm concerned. I'm not jealous. And I can't be reminded of something that has never stopped happening. That happens all over again, at bad times. And I can't be jealous now – who once was a jealousy expert. Who knew every refinement of jealousy, every nuance, every convoluted ingenious twist of the jealousy business. But she cannot talk thus to Teresa, because she never has done. Instead, she inquires keenly about the beaches, the shopping malls, the climate, and sees Teresa's relief that the minefield has been negotiated.

Today Harry's voice, his writing on an envelope, that California postmark, induce merely irritation. He has no power now – he is defused, unmanned. He is probably aware of this, and is accordingly offended. So he makes contact thus, tries to firm up a line between them. Pauline knows quite well what he would like. He would like a relationship that is subtly clandestine – a late flirtation with melancholy overtones. She has heard the proposition in his voice, has read it between the lines of his letters. And she has been filled with nothing more than mild outrage. Oh no, she has thought, oh dear me no.

She sees Harry now as some feckless child whose excesses prompt weary boredom. He has become a shadow Harry – the potent Harry is the one who exists only in her head. This Harry, the forever emotive Harry, is lodged there for ever in some crevice of the mind, to come looming up and stop her in her tracks. He looks at her across a breakfast table. 'So . . .' he says. 'Surprise, surprise.' He rears above her in the bed, looking down with eyes that do not see her. He turns from an open window and says, 'I'm sorry, Pauline. These things happen. There's nothing you can do.' Harry has gone, long since, but is forever there.

The rose is now tamed. Pauline straightens up, surveys her garden, satisfied, and goes inside. Later she will dig over Teresa's bit. Teresa has quite enough on her plate this weekend.

The day tips over into afternoon. Pauline is busy. Once she glances out of her bedroom window and sees Teresa in the garden with Carol. Teresa is occupied with Luke; Carol sits on a rug with a newspaper in her hand and her face tilted towards the sun. Maurice and James are presumably closeted upstairs with Maurice's manuscript.

That evening, Teresa serves roast lamb, followed by fruit salad. They eat in the kitchen. World's End blinks and hums around them, its appliances in fine fettle. Outside, there is quiet. Just the sound of the wind in the hedge and, if you listen hard, the distant murmur of traffic on the main road. By the time they reach the cheese course Maurice has opened a third bottle of wine.

Teresa is wearing what she has worn all day (the shoulder of her shirt is dappled with food stains – evidence of Luke). So do the men. Pauline has put on a different sweater. Carol has changed into cream silk pants with loose apricot tunic top and a pair of hanging silver disc earrings. Her face is tinged with pink. James, looking at her fondly across the table, says, 'You've caught the sun, you know.'

'I meant to. That's what you come to the country for, isn't it?'

'This is a great place,' says James to Pauline. 'How long have you been here?'

Pauline tells how she acquired World's End, ten years ago. Hitherto, the conversation has centred upon Maurice's book. Maurice has been entertaining about some of the issues raised. He has been quizzical and provocative about his exhaustive examination of contemporary museum strategy. There has been an animated discussion about what the book should be called – *Profit from the Past* is the putative title right now, apparently.

'I aspire to somewhere like this,' says James. 'You don't know if it's summer or winter, stuck in London all the year round.'

'Ah,' says Maurice. 'Interesting.' He gives James a thoughtful look. 'You feel better in the country, then?'

'Well, yes – of course.'

'Why?'

'Fresh air,' says James. 'Space. All that.'

'Closer to nature?'

James is wary now. 'If you want to put it like that. Surely most people feel that way, at some point or another?'

'Of course,' says Maurice. 'We all do. Deep conditioning. Centuries of cunning sales talk, from Chaucer to Wordsworth.'

Carol laughs appreciatively. James looks a trifle put out. He helps himself to another glass of wine and says he's glad to hear he's not the only one to have been sold the natural scene, and he'd still fancy a place like this if it came his way.

'Tedious stuff, nature,' says Maurice. 'A process of weary repetition. The ultimate conservatism.' He is a little drunk, Pauline realizes. Nothing unusual. Maurice drinks a fair amount, fairly often.

Carol laughs again. 'That's original.' She too is perhaps a little tipsy. She is enjoying herself, anyway, that is clear.

'No,' says Pauline. 'It's been said before. Anti-romanticism, that's all.'

'You're a rotten cynic, Maurice,' says James amiably. He seems to have recovered his good humour, if it was ever really lost.

Teresa now turns from the sink, where she has been stacking plates. 'Maurice is showing off, I'll have you know. He woke me up this morning to tell me to listen to the cuckoo.' There is an uncharacteristic asperity here, both in tone and content. Only Maurice and Pauline are aware of this. Maurice appears uninterested. Pauline takes note.

'Ooh . . . you fraud, Maurice,' says Carol.

Maurice grins – undismayed, it would seem. He drinks some wine, and looks around the table. 'Everyone all set for Bradley Castle tomorrow?'

'Definitely,' says Carol. 'It sounds hilarious. Can we go to the Medieval Feast?'

'Only available on Saturday nights, alas,' says Maurice. 'We shall have to make do with the Robin Hood Experience. Ten o'clock start, Pauline?'

'No thanks,' says Pauline firmly. She rises. 'I have other things in mind, I'm afraid – you'll have to excuse me. And I'm off to bed now. Goodnight, all.'

Outside, she pauses for a moment on the track. It is a fine night, with a quarter moon hanging above the hill – insubstantial, like a scrap of paper. At various points the blue-black sky flames with orange, just above the horizon, marking the nearest centres of population. World's End itself stands amid the dark mass of the fields, glowing with light, incandescent, inviting. There is no other light to be seen, except the occasional moving beam from the road. Pauline goes inside and locks her door.

When first she began to use the cottage, at weekends and for holidays, she was a little worried about the isolation. So far, the only intrusion has been the theft of a lawnmower from the outside shed when Pauline was absent. The thieves were presumably deterred from having a go at World's End itself by the prominently displayed burglar alarm which links the cottages to the police station. The police attributed the theft dismissively to local boys, and the shed is now kept padlocked.

The burglar alarm often surprises visitors, fresh from the perils of the inner city. 'Here?' they say, looking round at the placid landscape. There is an assumption that tranquillity of scene must reflect a comparable muting of criminal propensities. Presumably they expect the occasional outbreak of apple scrumping, to be dealt with by a village bobby on a bike. The countryside, for some, is still locked into a time warp, a benign nirvana of eternal summer in which you might come across a party of hikers in shorts having a picnic by a haystack, under the blue skies and puffy clouds of a Shell poster.

Maurice, of course, pounces with glee on such nostalgic misconceptions. His concern though is with the fostering of such mythologies in the interests of commercial exploitation. Pauline is more taken with the gulf between the image of the country and the actuality, perhaps always more startling to those who live there for the wrong reasons, themselves duped by the truth. The countryside is a landscape of mayhem, and always has been – a place in which birds and animals are being shot, strangled, chased or dug up and bashed to bits. The countryside is deeply traditional, as is well known, and these are the deep traditions. One can of course be thankful that nowadays beggars are no longer dying in ditches or foundlings being abandoned in churchyards. Inhumanity flourishes still, but at least there is official mitigation of conspicuous distress. Even the hunted foxes and the battered badgers have their lobby, for what it's worth.

On Saturday nights the local young go marauding in the agreeable centre of Hadbury – '. . . no. 14 High St (now Barclays Bank) of mid18c, with handsome portico, the Ship Inn late 17c with mullioned windows and some pargeted plasterwork . . .': Pevsner. Mainly they smash car windows and throw beer cans at shop fronts. Last month a posse of youths intent upon destroying the façade of the Co-op with a hammer were interrupted by a sixty-one-year-old man who was unwise enough to remonstrate with them. Affronted, the lads turned the hammer on him instead. He was beaten unconscious and remains in hospital with fractured skull and multiple injuries.

Pauline reads of such things in the local paper, alongside accounts of school fêtes and wrangles about planning permissions. A photo of laughing toddlers in the paddling pool donated by the Rotary Association is lined up beside another of the heap of compacted metal which records the latest pile-up on the main road which runs through the valley – the World's End valley, the valley of the wheat field and the hill crowned by a line of trees. The road is an old road with single lanes, too narrow for the volume of traffic it now carries, traffic heading north for such places as Birmingham and Coventry as well as the vehicles of local residents like Chaundy, making his way from one industrial enterprise to another, or Pauline, heading for Hadbury to do her shopping. Tourist coaches ply the road, going to Stratford. The ranks of heads swivel as the coach passes through the valley, its occupants riding high above the landscape that they observe through tinted glass from their air-conditioned container. And what do they see? A landscape that is beautiful? Or quaint? Or merely alien? Is their attention seized by buildings, or the crops grown, or the names on road signs or the logo of the Happy Eater on the roundabout?

Pauline has lived in many places. She does not consider herself as deriving from anywhere in particular. Her voice does not define her, as it defines many of the people in these parts. She grew up on the south coast, at Worthing, where her father had a medical practice. Subsequently, she has lived where circumstances have taken her. A northern university. A job in Manchester. During the Harry years she was in the south again, living in the cathedral town which found itself host to one of the new universities of the day, at which Harry was a rising star. Harry was in the right trade at the right time. Academia had become fashionable all of a sudden. The academic was no longer a shabby figure, respectable and profoundly tedious, but a bright and brittle fellow beloved of the media, game for television discussion programmes and swingeing pieces in Sunday newspapers. The student was born, as opposed to the undergraduate. And Harry was the man to seize the moment. He revelled in it. He was in demand everywhere. His particular line of popular history struck a fashionable note. The Americans got to hear of him – there was a sabbatical term at Harvard, jaunts to conferences in California. He played the system, juggled with job offers, and swarmed the promotional ladder. Senior Lecturer, Reader, Professor at thirty-eight.

And thus Pauline has learnt to acclimatize, to live in a leafy suburb or a city street, to up sticks and move on when need arises. She has preferred some homes to others, but is not fettered by bricks and mortar. She now divides her time between her London flat and World's End, suiting inclination and convenience. She can work from either place, with equal ease.

She thinks about all this, lying in bed waiting for sleep, a little too keyed up by wine and talk. She thinks of the anachronistic shell around her, the accommodating stone which slips imperviously from century to century. She thinks of all those others who must have sought sleep in this room – or fell into it, most likely, clobbered by toil. It is midnight, and she is restless, thinking no longer of the place or the people but stirred by something nameless, some apprehension she could not possibly identify. She switches on her bedside lamp, and the room is filled and warmed by its dusky light. She turns on the radio: the newsreader is talking of events in India, in the United States, in the Philippines. The world is at her fingertips, here at World's End. She can sense it, reaching away out there, in darkness and in light, empty spaces and seething cities, all of it talking, talking.

Once, in another time, she drove across the United States with Harry. The trip seemed to go on for weeks. Now, it is reduced in her head to conflicting impressions of space and intimacy. The infinite horizons and that endless road vanishing beneath the bonnet of the car, sliding up once more in the rear-view mirror. The car itself, bulbous and finned, an exotic monster. The blanket of trees in New England, wheat fields the size of an English county, canyons, mountains. The faces and voices of people in motels and petrol stations. The car radio was their lifeline, their access to this astounding and mysterious place through which they crept. Its voices sang and babbled hour after hour, seeming outrageous, sophisticated, absurd and unreachable. They felt as though they had arrived on another planet. Pauline was twenty-two. Harry was a year older, working on his doctorate, heady with achievement and ambition. Each night they fell on to the bed in sleazy motel rooms and made ferocious love. Pauline would wake to stifling dawns on mangled sheets that reeked of sex, hearing bizarre bird sounds from beyond the window. At three o'clock one morning, somewhere in Colorado, Harry said, 'We'll get married in the autumn, shall we?' He lay smoking a post-orgasmic cigarette, his hand resting friendly on her crotch. 'I'm crazy about this country,' he said. 'One day I'm going to fetch up here, for keeps.'

Pauline switches off the Radio Four news and extinguishes the world. Now she is alone again with the sounds of the night – the distant rumble of an aircraft, the wind in the apple trees. She consigns Harry to another night in Colorado, more than thirty years ago. She hears a window open next door – someone else is awake, restless.

Chapter Five

'The Robin Hood Experience was really stupid,' says Teresa. 'You walked through this wood and people in fancy dress kept bobbing up among the trees and shooting arrows at each other.'

'Do they hit?'

'Oh, no. And anyway they weren't proper arrows. James picked one up and it had a rubber tip. There were horses, too. Luke enjoyed that. Maurice loved it, of course.'

'From a scholarly point of view, presumably?'

'Oh yes. He's doing a whole section on these over-the-top tourist places.'

Pauline and Teresa are driving to Hadbury. Teresa needs a sun hat for Luke and some household things. Pauline must stock up on fax paper. She wants also to replace a cracked glass shelf in her bathroom cabinet and to buy a new toaster. Hadbury will supply all these requirements. Luke has fallen conveniently asleep in his car seat as they move from the World's End track to the main road and thence past the corn fields and the sprout fields and the oilseed rape and the ochre stretches of set-aside, the villages and the petrol stations and the Happy Eaters until at last they reach the maze of roads and road signs that indicate that they have arrived at the market town.

Hadbury is held in a vice of ring roads, bypasses and industrial estates. In the centre of this expansive layout – roundabouts, dual carriageways and an acreage of tarmac – crouches the town itself, with its market cross, its two churches and its high street of prosperous eighteenth-century houses, most of them now doing duty as banks or building societies. This nucleus is quite eclipsed by a satellite empire, tidily signposted at each outlying roundabout: Willow Way Industrial Estate, Oxpens Hypermarket, Meadowlands Trading Estate. Plenty of room out here – a glittering savannah of car parks, encircled by ranch-emporia. Tesco, Allied Carpets, Comet, Homecare. It is as though the original town were now protectively encased within this *cordon sanitaire* of commerce, preserved as a curiosity though patently long past its sell-by date.

It is for this discredited centre that Pauline heads, ignoring the allure of the tarmac savannahs. She achieves a parking space. Luke is decanted from the car, put into his buggy, and they set off for Businesslines and Mothercare, both of which are slotted into the redevelopment of the Buttermarket. Hadbury is active, even on this Monday morning. The pedestrian precinct at its heart is busy with people – most of them women, most of them young, many of them pushing a buggy. Pauline and Teresa fit nicely; there are similar groups all around – mother, daughter and small child out shopping. Babies and toddlers on all sides – lolling asleep under sun canopies, gazing regal from frilled pillows, lurching along the pavement or carried in slings.

'I thought there was supposed to be a fertility problem these days,' says Pauline.

Teresa agrees that this is not evident in Hadbury. 'Maybe the country's different.'

'Ah,' says Pauline. 'Urban blight again.'

For something has happened to reproduction, it seems. The sperm count of the European male has significantly declined. Young women no longer conceive as a result of one kind look. Or some young women don't. Teresa's friends sail childless through their twenties and then fly into a panic as they hit thirty. Their child-bearing years are ebbing away and now that they are good and ready nothing happens. They fail to get pregnant, month by month. It is all the fault of the pill, apparently. The great good pill, which has bared its teeth and turned nasty on the women it once saved.

Listen, Pauline says to Teresa and her friends, you think you've got problems? What do you imagine it was like for us? Always in a stew about getting pregnant. Checking your pants every half hour if your period was a day overdue. And then the pill came along and straight away they start muttering that it'll give you blood clots and you'll die at forty. So you've got to choose between babies or an early death. Some of us have *never* taken the pill.

And they look at her blankly. The climate of anxiety is as fickle as sartorial fashion, she sees. They cannot know about the freight that word once carried. Pregnant. To be spoken fearfully to a girlfriend. Confessed to a parent. Owned up to at clinics and doctors' surgeries. If these young women are pregnant they say so, loud and clear. It is a physical condition, not a state of mind.

She says to Harry, 'I'm pregnant.'

He looks at her. She cannot tell from his expression what he thinks or feels. She could have been announcing that she was off out to the corner shop.

'You're pregnant?' he says. 'Well, well, well. What happened?'

They have been married for eleven months.

'What *happened*! What on earth do you mean?'

'You've been using a diaphragm, haven't you?'

She stares at him. She realizes that she is talking about one thing and he about another.

'They sometimes fail, don't they?' she says. 'Eighty per cent reliable, that's all.'

52

'So . . .' says Harry. 'Surprise, surprise.' He reaches for the coffee pot, fills his cup, waves the pot questioningly over hers.

After a moment she says, 'I'm having a baby, Harry. A child.'

Teresa is manoeuvring the buggy through the open doors of Mothercare. They move amid a forest of tiny garments – Babygros striped like rugby shirts, miniature boiler suits, doll-size anoraks and parkas. Infancy is a serious matter, today. Beyond are thickets of equipment – cots and buggies and high chairs and playpens.

'And another thing,' says Pauline. 'What's become of abortionists? There's a whole profession been wiped out. They were everywhere, time was.'

Teresa has paused to inspect a display of sun hats. She shoots Pauline a reproving glance. A Hadbury granny is observing them through a rack of minute trainers.

Pauline lowers her voice a notch. 'There were two kinds. There were cheapo ones who hung out in flats south of the river or semis in Enfield or Hackney. Cheap and nasty, you took your life in your hands. Anyone who possibly could – who could scrape together a hundred pounds or more – went to one of the bent doctors. Brass plate and a West End address. A hundred pounds was a hell of a lot of money, then. The world was full of people running around desperately trying to raise a hundred quid. Cash, on the spot, in pound notes in a plain envelope. Hand it to the receptionist when you arrive.'

Teresa looks up from the small dome of navy denim that she is examining. 'God . . .' Then, 'How d'you know all this, Mum?'

'Oh, everyone knew,' says Pauline. 'And you can't put that thing on Luke. It's more suitable for a baseball player than a baby.'

They find an acceptable sun hat. And a couple of T-shirts untarnished by either teddy bears or the logo of sports equipment. They pay, and move out again into the Buttermarket.

They go into Businesslines, where Pauline stocks up. Luke is by now complaining, and is plugged into a bottle of juice while they sit for a while on the bench in the centre of the shopping precinct.

'I forgot to tell you,' says Pauline. 'I had a letter from Harry.'

They have referred to him thus for many a year. 'Your father' seems either accusatory or inappropriately formal. And Teresa abandoned 'Dad' long ago.

Teresa busies herself with Luke, whose nose needs wiping. Her expression is guarded. 'Oh?'

'He's coming over this summer,' says Pauline. 'He'll be in London for a couple of weeks. He hopes to see you. He'll give you a ring when he's got his dates fixed, he says.'

Teresa frowns slightly. 'We're going to be down here, really. Not in London.'

What Pauline does not mention is that Harry was putting out a feeler in her direction also. A delicate and cautious feeler. Could you maybe manage a lunch or a dinner while I'm over? She will of course ignore this feeler, will allow it to wither as she has allowed other similar approaches to wither. He never learns, does Harry. Or maybe he still believes in his infallible persuasive powers.

'This summer is crucial for Maurice,' Teresa tells her mother. 'If he can get all his rewriting done, and check his references, and then work on the introduction and the bibliography, then they may be able to get it to the printers this autumn. So the summer's vital, really.'

'Hmn . . .' says Pauline. And then, 'It's only a book.'

Teresa is shocked. 'Well,' she begins, 'I should have thought you, of all people . . .'

'On the contrary,' says Pauline. 'I have *no* respect for print. I know where it comes from.'

Teresa looks sceptical and Pauline laughs. 'Don't worry, love – I'll keep my heretical opinions to myself. Are those two coming down again this weekend?'

'I'm not sure. I think probably not till the one after.'

'Just as well,' says Pauline. 'You're not going to want them round your neck *all* the time.'

Teresa is defensive. 'I don't mind. I like them. And otherwise Maurice would keep having to go up to London. This is much more cost-effective, time-wise.'

'You're picking up the most appalling language,' grumbles Pauline.

The voice of James, she suspects – amiable James. Maurice would never stoop to that. He is much too fastidious. Maurice avoids all that is modish, and thus achieves an idiosyncratic personal stylishness that is somehow outside the expectations of contemporary manners.

'You'd better not let Maurice hear you talking like that,' she adds.

But Teresa has had enough of this conversation. She straps Luke into the buggy once more and proposes that they should get on with what they have to do.

Teresa never talks to Pauline about Maurice, except in the most practical sense – to report decisions, opinions, actions. And very proper too, thinks Pauline – who wants that dire traditional feminine conspiracy? No doubt right now all over Hadbury young women are complaining to older ones about their menfolk, and listening to competing accusations in return. She thinks momentarily of her own mother, to whom she never spoke of Harry. Except once, just once.

And Teresa is in love, of course. Each time Pauline is reminded of this she shivers. It is as though she herself stood on some safe shore and watched Teresa struggling in the surf.

She observes Teresa's state with awful recognition. She knows what Teresa is feeling and knows that Teresa would not for one instant wish to feel otherwise. Teresa is happy, gloriously happy. Of course she cannot talk about Maurice. Maurice is not a person but a climate. He is beyond comment or criticism.

'. . . frozen yoghurt?' says Teresa.

'Sorry?'

They are in Marks and Spencer, surveying a food cabinet.

'I said have you ever tried frozen yoghurt? Instead of ice-cream.'

They discuss frozen yoghurt, briefly. Luke is now in a condition of continuous protest. He has had enough of this expedition. He writhes and roars and weeps. He is a soul in torment, you would think, not someone who is merely bored and tired. And Pauline thinks with wonder of that forgotten turmoil of the emotions. There he is – he shares their days but lives elsewhere, in a place of flaring sensibility, in which anguish supplants ecstasy minute by minute. How can it be endured, survived – this switchback of feeling? Or is it perhaps a violent training for what is to come? A brutal education – a frenetic, accelerated version of what lies ahead.

Pauline realizes that she has not cried for years. Well . . . the occasional tear of sentiment, perhaps. But not real, raw, bleeding tears of pain. She has not sobbed herself into exhaustion, seen her face red and swollen, tasted the salt of misery. Not for years. And does this mean that she has been unremittingly content? That she has coasted along in a state of emotional neutrality? Of course not. Nor does it mean that the fires are banked. It means simply that you weep less frequently as you get older.

And now Luke is suddenly asleep. He has slipped from passion to oblivion, slumped there in the buggy. Pauline and

Teresa are able to complete their shopping in relative tranquillity and head for home.

Maurice is outside the cottage when they arrive. They can see him from afar, standing there holding the portable phone. There is tall grass on the track now which brushes the underside of the car with the sound of rushing water. The car surges through the young wheat and arrives at this island, this haven above which hangs a lark, bubbling invisible in the blue morning. Pauline switches off the car engine, and then there is just the lark.

And Maurice, who says, 'Had a good time, girls?'

He is in high good humour, they see, and this is said to tease. Neither Teresa nor Pauline rise to the bait. Teresa eyes the phone. 'Did someone ring?'

'People are always ringing,' says Maurice. 'When do they ever not ring?' He stands there, exuding well-being, until Teresa proposes that he should help carry things in. He moves at once to do so, he is all compliance. He puts the phone down on the garden wall and gives her a smile that displays compunction, apology, affection – a smile that is designed to disarm, and does so. Pauline sees Teresa's body relax. Teresa's back is turned towards her so she cannot see her expression but she knows how Teresa is looking, how her face will have softened, how her eyes will seem larger as she absorbs Maurice's smile, as she basks before it.

Pauline gathers up her shopping from the car and goes into her cottage, closing the door behind her. She puts her bags down on the kitchen table and stands there distracted, as though she were listening to something. She is no longer at World's End, it would seem. Some long arm has reached out and dragged her elsewhere, and what she sees or hears has made her face taut and pinched.

She stands thus amid the tranquil kitchen sounds and then the moment passes and she is back again, unpacking the new toaster, stowing food in the fridge. The green digits on the front of the cooker have marked up a few seconds, that's all. Nothing has happened here except the passage of time, and, for Pauline, some echo from elsewhere.

The builder's men who gutted World's End turned up various pieces of detritus which they produced for her inspection. The bowl of a clay pipe, shards of Victorian china, metal buttons. These fragments are now in a bowl on the kitchen dresser, filmed with dust and oddly tenacious. It would be unthinkable to throw them away – and yet someone once did. Discarded, lost, in the midst of busy lives. And hanging on stubbornly today in the little Italian majolica bowl on the middle shelf of Pauline's pine dresser.

The dresser was bought from a dealer who specialized in touring Ireland in order to purchase outmoded furniture from country folk at knock-down prices. It had been taken to bits, dunked in some aggressive chemical bath, reassembled and tricked out with new brass handles. It is a useful object and pleasing enough to look at but has to Pauline no particular resonance beyond the price she paid for it and the struggle there was to get it into the room. The majolica bowl, on the other hand, is loaded. The majolica bowl has been in her possession for nearly forty years.

When Pauline was eighteen she went with a girlfriend to Italy during the summer before she was due to start at university. Neither she nor her friend had been abroad before without their parents. Pauline was an only child. Her adolescence had been anxiously supervised by her mother, who had little else to do. Pauline did not see much of her father, a busy doctor, and had a restless and often barbed relationship with a mother whose approach to life was one of deep caution and mistrust. All her mother's energies were devoted to sidestepping the malevolence of fate. You avoided unnecessary car journeys for fear of accidents. You dosed yourself unrelentingly with prophylactics. You were wary in your dealings with others, lest you fall in with those who might make demands or turn out to be undesirable associates. It was a stance that had exasperated Pauline at eight, never mind at eighteen. Why can't I? she cried, throughout her childhood. Why shouldn't I? Her own efforts were concentrated upon outflanking her mother, upon finding ways to circumvent the restrictions imposed, upon living instead of holding life at bay.

The trip to Italy took place after interminable arguments and negotiations. Eventually Pauline's mother capitulated, with the extraction of various promises. No hitch-hiking. Cash and documents to be strapped to the person at all times. Never become separated.

As they moved south the girls felt themselves ripen and expand. By the time they reached Naples they were tanned and exuberant, on the rampage, heady with sun and food and cheap wine, with their own bouncing hormones and the admiring glances of young men. Pauline's friend, who had been considered rather fast at school, said, 'I can't seem to think about anything but sex,' and Pauline nodded. After that it was unspoken, but understood. They allowed themselves to be picked up – with circumspection at first and then with increasing abandon. They dallied with a couple of German students at Pompeii, but found them insufficiently compelling and dropped them. And then, on a beach, they took up with a pair of Italians. Charming. Attentive. And ultimately irresistible. For two days the four of them flirted and skirmished in and out of the sea, in the local cafés, on the steps of the girls' cheap hotel. On the third evening, by tacit agreement, they split up into two couples.

Pauline was a virgin. Her school friend thought she probably was, but there was an element of doubt. Afterwards, they did not compare notes but spent the rest of the holiday waiting in terror for their periods. When the friend was reprieved first, bouncing out of the lavatory in the *rapido* to

Milan to say, 'I'm OK! I'm OK!' Pauline almost hated her. She had found this initial sexual experience as disappointing as tradition demanded, but could see that the process could have definite possibilities. She was torn between the excitement of this perception and the panic about her awaited period. Which arrived at last on her first day back home, just after she had arranged upon her dressing table the majolica bowl bought her as a memento by the Italian youth whose features she could no longer remember.

Thus the majolica bowl, which has somehow clung on all her life, as a repository for paper clips or rubber bands, and now for these archaeological trifles. It would be forever associated not so much with the vibrant young Italian who gave it to her as with her own surge of relief when she knew she had got away with it, she was not pregnant, she did not have to pay the price. She had arrived home in a state of jitters, hardly able to speak to her mother, who hung around her lynx-eyed, knowing something was up. And the next day she had been aglow with relief, a new woman, life stretching rosy ahead. Had her mother wondered, guessed?

Pauline understands her mother's feelings now. She understood them long ago, in that moment of astonished insight when she held her own child and realized that there is a further dimension to love. The perception did not bring her any closer to her mother, whose assumptions and expectations were so far removed from her own as to create an unbridgeable chasm. But she was able to see why her mother had behaved as she had, why she lived in a state of perpetual dread. That Italian holiday must have cost her dear. And of course her worst fears had been realized, as she may have suspected. Well – perhaps not quite her worst fears. There are greater catastrophes than lost virginity.

Today at World's End the majolica bowl is not an echo to halt Pauline in her tracks so much as a continuous low murmur. It has the insistent subliminal hum of a physical object that has survived from then to now and continues quietly to reverberate. Pauline registers this reverberation as she moves the bowl to one side in search of the key to the window lock, which should also be here on the middle shelf . . . And yes, here it is, lurking behind a postcard of San Francisco, sent by Hugh, off on some book-related expedition earlier in the year. She opens the small window at the side of the room, which has not been opened yet this summer, and the sound of that lark comes flooding in. Along with the banshee wail of a police car on the main road and the throb of an invisible tractor somewhere beyond the brow of the hill. Pauline's kitchen resounds from within and without, as she moves around preparing herself some lunch – washing a lettuce at the sink, chopping a tomato, thinking of neither the majolica bowl nor the tractor but of the manuscript on her desk, at which she must work this afternoon.

Chapter Six

'Odd to see Maurice as a *père de famille*,' says James.

'If that's what he is,' says Pauline.

They are driving to Worsham. The party has split up, because there is not room for all of them in one car. Pauline has joined the outing without enthusiasm. She knows Worsham – a tourist honeypot, which is of course why Maurice wants to look it over. But she has not left World's End for the best part of a week, and it is a fine day, and Maurice is insidiously persuasive. He has this curious need for an entourage. He likes company – the more of it the better. And as they milled around the cars, installing Luke in his car seat, settling who would drive, Maurice elected that Pauline should be James's passenger, since she knew the way.

'Well, I suppose one baby doesn't make a *famille*.'

That was not what Pauline meant, but she lets it pass.

'Actually, I'm rather beginning to see the point of children myself,' James tells Pauline. 'Not right away, maybe – but in due course.'

Oh dear, thinks Pauline. In that case you'd better consider a change of partner. In due course.

She is beginning to warm to James and suspects regretfully that he is an innocent, which means that he may get a bashing in his profession, one which becomes rougher by the year. He works as editorial director of an imprint that is under the umbrella of one of the big conglomerates.

'No hurry,' continues James comfortably. 'Of course

it was a bit different for Maurice. He's forty-four, after all.'

'As I understand it, the human male is capable of reproduction well into the seventies.'

James shoots her a sideways glance, unsure how to take this. 'All the same, most of us would prefer not to put it off quite as long as that.'

The roads are busy, on this high summer Sunday, and they have lost sight of Maurice's car, which is somewhere ahead. Large numbers of people appear to be cruising the landscape in search of diversion. And everywhere there are banners and hoardings by the roadside which announce what is on offer – rural fayre, clay-pigeon shoot, self-pick strawberries. Half the population apparently earns its living providing the other half with something to do. Pauline points this out to James, who leaps upon the point with enthusiasm.

'Exactly. So Maurice's book is absolutely right for now. It'll be one of our lead titles for next autumn. Provided we can get it into production in time. If the TV angle works out this could be an important book. Which is why I'm hanging around Maurice this summer. Make sure he keeps at it. Maurice does rather tend to get distracted – shoot off after some new interest.'

'I'd noticed,' says Pauline.

'It's part of his fascination, of course. That ability to get hooked on the most unexpected things. And then write a clever book about it. We have a hunch he's going places, Maurice.'

Pauline asks James how long he has known Maurice. She sees that he is under the Maurice spell.

'He came to talk to us about the book three years ago, when he was just getting his ideas together, and of course we jumped at it. It's been one of the best things that's come my way, working with Maurice.'

'Go right . . .' Pauline interjects. 'We're nearly there.'

James turns off on to another road and into another line of traffic. 'HarperCollins are doing it in the States. They're really keen. The American section of the book is strong – he's got some sharp stuff on historic theme parks. Very witty, very Maurice. It's going to be a strong book – I'm really excited about it.'

Oh, books, books . . . thinks Pauline. Pernicious things.

'I once started to burn a book,' she says. 'In typescript.'

James glances sideways at her, startled.

'Don't ever breathe a word, or I'll be done for, professionally.'

'I swear. Why did you only start to burn it?'

'Deep conditioning got the better of me.'

'Whose book was it?'

'My husband's. Former husband.'

'Oh,' James sounds disappointed. 'I thought it would have been one of your authors.'

'Better go left here,' says Pauline. 'There's a car park, I think.' For they have arrived at Worsham, and must confront the problem of how to detach themselves from the car and become people rather than traffic. James will not now hear of the burning of the book. 'There are the others,' he says. 'They're going that way too.'

It is quite difficult to burn a book. She takes the first page – page one of Chapter One – and crumples it up in her fist. She puts it into the grate of the tiny Victorian fireplace which is a decorative feature in this restored and centrally heated terraced cottage in a small cathedral town. She strikes a match and puts it to the ball of paper. It flares up. Some feathers of charred paper float out on to the rug. She goes to the table and takes page two from the pile of type-script, crumples it, places it in the fireplace, strikes another match.

Each time she revisits this scene it becomes like a Dutch interior. She sees it with interested detachment: the quiet room across which lies a wedge of sunlight from the open door, beyond which can be seen the pram in the garden, in which a baby sleeps, the young woman who stoops before the fireplace, doing something with paper and matches.

The scene that Harry saw, when he walked into the room. Except that by then she was sitting at the table.

He halts, sensing that something is awry. 'What have you been doing?'

'I've been burning your book,' she says.

And he goes white. She has never seen anyone do that before. His face changes colour before her eyes – bloodless, drained. He cannot speak. He simply stands there, staring spectral at the fireplace, at the black mound therein, at the charred feathers on the rug. And then his glance swivels to the table. He sees the pile of typescript jutting from under the newspaper. He puts out a hand.

'Don't worry,' says Pauline. 'I couldn't go through with it. I'm too well brought up.'

He is examining the typescript, feverishly. He sees that only the first two pages are missing. The blood comes back into his face.

'But I made a start,' says Pauline. 'The spirit was willing. It was the flesh let me down.'

He looks at her now, instead of at the typescript.

'Why? *Why* – for Christ's sake.'

She looks back at him. 'You know,' she says.

Worsham is everything that Maurice had hoped for – awash with people. The pavements of the wide central street are teeming, as the crowds move slowly past the antique shops and the picture galleries and the pubs with flowered façades. Maurice has shot off into the Information Centre to pick up some brochures, of which he has a collection that must by now be of national importance. Carol has drifted after him. Teresa is administering juice to Luke.

'What was your husband's book about?' says James. Perhaps he feels it is more tactful to ask that than to ask why she wanted to burn it. Or maybe the interest is a professional one. They are standing outside a craft shop, desultorily inspecting expensive pottery and children's toys made of polished yew.

'Demographic history. An analysis of population trends in the seventeenth century.'

'Ah,' says James.

'Quite. Actually, an interesting book. He was in the vanguard of academic fashion at the time.'

Maurice has now joined them and is leafing through a handful of brochures. 'Right. First stop, the Model Village.'

'Model of what village?' inquires James.

'Any village. An apocryphal, ideal village. All done to scale, it says here, but waist high, and you can peer in through the windows at exquisitely reconstructed nineteenth-century interiors.'

'Must we?' says Teresa. 'There's a great queue. I saw it as we came past.'

'I suppose you and Luke might be let off.' Maurice lays a propitiating hand on her shoulder. 'Go and buy yourselves an ice-cream.'

'Count me out too,' says Pauline.

James and Carol elect to go with Maurice. The three of them vanish in search of the queue for the Model Village while Teresa and Pauline wander up the main street.

'Not ice-cream,' says Pauline. 'A nice cup of tea. In some superior joint with tablecloths and tea strainers.'

Worsham is doing good business. Raking it in. Each of these visitors will spend something, presumably, if only on refreshments and a postcard. Quite a few will fall for a pot of allegedly home-made chutney, or framed assemblage of dried flowers, or a patchwork cushion. Acquisition is one of the purposes of a day out, after all – the acquisition of new sights bolstered by something a bit more tangible. And Worsham has centuries of marketing experience – it has been a trading centre all its life, though traditionally for more essential commodities than dried flowers. Never mind – at least it has demonstrated economic flexibility along with an exemplary capacity to cash in on its assets. The limestone buildings that line the High Street are perfectly groomed; there are no offensive contemporary intrusions. Worsham knows quite well what it is selling.

'Horrible place,' says Teresa, arranging Luke in the elegant pine high chair supplied by the tea shop. 'I'd rather live in Brixton.'

'Hush,' says Pauline. 'You'll get us thrown out. Shall we go the whole hog and have anchovy toast and home-made Dundee cake? Actually,' she goes on, 'I'm afraid you rather suit the surroundings.'

Teresa is wearing a calf-length dark red dress with sleeves and high bodice which she made herself from a pair of curtains she bought from an Age Concern shop. This, along with her hair tied back into her nape, gives her a vaguely Victorian look. She seems in striking contrast to most of the other young women around, who wear trousers, T-shirts, cotton skirts and tops. Carol is dressed in beige linen shorts with a sharp crease and a matching waistcoat worn over a white shirt. Teresa has always bypassed fashion, going for clothes that she has contrived herself or come upon accidentally – she is a frequenter of market stalls and jumble sales. This is not so much thrift as a rejection of standard fare; she prefers to pick and choose and come up with an effect which is *sui generis*. Also, she has a passion for esoteric textures and patterns. The red curtains were a nubbly raw silk, which was the initial attraction.

Pauline's comment has disconcerted her. She looks at her reflection in the window of the tea shop, and then into the street beyond: a Kate Greenaway girl floating above a line of Beatrix Potter shop façades. She pulls a face.

Pauline is contrite. 'Only in the superficial sense. I shouldn't have said that – now you'll be put off that dress, which I happen to like.'

Their tea arrives. Luke discovers a taste for anchovy toast. He falls silent, absorbed in this new sensation. The women can indulge in unfractured talk. Pauline wonders if maybe Teresa should get into the local craft scene. No way! replies Teresa indignantly. Pauline points out that anything goes, so far as one can see. 'People will apparently buy whatever is there. Why should they be restricted to a diet of oven gloves and hand-thrown mugs? All they want is something they don't actually need. You've turned out some very appealing junk, in your time. What about those papier mâché birds you did for that Selfridges window display?'

'They took hours and hours,' says Teresa. 'I haven't got an hour a day, with Luke.'

Pauline concedes that this is true.

'And anyway by the autumn we'll be in London again.'

'It was a fleeting thought,' says Pauline. 'Forget it. I've been infected by all this getting and spending and feel we ought to join in.'

'Actually I've been thinking that when Luke's old enough to start at a nursery I'll take on some commissions again. I could be working part-time at least. Unless I have another baby.'

Pauline eyes her. 'Unless . . .' she agrees, non-committal.

'I'd rather two than one, really.'

Pauline says that two is not a bad idea.

Teresa now looks warily at her mother. There is something unstated that hovers, that has perhaps hovered before. 'Did you ever . . .' she begins.

'Whoops!' exclaims Pauline. Luke has dropped his piece of anchovy toast. He wails. There is a flurry of consolation and substitution. The moment passes.

And it is time to meet up with the rest of the party. Pauline and Teresa leave the tea shop. Luke is put back into his buggy, protesting – he has other plans, it seems, and there is a tussle as Teresa straps him in. They walk back up the village street to the agreed meeting place outside the wood craft shop where they stand for a few minutes until Maurice, James and Carol appear, all smiles, evidently well pleased.

'It was *really* kitsch,' says Carol. 'I loved it. Like doll's houses – you wanted to get inside and live there. Tiny oil lamps on the tables and a little mangle with a sheet in it, and a miniature washing-tub. Heaven!'

'Exactly what you were meant to feel,' says Maurice. 'I quite agree – it was entirely satisfactory. A perfect instance of the diminution of the past for purposes of touristic exploitation. Quite literally, in this instance.'

Carol giggles. 'Well, it exploited me all right. There was this cricket match,' she tells Teresa and Pauline, 'with miniature deck chairs for the spectators and little figures in white flannels.'

'Don't forget the four-inch bats,' says James. 'And the ball. And the real grass.'

'Where's Luke?' says Pauline sharply.

The buggy is empty. They have been standing in a group as they talked. Teresa had her back to the buggy, one hand upon the handle. A party of French schoolchildren has just jostled past. The pavement is crowded on all sides.

Teresa freezes. Then she darts frantically off. Pauline

follows. She hears Maurice shout, 'We'll go and look the other way.'

Pauline glances again at the empty buggy. She sees the straps hanging loose and remembers that earlier tussle. During which, presumably, Teresa failed to click home the catch so that it has fallen open, enabling Luke to climb out.

It is a full minute before they see him. A long full minute. He is between two parked cars, holding himself steady on a bumper. In the instant that they catch sight of him, he loses his grip on the bumper, falls to his knees, picks himself up and staggers out into the road, into the traffic which passes in a steady stream.

He is fifteen yards or so away. It is not Pauline or Teresa who reaches him but a man who shoots suddenly from the pavement, a middle-aged stranger who grabs Luke by an arm at the moment that a car swerves past him. When they get there Luke is crying and the man has picked him up and is awkwardly holding him. The first thing that he says is 'Sorry . . .' – presumably on account of Luke's screams.

Teresa takes Luke. She is shaking so much that she cannot speak. It is Pauline who says the things that should be said to the man. He is deprecating, he shrugs, he doesn't want too much made of this. 'All's well that ends well,' he says. And then he melts away.

They hurry back the way they came. Pauline sees Maurice's back view. She shouts. He turns. He comes towards them. James and Carol too arrive from somewhere. 'Oh good – you've found him,' cries Carol.

Maurice is rattled. Or rather, he has been rattled – distinctly rattled. But now that he sees everything is all right he is instantly restored. 'How did that happen?' he asks Teresa. 'Don't tell me he's learnt to undo those straps.'

Teresa does not reply. She stands there holding Luke and

they all see suddenly that she is crying. Her eyes glisten, her mouth is contorted.

Maurice pats her on the shoulder. 'Come on . . .' he says. 'It's all O'K. Nothing happened.'

Tears run down Teresa's face.

James and Carol stand eyeing Teresa. They are embarrassed. At least, James is embarrassed. He looks away. He wipes his hair off his forehead and fiddles with his car keys and pretends not to see Teresa weeping. Carol simply watches. She is not so much embarrassed as puzzled. She is wondering why Teresa is making such a fuss. There is a complete absence of empathy. Carol has no perception of what it is that Teresa is feeling, or of what it is that Teresa has felt over the last four minutes. She is seeing a person who is absurdly crying over something that has not happened.

'I think maybe we've all had enough of Worsham,' says Pauline briskly. 'Home, I suggest.'

No one objects. They head for the car park. Teresa pushes Luke in silence until eventually she starts to respond a little to James's determined chat. Pauline walks beside them, encouraging James, watching Teresa – who is surfacing, she sees, emerging from that black pit of horror glimpsed. Maurice and Carol walk a few paces ahead. Snatches of their conversation float back – anodyne, unexceptional.

At the entrance to the car park they regroup. Carol moves aside to sit on a wall and adjust her sandal. James is still telling Pauline and Teresa an anecdote – kindly improvised to distract and entertain. Teresa listens, a half-smile on her face now, her eyes upon Luke.

Maurice stands nearby – just waiting, it would seem. Pauline glances away from James and sees that Maurice's look is upon Carol, who is absorbed still in this problem with the sandal. There is a concentration about this look – an intensity

– that she has seen before. In Maurice's eyes above a glass of red wine. In someone else's eyes, at another time. She both sees the look and feels it like some chill shadow.

She says, 'Maurice, you take Teresa back. I'll go with James and Carol.' She speaks loudly, so that she is heard by all.

'Right,' says Maurice, jolted by her tone. He grins at her, at Teresa.

Carol stands up. 'Actually,' she says, 'I'd thought . . . Oh, OK, then.'

Thus they return to World's End, together and apart. Pauline finds that she is suddenly exhausted, clobbered like Teresa by what did not happen. She sits there in the car, hardly hearing what is said, seeing only Luke who potters out into the flashing road, and the face of that fortuitous stranger, who says 'All's well that ends well'. James and Carol talk on, because it is not polite to remain silent during a car journey with an acquaintance, and Pauline contributes from time to time, in a desultory way. Carol talks of the flat that she and James are considering buying together. Their relationship is only a year or so old, it seems, but moving in the direction of heavier commitment. She talks of her job. She too works in publishing, in a somewhat subordinate capacity and without great fervour, Pauline detects. She recognizes Carol. Not Carol personally but Carol as a species. She is a literary groupie – one of those who leech on to writers, who are passed from hand to hand among poets, and for whom publication and a degree of fame spell sexual magnetism. Pauline has worked with several Carols. They do not last long because they lack efficiency and ambition – they are only there for the pickings. They do not want to go to bed with a book, but with anyone who wrote one.

'What are you editing just now, Pauline?' Carol inquires.

Her attitude to Pauline has shifted. It has moved from casual dismissal (middle-aged, someone's mother) to mild dislike tempered with a certain caution. She perceives that Pauline is possibly a force to be reckoned with.

Pauline describes briefly the manuscript that is on her desk at the moment, which is in fact something of an oddity – a novel with a medieval setting and elements of fantasy, a curious marriage of myth and realism.

'Is it good?' says Carol, with brisk professionalism.

'I don't know,' replies Pauline. This is the truth.

'Do you like it?' asks James.

Pauline considers. 'I like the idea. Sometimes I have doubts about the language. The author's quite young.'

Carol has lost interest. She is off now on another tack. She is solicitous about Teresa. Thank goodness nothing happened to the baby. I had no idea they could move so fast, she says. He was half-way up the street, wasn't he? She talks of Luke with interested detachment, as though he were some kind of unfamiliar animal. My sister's got one, she says – a bit older, I should think, and he's like that too. I mean, someone's got to be watching *all* the time. I couldn't manage, she says, I just know I couldn't.

'Needs must when the devil drives,' says Pauline. 'I suppose.'

'What? Oh, I see. Well, maybe. Anyway, I just know I'd be hopeless. Actually –' Carol becomes confidential, flatteringly confidential – 'I was pregnant once, a couple of years ago – James knows all about this, it's before we met, when I was with someone else – but it didn't come to anything. I . . . sort of miscarried.'

'Bad luck,' says Pauline.

'Well, in fact I was awfully relieved really though of course it's always a bit traumatic. But I simply wasn't ready. Not then. Sometime, maybe. Anyway, there it was.'

There it was, thinks Pauline. Easy come, easy go. An admirable resilience. Very healthy. A great mistake to dwell on these things.

A great mistake.

She is walking down a leafy street in north London, feeling sick. Spring is bursting out all over, unstoppable, unquenchable, blackbirds shrieking in the gardens, the blossom boiling on the trees. And she is walking towards this address which is written on a piece of paper in her bag. She checks every now and then that the envelope is there also, the envelope stuffed with £5 notes. For she has done what it would have been better not to have done, and now must pay the price. The price is £100. For a start, for the first instalment.

Future demands will follow. At irregular intervals. Rising out of the darkness in the small hours, the ghost child standing silent by the bed, for ever there and for ever terribly not there. The not-child who grows up not as ordinary children grow up, but as a perpetual absence. Who has shadowed Teresa over the years, unknown to Teresa but known always to Pauline – the other, older child who is mirrored continually by children that Pauline sees. Who would be like that now – or like that.

And who surfaces for an instant today, but as some eerie reflection of Luke. A Luke who can never exist. Pauline shrinks. The familiar chill, unchanging over the years – private, incommunicable, intense. And then the moment passes, the ghost has gone. Pauline collects herself and replies to James's question. 'Yes,' she says. 'Go right here, and then it's next left.'

Chapter Seven

'Chris Rogers?'

'That's me.'

'Pauline Carter. Your copy editor.'

'Oh – right. Could you just hang on a moment?'

There is background noise of children, a running tap, a radio. Some of this is eliminated and Chris Rogers returns to the phone. Pauline knows nothing of him except that this is his first book and he lives in mid-Wales. She explains that she is half-way through her work on his manuscript and it might be a good thing to sort out a few queries at this stage. She asks if he has a fax.

'I do not,' says Chris Rogers. From his tone of contemptuous rejection you would think that she had asked if he had a Kalashnikov rifle.

'Never mind. I'll send it first-class post.'

'That'll probably get here.'

'It's lovely country where you are,' says Pauline encouragingly. She has looked it up on the road atlas – a pin-prick in Powys.

'It's cheap country, is what it is,' replies Chris Rogers. He explains that he and his wife rent a cottage that no one else wants half a mile up a rough track in an empty valley. 'I reckon country doesn't come much cheaper.' This seems to be a matter of pride.

'And scenic into the bargain,' Pauline offers.

'Scenic you can keep,' says Chris. 'Downtown Manchester,

that's where I'd like to be. It'll be a long time before we achieve that. At the moment we aspire to Swansea. I don't suppose this book's going to make me rich, is it?'

Pauline knows that it isn't. She hesitates. 'Well, of course it's very difficult to . . .'

'Not to worry. Anyway, I've just spent fifty quid on a load of firewood for next winter. More to the point – how did you get on with it? Does it make sense? Are there a lot of spelling mistakes?'

Pauline mentions a few queries she needs to raise with him. 'But it's all in the notes I'll send you. I have had a bit of a problem with the names of characters. Talusa, for instance.'

'I made them all up.'

'Well, yes – I guessed as much. But sometimes you give that one *l* and sometimes two.'

'Which do you fancy?' he inquires.

The background noise has built up once more to an insistent clamour. 'Excuse me while I slaughter a child,' says Chris.

'Don't bother,' Pauline tells him. 'I'll get all this off to you today and then we can talk later in the week.'

She rings off. The cottage in Powys vanishes, extinguished as she lays down the receiver. She puts her notes into a large envelope. The postman has already been so she will have to take it along to the village to catch the second post. She writes POWYS on the envelope in felt pen in large letters and then looks out of the window at her own section of landscape, struck by the fickle nature of space. That pullulating cottage and the unknown young man are simultaneously within arm's reach and a hundred miles away. While she talked to him the noise of his children playing was overlaid by the rumble of a tractor on the track in front of World's End. And as she listened there had drifted into her head an image of Teresa as a small child squatting on a toy-littered floor staring up at Harry who stands at a window with his head cocked over the black receiver of a telephone. Time and space were for an instant fused.

The tractor has come to a halt further down the track, its driver now in discussion with Chaundy, who is on patrol in the battered Peugeot. This tractor is the flagship of Chaundy's fleet, a shining scarlet monster in which the driver rides high in a cab of tinted glass, perfectly insulated from his surroundings. He can cruise the fields in a state of absolute detachment, like an astronaut in a capsule. Rumour has it that some of these vehicles are equipped with television sets, though Pauline has never been able to confirm this. She watches Chaundy conclude his instructions and get into the Peugeot. The tractor driver gets back into his capsule and roars away towards the main road. Chaundy drives slowly past World's End on his way presumably to the battery chicken complex over the brow of the hill. Nobody working this landscape ever proceeds on foot. The only walkers who pass World's End come from elsewhere, ramblers on whom Chaundy wages war, disputing rights of way and erecting thickets of barbed wire.

And now Pauline gets into her car to go to the village, which is just over a mile away. She has occasionally walked there, but this is inconvenient in terms of time taken and also the fact that the only route lies along the main road, not an agreeable pedestrian route. So she drives, parking the car outside the branch of the Mace Store which is now the village shop and post office. The village is impoverished, in terms of facilities. The school closed down several years ago. Mace is said to be struggling, unable to compete with the allure of the Hadbury superstores. Only the pub survives, because it has upgraded itself from its former local and homely role to reference book status. It is in the *Good Pub Guide* and Egon

Ronay. It serves gravadlax, couscous and gazpacho. Its façade is a cascade of petunias, lobelia and fuchsias fattened to monstrous proportions on Phostrogen.

Pauline spends some time in Mace, having her package weighed, buying stamps and stocking up with a few other things in order to save a trip to Hadbury. As she comes out she pauses on the step and sees Maurice emerging from the phone box opposite.

She is momentarily taken aback. She had not noticed his car – indeed he must have arrived while she was in the shop. And why does he need to use the village phone? If theirs was out of order he could have used hers.

'Hi!' says Maurice. 'We could have given each other a lift.'

'Is something wrong with your phone?'

'No, no. I came for some stamps and suddenly remembered a call I should have made. Let's have a coffee.' He waves towards the pub.

They sit outside. It is a fine morning, suggesting real heat later on.

'You know something . . .' says Maurice. 'This threatens to be a good summer, weather-wise.'

'So it seems.'

'Worth several million to the British Tourist Board. And with the useful knock-on effect that a quite wrong impression of the climate will bring a further spate of foreigners next year.'

'I suppose so.'

Maurice drops this topic, noting Pauline's abstraction, or lack of interest. He is sensitive to other people's moods, though it is not a sensitivity that necessarily makes him switch course. But he changes tack now in a diversionary move that enforces Pauline's attention.

'Where were you living when Teresa was Luke's age?'

He does indeed have her attention, because the question has focused uncannily on her own preoccupations. She names the town in which she lived with Harry, when Harry was forging ahead in the academic stakes. The town in which she attempted to burn a book – but she will not tell Maurice about that, because he would be rather too interested. 'Why do you ask?'

'I was wondering if it was town or country. Teresa was claiming this morning that she's never lived in the country before.'

'She hasn't – bar the occasional holiday. Neither have I. And none of us really lives here, either. We perch.'

'Quite so.' But this is not to be a discussion of *rus* versus *urbe,* apparently. Maurice is now in pursuit of something else. 'Do you think motherhood changed you?'

Pauline looks sharply at him. It seems that he really wants to know. 'Who am I to say?'

'Teresa is different.'

'Different in what way?'

'More . . . applied,' says Maurice. 'More concentrated. Less . . . diffuse.'

'You make her sound like a chemical experiment.'

Maurice grins. 'But you see what I mean, I'm sure. An interesting process – watching someone you know well go through a process of change. Can you remember it happening to you? Within sound of the cathedral bells. Did you live within sound of the cathedral bells?'

'No,' says Pauline. It is not clear which question she is answering. Or indeed if she is answering a question at all or merely blocking Maurice's line of conversation.

Maurice perceives that he has fallen upon stony ground. He gives her a look – a good-humoured, foxy look which tells her he knows there is no point in going on with this, that he concedes she has every right to clam up if she wants to but

79

that he has noted her resistance and finds it of interest. Pauline feels both irritated and in some obscure way outmanoeuvred. Maurice is now talking about a visit he made last week to a new tourist attraction – the re-creation of an industrial site in the Black Country. He is shrewd and entertaining. She is entertained, despite herself. Maurice is laying himself out to please, and she is pleased, also despite herself. They sit in the sun, finishing their coffee outside the pub, beside an old wooden wheelbarrow filled with potted plants and a cartwheel from which gushes lobelia and African marigolds.

'Well,' says Maurice, 'I'd better get my stamps before I forget what I came for.'

They part company. Pauline gets into her car. She sees Maurice enter the Mace Store. She looks again at the village phone box. And then she drives back to World's End.

Pauline does not often think about that town. When she does, she sees it as two distinct places. There are the placid streets, in which women like herself push prams. There is the majestic presence of the cathedral, suggesting an impervious continuity. There is Harry's university, a campus on the outskirts of the town – stylish brick and concrete by the architect of the day, all done out with blond Swedish furniture, openweave curtains and swinging black-clad students who make Pauline feel middle-aged at twenty-seven. There is the house, a Victorian cottage with a little garden at the back and quiet rooms in which she looks after Teresa and waits for Harry to return.

An unexceptional place. Innocent, even. Once, a few years ago, she found herself nearby and made a detour to drive through the town. There it all was – the shop-lined streets, the great complacent pile of the cathedral. And there also was that other place which she carries always in the head, the place she has long left behind but which is always there. The place in which she holds a match to a crumpled sheet of typescript and in which Harry stands at the window holding the telephone to his ear, and turns towards her as she comes into the room.

Turns towards her and simultaneously puts down the receiver.

'Who was it?' she says.

'Wrong number.'

'But you were talking.'

'Of course,' says Harry. 'I was telling them they'd got a wrong number, wasn't I?'

They stare at each other. Or rather, Pauline stares. Harry simply looks – bland, a touch perplexed. 'What's wrong, love?' he inquires.

'Nothing,' she replies at last. She stoops to pick up Teresa. She goes through to the kitchen to give Teresa her lunch. She has this sick feeling, but does not think that she is pregnant.

Harry is not often there in the terraced cottage. He is here, there and everywhere but not a great deal at home. He is at the university, caught up in a whirlwind schedule of seminars and lectures and meetings. He is off to London for a bout at the BBC or a snatched day at the British Museum or the Public Record Office (for he must maintain the production of books and articles that will keep him at the sharp end of his profession). He is away at conferences. When he does come home he often brings people back with him – colleagues who make bright and brittle conversation or a posse of students who sit cross-legged on the floor and for whom Pauline has to make vats of spaghetti. Sometimes they smoke dope, to which Harry makes no objection. Indeed, he may well join in. The students dote on him. They find him clever and outrageous and challenging. Most of them would like to grow up to be Harry. This is a sign of the times indeed. Ten years ago students did not want to grow up to be academics. They wanted to be journalists or BBC producers or advertising agents (which is what most of these will end up as).

Pauline lives on the edge of all this. Sometimes, if she can find a baby-sitter, she goes with Harry to parties where the faculty and the students are democratically mingled and she feels out on a limb because she is neither – not young enough nor old enough. Most of the wives of Harry's colleagues are in the same position, and she often finds herself in a group with them, talking about children. They have all read Bowlby on child care, and believe that their children will be irremediably damaged if they abandon them for more than five minutes. They have also read Spock, who tells them that their children are always right, so they are both anxious and unconfident. They are young, and youth is riding high just now, but none of them feels particularly young. Unlike their husbands and the students, all of whom seem caught up in a continuous celebration, carefree and liberated, lords of creation. When Pauline is out and about in the town with Teresa in her pram, she sees that she and those like her are pushed to the margins of life, just like the pensioners who also potter between the butcher and the greengrocer.

She is not dissatisfied, though the day is to come when she will be. The climate of the times has not yet told her that she ought to be dissatisfied, and in any case she is happy. She has a husband with whom she is in love and a child that she very much wanted. She is sometimes bored. She would like to do things that it is impossible at present to do – read a book uninterrupted, go to the cinema, travel, do anything on a whim – but this does not amount to serious dissatisfaction. There is Teresa, all day and every day. There is Harry – sometimes.

One of the girl students once said to Pauline – impertinently, in Pauline's view – 'God – you are lucky to be married to Harry.' Pauline did not care for the implication of this: that out of an array of available women Harry had for some inexplicable reason picked her, Pauline. As it happens, Pauline was not short of suitors. Before she met Harry she had been deeply involved with an American research student: the consequences of this would be always with her. And there were others. When first she met Harry she had been much taken with the mutual friend who introduced them. She had thought Harry brash. And then Harry had made a dead set at her. The brashness became original and invigorating; the mutual friend began to seem rather colourless. Harry announced that he intended to spend the summer driving across the United States. 'Come!' he said. Or commanded. She went.

Thus, that cathedral town, which will be for ever locked into a particular time – so that Pauline was startled to find that the familiar High Street now had branches of Waterstone's and Ryman's. There was something vaguely treacherous about its mutation, as though it should have stayed as it was so that she could consign it to the past as she consigns those Harry years. For Pauline sees the Harry years now as a time of traumatic illness, a period of affliction, the long wasted era when she suffered from that now mysterious disease – love for Harry. Love? No, she thinks – balancing what she feels for Teresa, for Luke. Not love. An awful consuming need. Irrational obsession. Enslavement.

When Pauline arrives back at World's End she finds Teresa and Luke on the track outside the cottages. There is a large muddy puddle here, much loved by Luke. Luke is picking up sticks and dropping them into the puddle. Teresa is both watching him and gazing down the track. She comes to the car window. 'Maurice has been gone ages. He only went to the village for some stamps.'

'We met up there and had a cup of coffee. He's probably on his way back by now.'

Teresa's face relaxes. She has been imagining a car smash. Pauline knows this because she has gone through the same herself, many times – oh, many, many times. Now Teresa blossoms again, immediately. All is right with the world, and she turns her tranquil face to Pauline and talks at once of other things. She tells Pauline that Chaundy's tractor driver lifted Luke into the cab of his tractor, evidently a thrilling experience. They discuss a wild flower growing at the edge of the track, for which neither of them can find a name. Vetch, says Pauline – most things are vetch. Toadflax, proposes Teresa.

And Pauline, looking at Teresa, remembers Maurice's remark and sees that there is a difference in her. Pauline has grown used to this difference and therefore has hardly registered it. There is a new depth in Teresa, something still and settled. She seems not so much older as riper. She has acquired a bloom, like fruit. Pauline is startled now by this further metamorphosis of which she has scarcely been aware.

They stand talking in the sunshine outside World's End, as women have probably stood before, taking a breather from the day's demands. And beside them, in his own detached time capsule, Luke is locked into communion with his puddle of mud, learning about wetness, about softness and hardness, about buoyancy and the force of gravity and reflection and porosity. And eventually about pain, as he stumbles and bangs his knee on a sharp protruding stone. He howls. Startled birds erupt from the hedgerow. Teresa comforts him. She picks him up. 'Look,' she says. 'Look who's coming.' And there is Maurice's car, gleaming again amid the green surf of wheat. Luke stops crying, and manages a watery smile. Teresa glows.

Chapter Eight

It is June the 15th. Mid-year, mid-week, mid-morning. World's End sits amid a landscape of exuberance. The verge alongside the track is lush, brimming with red campion, knapweed, foaming drifts of cow parsley. The hedges are studded with creamy plates of elder. There is a feeling of completion – that the surging growth of May has peaked, is suspended now in its abundance. Only the wheat is still growing. The green pelts have become deep seas that billow in the wind. Pauline looks out on all this from her desk with appreciation. The place is different each day, transformed by weather and its own inexorable programme. She appreciates in particular the sky – sometimes stacked with columns of incandescent cloud, sometimes rippling with milky white cirrus, sometimes a primrose arc backlit by the setting sun. The weather is a spectacle, to be observed with interest as she turns the page of a typescript, opens a book or reaches for the telephone.

It occurs to her that she is probably the first person to live here for whom the weather is an aesthetic diversion. For those before her it conditioned the plans for the day, determined whether you were going to be wet, cold, baked or frozen. There may well have been those who managed nevertheless to note the luminosity of a cloud or the bright ripple of the wind across the wheat, but for the most part weather would have been a grim and capricious dictator. For Pauline, rain or sun merely decide whether or not she will be tempted from her desk to walk up the track and down the bridle-path that runs along the crest of the hill, whether she will sit for a while in the garden after lunch or spend all day at work.

She has been surprised by weather, these last weeks. By its versatility and by the grandeur of its effects. In cities the weather is incidental. She has been surprised too by time. At World's End time becomes two-pronged. There is the controlled and measured time of the flashing green digits on appliances, of the display panel of the fax, or the pages of her diary. And there is the time that happens beyond the window which unrolls in terms of leaves and flowers and the green stems of wheat, in terms of climbing temperature – a primitive and elemental form of time untamed by Greenwich or the Gregorian calendar.

And now suddenly it is the middle of June and she has not been to London for nearly six weeks. She ought to check out her flat. There are business calls to be made. She needs a haircut and would like to see friends. Hugh, in particular. She picks up the phone and makes various arrangements.

When, later, she tells Teresa that she will be away in London for a couple of days next week Teresa says, 'Oh, right – Maurice'll be back before you go then.'

'Maurice is going away?'

'He's got to go to London too. There are books he needs – and someone at the Tourist Board he wants to interview.'

'Why don't you go with him?' says Pauline after a moment.

'It isn't really worth it. He'd be out all the time, anyway. I might as well stay.' Evidently Teresa is perfectly happy about this. She shifts Luke to her other hip and goes on. 'And it's nicer to be here when the weather's so good.'

'Well – yes,' Pauline agrees. And indeed the sun continues to pour down, day after day – hazy sun on some days, sharp brilliant sun on others.

It shines the next morning, as Pauline watches Maurice depart. He has nothing with him except a battered Gladstone bag which is his briefcase. That Gladstone bag – acquired presumably in an antique shop – is typical of Maurice. It indicates a contemptuous rejection of standard consumerism: no smart briefcase or neat and practical holdall for Maurice. In fact, the Gladstone bag weighs a ton and must be rather inconvenient. Pauline remembers noticing it when first she knew Maurice, when Maurice was a casual and engaging acquaintance. He was about to leave it behind in a wine bar and she had picked it up to hand it to him and said, 'My God – what have you got in this thing?' 'A book,' Maurice had replied. 'And possibly a newspaper.' And had grinned, the grin conceding the impracticality of the bag while quietly flaunting it.

The Gladstone bag is put into the back of the car. The car is a dark blue Vauxhall Astra. Pauline is conscious of this because she discovered recently that Maurice did not know what make of car he owned – he had had to ask Teresa, while in the process of filling in some form. This dismissal of a universal preoccupation is also typical of Maurice. Most people take a proprietorial interest in their car, therefore Maurice does not.

Maurice kisses Teresa. He kisses Luke, who stares at him with an expression of blank amazement, as though he has never seen him before. Presumably Luke is away on some mysterious and inconceivable level of perception. Maurice starts the engine, waves, and the car moves slowly away down the track and is eventually swallowed up in the wheat. Teresa stands watching. Pauline watches from her window. She thinks about Maurice, and it comes to her that the Maurice she now knows is irrevocably detached from the Maurice she once knew, who seems in retrospect a weightless figure – just someone she had come across and found agreeable, no more, no less. The new Maurice is loaded with implications – nothing he says or does can be seen in the same way.

*

She began to realize this at the wedding. Maurice and Teresa were married in a registry office. Those present were two friends as witnesses, and Pauline. Maurice's mother, a widow in her late seventies, lived in Carlisle and had felt that the journey would be too much for her. Their small group put up a poor showing in the waiting room at Finsbury Town Hall, as other wedding parties came and went, dressed to kill and attended by droves of bridesmaids in frothy dresses. Maurice was enthralled. He sat there talking about the sociological implications of the occasion. He pointed out that the most flamboyantly and expansively presented groups were Afro-Caribbean or Asian, and that the more middle class the wedding the more sparsely attended it was and the more ill-clad the participants, as though they were embarrassed by the whole procedure. Maurice himself was wearing exactly what he would wear on any other day. Teresa wore a 1920s evening dress from an auction sale and looked like someone who had wandered off the set of a Noël Coward play.

The reception was thronged. Scores of people filled all three floors of the large Onslow Square house lent by some well-heeled friends of Maurice's. They spilled out into the garden and stood laughing in the intermittent rain. They sat on the stairs drinking champagne. Pauline was startled, pushing her way through in search of the occasional familiar face. It was as though the whole of Maurice's previous un-known life was laid out in terms of these strangers and she felt a curious dismay. The small gaggle of Teresa's friends hung together in a corner, looking very young. At one point Pauline found herself in a group with the mistress of the house, who leaned against her marble mantelpiece tolerantly inspecting the crowd. 'Well,' she said, 'isn't this amazing! Maurice, of all people – who'd have thought it!' Someone introduced Pauline and the woman turned her attention upon her with what seemed like amusement. 'Your daughter? Congratulations! She's sweet.' Later, the woman's husband, rather drunk, said, 'Of course Maurice is an old flame of Shirley's – from way back before she married me.' He laughed indulgently. Pauline looked across the room and saw Maurice as though she had never seen him before – a man she hardly knew with whom she was now inextricably associated. Teresa stood beside him, seeming both happy and bemused. I did this, Pauline thought. I didn't mean to, but I did.

Teresa and Luke go back indoors. As they do so, Teresa glances up and catches sight of Pauline. She waves and gestures. 'Coffee?' she is saying. Pauline nods.

There is a letter with the California postmark on Teresa's kitchen table. 'You were right,' she says. 'Harry wants to meet when he's over. I suppose I will have to go to London then. But it's not till August.' She glances at her mother. Teresa is delicacy itself where Harry is concerned. The delicacy seems touched with guilt, almost as though she were indirectly responsible for Harry – or rather, for what Harry implies.

'Of course you must,' says Pauline sternly. 'He definitely ought to see Luke.'

In fact it is clear that Harry is queasy about being a grandfather. It is a label he evidently finds disconcerting – he had not realized he had got so far in life and his pleasure in Luke's existence is qualified by a certain dismay. This makes Pauline ghoulishly keen to insist on the relationship.

Harry had expressed a wish to attend Teresa's wedding. It was Teresa who vetoed this, for which Pauline was grateful. And in the event Harry has only once met Maurice, over a lunch described by Teresa as uneasy. When Pauline pressed her on this she became evasive. No, it wasn't that they hadn't taken to each other, it was more that in a way they had but somehow didn't feel they wanted to. 'I can't explain,' she said, ending the matter. 'But I wouldn't want to do it again, and I don't think Maurice would either.' And Pauline had understood. She had seen it all as though in a shaft of light – the three of them at a table, Teresa between the two men who eye one another and see an uncomfortable reflection.

Harry is twelve years older than Maurice, but he has worn well, by all accounts. Maurice would have seen in him an unwelcome reminder that he, Maurice, is no longer to be counted among the young, that he has crossed the divide, that he is of Harry's generation rather than of Teresa's. He would have felt one of those surges of panic. Would have wanted to distance himself from Harry, to push the disagreeable raw fact to one side. Pauline does not have the same effect on him because although standing in the same relation to Teresa she is a woman, and also a person previously known. Pauline's age is somehow less relevant. Maurice would have talked copiously to suppress his dismay.

And Harry, looking across the table at Maurice, would have seen a reflection of the self he is leaving behind, the Harry who still had a foothold in youth, who was still – just – something of an *enfant terrible*, a gadfly to his elders, a subversive element. He would have been reminded that within a short while he could become a grandfather, for Christ's sake. He too would have talked effusively, and no doubt in the process the two of them struck up some sort of accord, for they are both clever and responsive men. They would have responded to one another, recognized a potential affinity, and recoiled from the idea of it.

'It's two months away,' says Teresa serenely. 'August. I can't start thinking about something that's going to happen in August. There's the whole summer ahead.'

Two days later, Pauline observes the return of Maurice: the smiling emergence from the car, the kiss for Teresa who has come out to greet him, the lugging into the cottage of the

Gladstone bag – now evidently even heavier. And two days after that Pauline herself gets into her car and heads up the track.

The drive from World's End to central London takes about two hours. Pauline has done it so many times that she has ceased to find this abrupt transition strange. Indeed, like any other late-twentieth-century traveller she is indignant about delays – the tiresome incursion of roadworks, the irritating crawl in a traffic jam. The World's End track takes her to the main road which sweeps her round Hadbury on the girdle of ring roads and roundabouts, and eventually shoots her off on the sliproad which leads on to the motorway, on which she cruises until the landscape starts to thicken with roads and buildings, the traffic slows again and she is digested by the city's sprawl. Once, browsing in Hugh's office, she picked up an edition of Ogilby and saw the same journey translated into the emotive draughtsmanship of a seventeenth-century gazetteer – the road snaking onwards strip by strip, fringed by the neat insignia of church towers that would act as landmarks, the schematic trees and hills to indicate woodland or high ground, the rivers and bridges. Here were implications of time and space. Behind the stylized representations of a village or a range of hills lurked pot-holed roads, barren dangerous heaths, dust, mud and rain.

It is not raining today – indeed the sun is making the car uncomfortably hot. Pauline adjusts the air flow and opens the sun roof. She flips through radio channels, rejects them all and puts on a tape. The car is filled with Mozart. Thus cocooned, she skims past the village, around Hadbury, past the fields of wheat and hay, the distant cows and sheep like farmyard toys, the petrol stations swagged with plastic bunting, the thickets of road signs. Soon she is on the motorway and quite detached from the scenery which streams past at either side. She is a part of another element, the endlessly moving belt of traffic into which she is now slotted, locked into negotiation with this car or with that lorry, overtaking, slowing up, speeding on. The green and blue distances beyond and behind are irrelevant – her dealings are with the road and its occupants.

Thus she moves imperceptibly from the country to the city, exercised only by the behaviour of other drivers and the shift from the Mozart oboe concerto to a Ravel quartet. She tunnels her way into London and steps out of the car outside the late Victorian house of which the top half is her flat. This is the city – they do things differently here, though this is not always apparent.

Ten years ago, when the renovation of World's End was complete, Pauline hired a van with driver and associate to move down there the various pieces of furniture she had assembled. The driver got lost and had stopped off in the village to seek directions. When eventually the van arrived both men were in fits of laughter. They sat in the kitchen on packing cases drinking mugs of tea and spluttering with mirth because, it seemed, their Cockney inflection had been found incomprehensible in the village shop. They had had to repeat themselves several times before the query got through. Pauline found this tale somewhat incredible, but it seemed churlish to spoil their enjoyment of what was evidently perceived as rural insularity. They sat there in grubby vests, brimming with self-confidence and well-being, and laughed benignly. Outside, Chaundy's tractor driver, who looked much like they did, roared up and down the field, apparently poles apart.

Pauline unlocks the front door and climbs the stairs, adjusting herself as she does so, assuming the city like a change of skin. The flat greets her with a tide of garish slippery flyers on the doormat, shouting of pizza deliveries and Indian take-aways. It is hot. Dust boils in a shaft of sunlight. She opens windows, sweeps dead insects from the kitchen table, tips the flyers into the rubbish bin, moving briskly from room to room, checking her watch. She has switched to a different mode, without effort and almost without realizing that she has done so. She is on a new course, powered by lists and diary entries. World's End is relegated, shunted aside, suspended somewhere down the motorway out of sight and mind.

The restaurant is one to which they have been before, but not so often as to make it tediously predictable. Hugh likes to circulate between various favoured eating places. Pauline looks fondly at him across the table, thinking that to be with him is like putting on some loved and familiar garment which induces instant ease and comfort. There is not the faintest tingle of sex about this feeling, but it does have some eerie connection with the fact that Hugh is a man. She cannot much remember sex with Hugh now – there is just an impression of genial intimacy rather than of eroticism. The experience bore no relation whatsoever to sex with Harry, which is presumably why she is able to sit here with Hugh today in perfect amity. What there is between them has not been sharpened by sexual tension, and thus cannot corrode.

'What do you think about the idea of romantic love?' she says. 'Unquenchable, irresistible love.'

Hugh is busy with the menu. He glances at her over the top of it. 'Hang on a minute.' He completes his inspection, takes his glasses off and lays the menu beside his plate. 'As in Héloïse and Abelard? Romeo and Juliet? Dido? That sort of thing?'

'That sort of thing.'

'I hope you're not suffering from it,' says Hugh. 'I'm told it's very debilitating. You're not, are you?'

'I'm editing a novel about it.'

'Thank goodness for that. I'd have felt obliged to seek professional advice for you. Don't people just go to a therapist or something nowadays?'

'Don't be flippant,' says Pauline. 'It's a serious matter, and always has been. It happens. Which is why people go on writing about it, like this guy of mine.'

Hugh sighs. 'I'm sure you're right. I've been told before that I have a low emotional temperature. That's probably why I'm so fond of food. Talking of which – shall we order? The salmon sounds interesting. Or there's a pigeon breast concoction I haven't come across before. I think I'll give that a whirl.'

They order. Hugh is now in a state of warm complacency. He puts his glasses on again and studies Pauline. 'I must say you're looking extremely well. You've gone a sort of pale coffee colour, like a foxed book. It's most becoming.'

'Thank you. So you don't accept the idea of romantic love?'

'I never said that. I don't subscribe to any set of religious beliefs, but that doesn't mean I reject the concept of religion. It's got far too strong a track record. Is this a good novel?'

'I'm not sure. The setting's medieval – period unspecific. There's a Lady and a Knight, but he betrays her – he abandons her and she searches for him and in the end kills herself. And there are dragons and unicorns and werewolves.'

'I don't think this is my kind of book,' says Hugh.

'It isn't mine, entirely. But fortunately I'm not hired to pronounce on that. I just correct the spelling. But it grows on you. It's very sad. I actually cried. You don't often cry over a typescript. You're too busy creeping through it word by word.'

Hugh considers this point. One of Hugh's attractive qualities is that he is basically a serious man and he listens to what other people say – especially to what Pauline says. He considers the point while also considering the seafood salad which he is now eating. Eventually he observes that he cannot comment on that since typescripts do not come his way, but that the assumption must be that if words have validity then they will have it regardless of the medium. There is no reason why type should not have the impact of print. He asks if Pauline's crab terrine is all right.

'Delicious. But print *is* more persuasive. It has authority. It's because you know type can still be tampered with. And it's my job to tamper.'

'I suppose so. Can I try a bit? The terrine, I mean.'

Pauline offers her plate. Hugh helps himself to a forkful of terrine. 'Mmn. Very nice. I should have had that – the seafood is a touch boring. So . . . how's Teresa?'

'Teresa's fine,' says Pauline.

Hugh looks closely at her, as though the reply was not quite satisfactory. 'Nothing wrong, is there?'

'Nothing at all. The weather's gorgeous. At weekends we go and look at tourist attractions in the interests of scholarship. Maurice's scholarship.'

'Oh dear,' says Hugh. 'I really do think you should come back to London.'

Pauline shakes her head. No – she will stay put. For various reasons. And this seems to be one of those few famous fine summers.

'Definitely something has got into you,' says Hugh. 'Never before have I known you talk about the weather.'

Pauline laughs. 'Then you'd better move things on to a higher plane and tell me what you've been doing.'

Hugh has been across the Atlantic, visiting clients. He tells Pauline about trips to Yale and to Toronto, where he negotiates the sale of rare books to great libraries, and to New York where he acts as a purveyor of choice goodies to a man who collects modern firsts. 'I've just filled the major gap on his shelf,' says Hugh. 'A *Ulysses* in pristine condition.'

'Does he read them?'

'Of course not, that's not what they're for.'

'I'll never really understand bibliophilia,' says Pauline.

'Nobody does. Mercifully there's quite a bit of it around or I'd be out of business. You're dealing with people who've got a bee in their bonnet. Perfectly normal in other respects. The New York fellow is a stockbroker. Stinking rich and an awful bore. He takes me out for a stupendously good dinner but the conversation's rather heavy going.'

Pauline pictures Hugh on these trips, padding around North American cities in his shabby clothes, with his raincoat over his arm and some arcane treasure in his briefcase. She thinks of him negotiating in air-conditioned offices, eating appreciatively in carefully selected restaurants. Getting into bed in hotel rooms.

'Where do you stay? In New York, for instance.'

Hugh looks startled, and then faintly embarrassed. 'Well, as a matter of fact there's a lady I stay with in New York. I've known her for – oh, ten years or more, I suppose. It's a long-standing arrangement.'

Pauline stares at him.

'The thing is,' he goes on, 'she does the most amazingly good breakfasts. She's an Italian lady who has a deli on the Upper West Side and she also runs a very informal B & B arrangement for a few regulars. Her waffles are a dream.'

'Hugh, I do love you,' says Pauline.

'I'm quite fond of you too. Is the salmon up to scratch? This pigeon affair is definitely interesting.'

Pauline pays courtesy calls at various publishing houses for which she does editorial work. She sits chatting to a former colleague for a while in the office where once she clocked in daily, tests herself for corporate nostalgia and decides that there is none.

'How's our Maurice?' inquires the colleague.

'Maurice is in good health, so far as I know.'

'And how's the great work coming along?'

'Very well, I believe.'

'James Saltash is putting it about that this is going to cause a stir, this tourism book. Controversial. Pulls no punches.'

'I don't doubt,' says Pauline.

'Interesting guy, Maurice,' says the colleague, after a moment. She eyes Pauline and veers off in another direction. 'So you're dug in down in the sticks for the rest of the summer?'

'That's right. I'm watching a field of wheat grow.'

'Life of Riley, it must be. Unlike the rest of us . . .' The colleague embarks with relish on an account of high jinks within the trade, designed perhaps to indicate what a lot Pauline is missing. 'What are you up to, workwise?' she asks kindly.

'Putting commas into a novel about unicorns,' says Pauline, and takes her leave.

No, she thinks, going down in the lift – no, you can keep it. The hurry and scurry, the wheeling and dealing. The gossip was good – I miss that. The salary cheque was more reliable than a string of small commissions. But you can still keep it.

She walks out of the building, a free woman. She has plenty of work lined up. The unicorns will be succeeded by a gargantuan account of the North Sea oil industry and a travel book on the Caucasus.

Nearly twenty years ago she entered this building – or rather, its predecessor – and became for the first time an employee. Her role was a humble one, and the building was elsewhere, a modest house in a west London street, the home at that point of the imprint which has now fallen into the imperial grasp of a large conglomerate. The house is superseded by a green glass column with a lushly carpeted entrance hall, and few of her former colleagues are still present. But, back then, it was with a tremulous sense of freedom that she had gone to work. She hardly knew what to expect, and wondered if she would be up to it, but she knew that day was a climactic one. The end of dependence, in every sense. She was stepping away from Harry, and into a new country.

Harry went to California, and Pauline went to work. In the event she found not only that she was well up to it but that she was rather better at it than most. Her role did not remain a humble one for long. She grew. She moved on and away. The Harry years fell back, removed into some other dimension, where they exist still as a narrative of which many details are lost, and just a handful of potent moments survive, about which nothing can be done.

Waking that night in her flat Pauline is disorientated. There is some racket outside that should not be there. Then she realizes that she is not at World's End, that this is the city, and the city talks day and night. People are shouting in the street – incoherent high-pitched abuse that goes on and on, in one voice and then another, an incomprehensible torrential exchange. She goes to the window and sees that the source is a bunch of young girls, adolescents, who eddy back and forth along the pavement, bawling at each other, coming together and drifting apart like a flock of birds. It is one o'clock in the morning. She watches them in dismay, hearing obscenities and hysterical accusations. Are they drunk? High on drugs? At last they drift round the corner and out of sight, their shrieking ebbs away and she goes back to bed, wide awake and insecure. The manic children have unleashed some nameless anxiety of her own and in the morning she has a compulsion to telephone Teresa, even though she is returning to World's End the next day.

'Hi,' she says. 'Could you do me a favour and just check

that I left my answering machine on?' And then, 'Everything OK?'

'Fine,' replies Teresa, perplexed. She has caught a whisper of that anxiety. 'Are you all right?'

'Perfectly,' says Pauline. 'See you tomorrow.'

Chapter Nine

Pauline looks out of the window – a World's End window. She is holding Luke, who points – a majestic, whole-hand gesture. 'Da,' he observes. There is my father, he is saying. And there indeed is Maurice, standing in the sunshine on the track talking to Carol. Maurice stirs the grass with his foot, and gestures as he speaks. He is presumably in full Maurice spate, engaged on one of those long and often compelling discourses. Carol is idly shucking a head of corn, a green head of Chaundy's corn which now has soft milky kernels. The sun glints off the neat gold helmet of her hair. She throws back her head and laughs.

An unexceptional scene, one might think. And now here comes James, and after another minute Teresa, and all four stand in the evening sunshine and then move towards the cars. They are going to the pub for a drink. Pauline has volunteered to give Luke his bath and put him to bed, because she will enjoy this and has no desire to join them.

She watches the four of them get into the car. James is driving. Maurice and Carol get into the back. The car moves away down the track. Maurice is still talking, Pauline sees. He has turned sideways towards Carol and his arm lies along the back of the seat behind her.

Pauline takes Luke into the bathroom and sets about the bathing process. She does and says all the things that have to be done and said – the running of the water, the undressing of Luke, the continuous commentary that is necessary to keep Luke happy and cooperative. Luke sits in the bath and bangs small plastic containers around. Pauline kneels on the bath mat with her arms over the side of the bath and demonstrates to Luke the physical properties of water – the qualities of whoosh and splash and pour – while thinking not of these nor indeed of Luke himself but of another child and another time.

The bath in that house in the cathedral town was made of cast iron, with claw feet. Lion's feet. Lion. That was one of Teresa's first words. Lion meant bath. The part became the whole. An antediluvian bath. Pauline has observed that nowadays baths like that are manufactured once again and are displayed in emporia which sell bathroom equipment with very expensive price tags. Back then the possession of such a bath was a stigma. The upwardly mobile young couple aspired to an avocado suite.

Pauline did not aspire to an avocado suite. She had other things to think about in the Victorian house with the lion-footed bath.

She stoops over the high awkward side of the bath and soaps Teresa's back. She feels the delicate wings of her shoulder blades and then the serration of her ribs. She knows every inch of Teresa's body – each plane, each groove, each cranny. If something is amiss – a scrape, a bruise, a rash – she feels an instant disquiet. Teresa's body is somehow more intensely personal than her own. It is as though it were a vulnerable extension of herself that must be protected from the onslaughts that Pauline's own skin and flesh have come to endure.

She examines a scratch on Teresa's arm – a pink thread. She sees and registers the scratch and registers also that it is insignificant, but without thought or attention. She cannot think or attend because of what she is feeling, because of the cold void in her stomach, because of the words that run through her head, over and over again.

'There's something you ought to know, Pauline,' says Louise Bennett, who is married to Harry's colleague Ted Bennett. 'About Harry. The thing is, apparently – Ted says, everyone in the department is noticing – anyway, the thing is, he's always with Myra. You know – Myra Sams, from International Relations. She's always in his office, Ted says. Or they're in the canteen together. I mean, maybe you already know . . .' Louise's voice trails away.

Pauline likes Louise. At least until that moment Pauline has liked Louise. Now, within three seconds, she no longer likes her. Nor Ted Bennett. Nor everyone in the department. That is all she can think of at this moment – how much she does not like Louise. The rest will come later. Oh, it will come.

'Yes,' she says. Quite calm, quite natural. 'Yes, I expect she is. She's helping him with his book. He was telling me – the other day. She knows a lot about French nineteenth-century population studies, so that's very useful to him.'

'Oh, I see,' says Louise. 'Oh, well . . .' She looks away. She starts busily to talk of something else. And Pauline hears not a word she says. Not a single word. She can think only of them. Her and him. Him and her. Talking about the book. Smiling at each other. Laughing. Doing whatever it is that they do.

Myra Sams. The first. That is to say, the first so far as Pauline was concerned – the progenitor, the prototype, the only begetter. She who began it all, whose name was the first to prompt that icy trickle within, that creeping nausea.

And where is Myra Sams today? Vanished, extinguished, quite undone. She is neither here nor there – she exists only in Pauline's head, as an emotive sound. Myra Sams. And indeed it is not her name which has prompted an echo of that time

102

now, as Pauline leans over the World's End bath to lift Luke
to his feet. An echo, a twinge – like the ghost of a toothache
when the real thing has gone.

'Up you get,' she says to Luke. 'Out now. Yes, yes. Up and
out.' She swings him up. She wraps him in the towel. She
chats, she sings. No, she is thinking. No, no, no. Not again.
Not that again.

She looks across the table at Harry. 'I've been burning your
book,' she says.

'Why? *Why?*'

'You know why,' she says.

Oh, books, books . . . she tells Luke. Terrible things, books.
Cause nothing but trouble. You keep out of the book busi-
ness, my lad. Commodity dealing for you. Or heart surgery.
Or the construction of oil rigs.

She puts Luke into his cot. Luke protests. She fetches his
bottle, and he reverts to infancy. He lies there sucking, his
eyelids drooping and then jerking open as she backs furtively
towards the door. He drops the bottle and wails. Pauline returns to his side, restores the bottle, murmurs reassurances,
creeps from the room, reaches the kitchen in time to hear
Luke wailing once more.

This process is repeated several times. At last Luke is silent.
Pauline plugs in the baby-alarm and settles herself in the
sitting-room. She sifts through the pile of books on the table
and rejects them all in favour of the newspaper. She reads for
a while. Her attention drifts and she looks around the room,
which records the presence of its recent occupants. Teresa's
straw hat hangs on the knob of a chair back. Luke's ball has
rolled under the table. On the mantelpiece is an alien pair of
sunglasses – reflective with gilt rims – that must belong to
Carol. The cream cable-knit sweater slung over the arm of

the sofa is presumably James's – it is far too considered a garment for Maurice. But the rather grubby cotton jacket with a rip in the sleeve does indeed pertain to Maurice.

Pauline waits for them to return. She knows this room intimately. And it is not right tonight. There is a whiff of something feral and disturbing, which is also a reverberation of that continuous elsewhere in the mind. Then and now have become uneasily confused. Simultaneously another Pauline waits in another room, waits for Harry to return from wherever he is and whatever he is doing – from the seminar that he is giving or the counselling of a student or the drink in the bar with a colleague. Or from some other activity which she does not want to think about but must – which she is driven to contemplate in excruciating detail, each image a torment.

She sees them face to face across a table, his hand on hers. She sees them making love, body to body. But most of all she sees them as she did indeed see them last week at a party, on the far side of a room, simply talking. Harry's back is turned so she cannot see his face, but she sees it through the eyes of Myra Sams and knows precisely what Myra Sams is seeing. She knows the expression that Myra Sams is seeing, the way Harry's mouth will tilt at one side, that quizzical look with his eyes slightly screwed up, the head a little on one side. It is the look he gives to those he has singled out for close attention. It is the look which once was directed upon her – over restaurant tables, in that car driving across America, in bed. She sees that look, and her insides run cold.

Pauline, Teresa, Maurice, James and Carol are in the grassy car park of this eighteenth-century mansion. Pauline is helping Teresa to stow Luke in the buggy.

'So what's your view, Pauline?' says Maurice. 'Come and

arbitrate. Why do people visit stately homes? We differ. James says it's just snobbery.'

'Not quite,' says James. 'I said it panders to a need to fantasize. You know – I too might have lived like this – that sort of thing. Personally I just feel resentful. I know damn well where I'd have been living back then – in a hovel. My great-grandfather was a ploughman.'

Carol puts on the gilt-framed sunglasses, which almost engulf her small face. 'Was he? You've never told me that. I think you're both being far too ideological. People just like looking at nice things. All that plushy furniture and the walls covered in pictures. They like moseying around saying imagine sleeping in a bed like that and look at that amazing staircase and asking if it's haunted. It's not envy – it's just curiosity.'

'Up to a point,' says Maurice. 'But there's surely an element of voyeurism and there's certainly a built-in invitation to make comments and social comparisons. It becomes a very complicated experience. You're confronted by the past, and by unfamiliar objects, and by suggestions of a distinctly alien way of life. People feel challenged. They can't just look, they have to react as well. And they know this in advance, because they've already been sold the concept of the stately home. So . . .' he looks provocatively at Pauline, 'why are all these people here? Why are we here?'

'Because it's Saturday,' says Pauline. 'And the weekend has to be filled in somehow.'

James laughs. 'There you are, Maurice! Perfectly simple.' Maurice grins.

'Could we move?' says Teresa. 'I'm going to have to find their loo first of all. Luke needs changing.'

They proceed along gravelled paths towards the house, which stands complacent amid carefully arranged trees. They climb the sweep of steps, buy their tickets and sidle away from the sales pitch of the National Trust lady at the door. Maurice has views about the National Trust, which will be given expression in the book. 'Sufficient unto the day . . .' he mutters with relish, aiming a deferential smile at the sales pitcher, who is now directing Teresa to the toilets and asking if she could please leave the buggy by the umbrella rack.

They tour. They move slowly from room to room, inspecting tapestries and china cabinets and elaborate pieces of furniture. Each room is host to a temporary drifting population, which itself becomes a part of the exhibit, so that Pauline finds herself gazing with equal attention at a Japanese couple and at the polished oak fruit and foliage of a carved mantelpiece. The Japanese couple take it in turns to manipulate a camcorder. The mantelpiece juxtaposes pineapples with acorns. Pauline wonders about both. Will she appear on this video, hijacked willy-nilly into some sitting-room on the other side of the world? Did the woodcarver think pineapples grew in the Midlands, or is this an elegant joke of interior decoration? She looks round for the others. Maurice has vanished, having dived off in pursuit of something that has caught his attention, which is what Maurice always does. Carol and James are looking out of the window at the emerald swathe of the lawn. Teresa is trying to interest Luke in a display of Staffordshire dogs.

There are many pictures. Most are concerned in some way with slaughter. In a hunting scene hounds pour decoratively over a hillside; the gay scarlet of the huntsman's jacket is complemented by the red flash of the fox as it leaps a wall. A still life of dead game birds has pheasants and partridges draped across the gleaming surface of a table, with swags of greenery and some apples strewn around, each detail meticulously rendered, the stippling of a feather, the bony surface of a foot, the smear of blood on a beak.

Pauline cruises these scenes of carnage, and finds Maurice suddenly at her side.

'I've never killed anything more substantial than a wasp,' he observes. 'Maybe one should try it sometime. Obviously one's missing out on a basic human experience.'

'Plenty of experiences I'd prefer to pass up,' says Pauline drily. 'If the people in this room thought about the implications of what they're looking at they'd be a bit more squeamish. Which includes us. Sanitized violence, this is.'

'Of course. A necessary ingredient of the heritage industry. The torture chamber cleaned up into a museum display. Colourful anecdotes supplied by tour leaders and guide books. Worth an entire chapter, I've decided. Nice remote violence – no more upsetting than something you see on the telly. Most of these people would throw a wobbly if they came across a road accident. Including you and me.'

Teresa has joined them. 'Luke's getting a bit fed up with this. I'm going to have to speed up the house part and get him out into the gardens.'

'Right,' says Maurice vaguely. 'You do that.' He crosses the room to examine a huge dark oil painting in which a young woman in floating garments aims a bow and arrow at a fleeing stag. Next to it a muscular figure struggles with a lion. Diana, thinks Pauline. Hercules. She follows Teresa through the next room, and the next, at a smart pace now. An immense tapestry depicting the birth of Venus. Portraits of eighteenth-century owners of the house dressed as Roman dignitaries. It occurs to Pauline that for those unfamiliar with the codes of classical mythology the reference system of this place must acquire a further dimension of obscurity.

Pauline and Teresa complete their accelerated tour of the house and emerge on to the terrace at the back, where Luke can be released to potter around. They are joined eventually by the others.

'Which way was the loo, Teresa?' says James.

'That way . . . No, not the first path, the second.' James sets off, hesitates.

Carol says, 'James has a wonderful capacity for getting lost. He gets lost a hundred yards from our flat.'

'Teresa,' says Maurice, 'do James a kindness and show him.'

'OK,' says Teresa equably. 'Hang on, James – I'll come with you.' She goes after James, with Luke astride one hip. Pauline wanders a few yards along the terrace, admiring a flower border, preparing to wait for their return. After a minute she looks round for Maurice and Carol. They are no longer there. They are not waiting, it seems. They were a few yards away, apparently stationary, and now they are not.

Pauline continues to patrol the flower border. It is some while before James and Teresa appear. Teresa has called in at the café to buy Luke some biscuits. 'Where are the others?' she asks.

'They must have gone on,' says Pauline. 'Maybe they thought they'd missed you. Probably they're looking for us. These gardens are vast.' She consults the plan in the brochure. 'Water garden . . . yew walk . . . fountain court.'

'No problem,' says James. 'We'll meet up with them sooner or later.'

The gardens are a crafty manipulation of landscape. The lawn forms a plateau which ends in a long balustrade, below which the hillside tips downwards in a sequence of grassy terraces and flower borders. At the bottom is the water garden, and the terraced hillside is flanked by high hedges which screen further enclosures. Pauline, James and Teresa pause at the end of the lawn to lean on the balustrade and get their bearings.

'We should go down there,' says James. 'Incredible great lily things – you can see them from here.'

The path at the side is very steep and looks slippery. Teresa points out that it will be hard to get the buggy up again.

'Maybe there's an easier way at the other side,' says Pauline. 'I'll have a look.'

She walks off. Luke has devised a game which involves dropping sticks through the balustrade. James is telling Teresa that Maurice has suddenly decided to rewrite a chapter, which is going to hold things up a bit, but no matter, Maurice is his own sternest critic and if that's the way he sees it . . .

Pauline reaches the far end of the balustraded terrace. The route down to the water garden does indeed seem easier here. She pauses to look over into a hedged space to one side, a grassy enclosure with a spreading maple tree under which a man and a woman are standing, face to face.

Maurice and Carol. They are distant. Expressions cannot be seen. But there is a stillness, a tension. Maurice is speaking – his hand sketches something. Carol has taken off her sunglasses and stands looking intently up at him. And then he puts his hands on her upper arms, one at each side, holding her, and they stand thus for a few seconds before he lets her go.

Pauline turns away. She walks back and meets James and Teresa coming towards her. 'No,' she says, 'it's just as steep this side. Why don't we leave the buggy here and carry Luke down?'

The water garden has creamy lilies floating amid shiny great leaf-pads. There are blue bulrushes and huge clumps of iris and interesting striped dragonflies. James and Teresa enjoy all this and Pauline apparently shares their appreciation. She too exclaims at the plant with gigantic leaves like some science fiction apparition. She shows Luke the pond skaters and the red gleam of goldfish coasting among the water-lily leaves.

And now here are Maurice and Carol, appearing from the

path that leads to the terrace above. '*There* you are . . .' exclaims Carol. 'We couldn't think where you'd got to. We were hunting for you up there.'

'Hi!' says Teresa. 'Look at these amazing dragonflies.'

'Like miniature helicopters,' says James. He puts his arm round Carol. She leans up against him, squinting into the sun, smiling. She fishes the sunglasses from the pocket of the oversized green shirt that she is wearing over white jeans and puts them on again. The shirt engulfs her as do the sunglasses, making her look like a child who has borrowed adult gear. Pauline stares at her. Oh, I know you, she thinks, I recognize you. You are neither here nor there in the long run, but right now you are very much here, and I see you, and those who will come after you, and I am sick to my stomach.

Teresa is squatting by the side of the pond, holding Luke by the back of his trousers so that he will not fall in. 'Da!' says Luke, indicating the dragonflies, the fish, the lilies, this entire glinting flashing quivering experience. 'He's loving this,' says Teresa to Maurice, who is looking down at them. She is wearing her straw hat, which throws chequered shadow on her face – her cheeks and nose are meshed in sunlight. She beams up at Maurice. 'Can you take him a minute?' she says. 'I want to get that stick.' Maurice stoops to hold Luke. Teresa picks up a stick and reaches out to nudge gently a clump of grass in which crouches a brown stone. The stone jumps into the water. Luke gazes in astonishment. Teresa laughs delightedly. 'His first frog,' she says. 'Toad, surely?' says Maurice. 'Aren't frogs green?' 'Frog, toad, whichever . . .' Teresa is aglow, happy, seized by one of those sudden surges of contentment to which she is prone. 'I'm glad we came here,' she goes on. 'It's a great place. Don't you think so?' 'Great,' agrees Maurice. 'Look! Your frog's under that lily leaf now,' says Carol. 'I can see its foot.' And there they all are, gathered in this benign place on this exquisite blue summer day, looking at a frog in a pond.

'I swear to you,' says Harry. 'It's over.' He is gazing very directly at her, biting his lip – a look that is uncompromising and unflinching and which suggests compunction and apprehension. A complex look. A look that Pauline has not before experienced. This is in itself unnerving. She is unnerved.

She says nothing.

'Finished. Kaput. Next term she won't even be here. She's got a lectureship at Leeds.'

'*Why?*' says Pauline at last. 'Why her? Why anyone?'

Harry looks down. He pulls a face that implies shame, embarrassment, perplexity, take your pick. 'I'm susceptible, I suppose.'

Silence. Harry's hand creeps towards Pauline's. He lays a finger on her wrist. One finger. She does not move. The finger tentatively strokes.

Harry and Pauline are walking in the woods. Teresa is riding on Harry's shoulders, her short legs clenched round his neck, her hands clasping his forehead. Her face is alight, this treat does not often come her way, outings like this one are rare, such are the demands on Harry's time. But today he is theirs, the family man, and this is the family outing, in these late autumn woods with the smouldering leaves hanging still from the trees. This is one of those times that will seem even better much later, thinks Pauline. It is perfect now, but it will be more perfect yet when it is stowed away in the head. Harry is holding her hand. Teresa is singing – a tuneless chant with jumbled mumbled words. Pauline laughs.

'What's she singing?' asks Harry.

'"The Teddy Bears' Picnic". "If you go down to the woods

today . . ." Her version. They've got a record of it at the nursery school.'

Teresa breaks off. 'I want a teddy bear,' she proclaims from up there above their heads.

'You shall have a teddy bear,' Harry tells her. 'A big brown American teddy bear. I'll bring you one.'

'American?' says Pauline after a moment.

'I'm going to Washington after the end of term.'

'I didn't know that.'

'I thought I told you, sweetie. It's only for a week.' Harry squeezes her hand. He joins in the song. '"If you go down to the woods today,"' he sings, '"you're sure of a big surprise . . ."'

'You're Harry Carter's wife?' says the visiting professor from Stanford. He is looking at her rather closely.

'I'm Pauline Carter.'

'I met your husband briefly at the American Studies Association conference. The man of the moment, he was. Having himself a ball.' The professor seems to be recalling something that amuses him. He quells the lurking smile and again looks at Pauline as though she were a possibly useful item in a window display. 'But I don't seem to see him around the campus.'

'Harry's having a sabbatical this term,' says Pauline. 'He's working up in London a lot of the time.'

'Is that so? Too bad. I'd hoped to see something of him. Maybe you and I could meet up for a drink one evening then?'

'Maybe not, I think,' says Pauline.

'Christ!' says Harry. 'Thirty-six! Thirty-*six*! What's going on?' He stands naked in front of the bathroom mirror, inspecting himself. He does not seem, on the face of it, displeased.

'Time is going on,' says Pauline. 'I thought that was your trade. History.'

'I'd prefer it didn't get so personal. Thirty-six is pushing forty, and by forty I have to have a Chair.'

'You don't have to,' Pauline observes. 'You'd like to. Different.'

'Oh, sweetie . . .' says Harry, 'you are such a very accurate girl. Some might say literal-minded. But I dote on you anyway. By the way, I've asked some extra people to the party.'

'Who?'

'The new guy in French and his wife. A couple of research students. Oh – and a girl called Alice who works in the Vice-Chancellor's office.'

Chapter Ten

'I did wonder a bit about dragon's breath setting fire to a tree,' says Pauline. 'Would it?'

'I tried with a blow-torch,' says Chris Rogers. 'I borrowed my neighbour's and had a go at some old fencing. It started smouldering, and I reckon dragon's breath would be more powerful still.'

'In that case I stand corrected,' says Pauline.

'The problem really is whether or not the reader will accept dragons or unicorns at all,' Chris continues. 'And whether anyone's going to be interested in a story about undying passion. Bit of an unfashionable concept.'

'I think the setting is a distinct advantage. The fantasy helps you suspend disbelief. It's merely a quibble – the dragon's breath.'

'What about the death of the Lady?' asks Chris anxiously. 'Talusa's suicide. Does that work? I hope so. I sweated my guts out over that bit.'

'Oh, it's very powerful. Unbearably sad.'

'Are you sure? You sound a touch doubtful.'

'Oh no. You've done it just right. It's me reacting inappropriately.'

'Inappropriately?'

'Oh, well . . . she shouldn't have done it, of course.'

'Why?'

'Because in the fullness of time she would have recovered. She'd have ceased to give a hang about the Knight. Maybe she'd have got herself another Knight. Or found that she could get on quite well without one.'

'That is a very cynical view,' says Chris sternly. 'Are you sure?'

'Oh, I'm sure,' Pauline tells him. 'I'm fifty-five. I know about this sort of thing.'

There is a pause. 'Well, that's one way of looking at it, but it won't do for an allegory about romantic love, will it?'

'Of course not. Actually I rather prefer your version, even if it does mean killing off the Lady. It's a much stronger story.'

'Stronger than what?' enquires Chris, again after consideration. He seems to be a person who takes conversational exchange seriously. Pauline approves of this.

'Stronger than disillusion, I suppose. Not much of a story there – just a kind of fading away. Passion isn't supposed to do that. Good thing they didn't have any children, incidentally.'

'Out of the question. Or if they had they would have been irrelevant. The children, I mean.'

'I doubt that,' says Pauline. 'They tend to have an awful relevance. But I'm being very literal-minded. An occupational hazard. And entirely inappropriate in this context.'

'You're the editor. You're supposed to raise objections.'

'Copy editor,' she corrects. 'I deal in nuts and bolts, not large aesthetic judgements. That's been done elsewhere.'

'Hugo. Yes. Actually he had a problem with the Lady's death. He made me rework it in some places.'

'Well, it reads very well now,' says Pauline. 'Is your new book along the same lines?'

'No way. I'm through with that sort of thing. This one's sci-fi. Mainstream sci-fi for the devotees. But it's going slowly. I've just climbed to the top of our local mountain in search of inspiration.'

'Successfully?'

'Frankly, no. All I got was a blister, but the view was good.'

'Well,' says Pauline, 'I'll leave you to it. Send me the chapter you're rewriting once you've squared it with Hugo, and I'll go through it.'

'You'll be glad to see the back of me – chopping and changing like this.'

'On the contrary,' says Pauline. 'I'm looking forward to seeing what you've done with the flight through the forest. Please don't get rid of the werewolves.'

She puts down the telephone and looks out of the window. Teresa is on the track in front of the house, entertaining Luke, who weaves his way from one object of interest to another – a puddle, a clump of grass, a lichen-covered fence post. The wheat is no longer dark green but pale, the ears beginning to bend and seethe. The year has turned. That uprush of growth is done with. The place is full to the brim and somehow static. The trees droop over pools of shade. The fields have dusky margins of nettle. There are still the ochre rectangles of set-aside, but there are also occasional glimmering lakes of sky-blue flax, which like the flaring oilseed rape seem to have southern overtones, but more con-genial ones. When a rash of poppies floats against the blue it is as though the hand of an impressionist painter is at work here in the English landscape.

And it is hot. The summer is by now becoming legendary, a news item in its own right. Toppling records, incipient drought. Swarms of jellyfish in the Channel, basking sharks off the Cornish coast. Ice-cream sales at an all-time high, melanoma warnings with the weather forecast. One summer's day rolls into the next, indistinguishable days in which it is light still at ten o'clock, then the sky starts to drain and within a short while is a strange dark electric blue, and the trees and hedges are shadows in a monochrome landscape.

Teresa and Luke are fifty yards away along the track now. Teresa picks Luke up and sits him on the crossbar of the fence. Together they contemplate the wheat. Teresa glances at her watch. She is checking by how much the day has inched ahead, hitched as she is to infant time, that unique dictation of needs and moods, when an hour or a day can seem motionless, spun out into an interminable now. Pauline remembers exactly how it was, and feels as though in one crucial sense she inhabits a different time zone from Teresa, one in which the hours trip over themselves instead of stalking past.

Back then in the cathedral town she was an expert on child time. She knew with precision just how many hours could be consumed by an excursion to the park, by the shopping, by sleep, by a visit to a friend. Now she wants to explain to Teresa that it is all an illusion, that in fact the months are racing by and Luke with them, an irretrievable succession of Lukes, but she knows that this would make no sense to Teresa, who is in the thick of it. She inhabited then a different time zone from Harry. Her days were long, and one day mirrored another. Harry's days – well, Harry's days were a helter-skelter progress of seminars and meetings and sudden dashes up to London for a broadcast and unexplained sorties in all directions because there was a conference he must sample or someone he must talk to about an article or a grant or a job opportunity. The notion that academic life is an orderly and contemplative affair is quite misguided, Pauline came to realize. Harry bounded about the place and occasionally withdrew to his study for a few hours of feverish work, during which he must not be disturbed. The turbulence of his own existence was reflected by the life on the university campus, which seemed to be in a condition of permanent uproar. The students were always demonstrating or protesting, either about the state of the world or about what they perceived as their own unjust treatment at the hands of the authorities. Harry and his colleagues were forever locked into excited negotiations which would spill over into the house as the phone rang late at night or little posses of stern-faced students arrived to deliver ultimatums.

Pauline took a keen interest in all this, but realized that she was irrelevant. The students did not even see her, immersed in their own entrancing world of outrage. Harry saw her, daily, but recognized the house and its occupants simply as the reliable anchorage to which he returned when it was convenient in search of sustenance and recuperation. He would breeze in, exuberant or uncommunicative according to his state of mind, knowing nothing of her protracted days with their many hours in which to consider his alternative existence.

Pauline and Teresa patrol the pond in the park, feeding the ducks.

'Daddy?' says Teresa with animation, staring across the pond.

'No,' says Pauline, 'that's someone else's daddy.'

Your daddy is at Broadcasting House right now, which is a large building somewhere off Oxford Street, I'm told. Or on the other hand he may not be. He may be whooping it up in a pub with some of these intimate associates I do not know or he may be bent studiously over a book in the library of the British Museum or he may be in bed with this person Clare something who has rung up on several occasions lately and prefers not to leave a message. I do not rightly know where your daddy is. I note that most of your friends' mothers do know where their husbands are, pretty well, which is beginning to give me pause for thought, though your daddy becomes petulant and aggrieved when I murmur words to this effect. Your daddy points out that he is a brilliant and thrusting young man – he puts it slightly differently but that is what he means – much in demand, and that he cannot be expected to account for his every move. Your daddy implies that my concern is suffocating and proprietorial. When I am stung into making reference to an episode we will not go into here he looks wearily reproachful and says he thought that was dead and buried now. I am made to feel errant and unreasonable which is quite an achievement on his part because it is clear enough to me that the boot is on the other foot. So I end up confused, not knowing quite where I am – along with not knowing at all where he is. I begin to wonder if perhaps it is all in my mind, if perhaps I am indeed becoming slightly paranoid – that is a word which has been used when your daddy is feeling particularly self-righteous. So I do not press the point, and your daddy usually ends up making love to me because he knows full well that will shut me up.

I love your daddy, unfortunately. None of this would arise if I didn't, I presume. What I am feeling these days is one of the appalling side-effects of love. At least I suppose love is the right word. This too gives me pause for thought because what I feel for you is also generally known as love but it is profoundly different from what I feel for your daddy. I would kill anyone who laid a hand on you but where your daddy is concerned there are circumstances under which I suspect that I might kill him. I am obsessed with your daddy. I think about him most of the time. But I am quite clear-eyed about him. I see that he is egotistic and self-regarding and entrepreneurial. When I consider your daddy with detachment I do not entirely like him. I think he is clever and stimulating but I do not altogether admire him. I love him, which is different. Good sense and indeed self-interest seem to be set aside. And yet I am an intelligent woman, or at least I believed I was. I cannot contemplate the thought of life without your daddy. I cannot contemplate the thought of him being with anyone but me. And this means that your daddy always has the upper hand. He can defuse me with a word or a look.

Take last weekend. We were going to drive to the coast and have a picnic up on the downs. You are partial to picnics. So am I, come to that. We were looking forward to this outing, both of us. And then on Friday evening, late, long after you were in bed, your daddy recalled suddenly that he had not remembered to mention that he was going to have to go to London because there was this symposium at UCL which he really could not afford to miss. I protested. I dare say there was an extra edge to my protestations because last week there had been one of those phone calls from this person Clare something who is so oddly averse to leaving messages. Perhaps your daddy was aware of this edge because he was unusually contrite, unusually anxious to propitiate. He got us both a drink and talked about this plan he has to take a house in France for the summer and he looked at me with that look that unsteadies me entirely. He looked and I was unsteadied and then we went to bed, but not to sleep. So it goes.

Teresa has lifted Luke down from the fence and they are now coming back along the track, very slowly, at Luke's pace, with many stops and starts as Luke pauses to examine a leaf or a blade of grass, falls over, sits down for a while. Teresa waits for him, patiently in attendance. She looks towards the cottages and becomes suddenly alert. A door bangs. Maurice has appeared and strolls towards them, a cup of coffee in his hand. Taking a breather, it would seem. Pauline watches for a moment and then reaches abruptly to switch on her computer. She starts to sort through a pile of correspondence.

Pauline lies in bed. The bed is striped with thin brilliant bars of sunlight. It is early morning, and the shutters are closed, but the light still pours through. Teresa is asleep. Harry has risen early to work. His typewriter pecks away in the next room – peck, peck, peck, then ping and shunt, then peck, peck, peck again. That is the only sound – that and the endless rasp of insects outside. It is very quiet here in the house in France, which is turning out to be as she had expected in some ways but not in others.

She had not understood about Mrs Gatz. Harry has not exactly taken this house – rented it, paid cash for it. He has been lent it by Mrs Gatz. Mrs Gatz is rich. She is a patron. She patronizes those who are up and coming – academics, writers, artists. Harry met her in the States, apparently, and is now included in her constituency of patronage. Mrs Gatz herself occupies a much bigger house nearby – a sort of small château indeed – and some of the patronized are installed there with her. Harry and Pauline have been allocated this house, on account of Teresa, no doubt (it is apparent that Mrs Gatz is not all that enthusiastic about children). Thus they have a degree of privacy and distance from the fervent life of the château, but Harry is expected to appear there with regularity, to join the late-morning gatherings round the swimming pool and the long evening drinking sessions on the terrace. And Pauline also, by extension. Those patronized have certain obligations. Mrs Gatz has thoughtfully fixed up a girl from the village who will come in to baby-sit, but the girl is fifteen, bovine by disposition and patently of low intelligence. Teresa hates her and Pauline is uneasy about her, so she does not accompany Harry very much in the evenings. She sits here in the house and drinks some of the *vin du pays* provided and thinks about the ways in which this summer in France is not turning out quite how she had hoped.

It is not exactly the family holiday Harry had seemed to be proposing. It is not the rare opportunity for them to spend time together, freed from the demands of the university and Harry's relentless diary. It is indeed the occasion for Harry to get down to some work, and that of course is the purpose of Mrs Gatz's generous patronage. She is a facilitator. She is in the business of facilitating production by the young and promising. They are to write and think and paint and sit around brilliantly exchanging ideas and thereby entertaining Mrs Gatz, who is easily bored.

So Harry gets up early and pecks away vigorously at the typewriter. The pile of typescript rises, and with it Harry's spirits. Harry is having a good time. He loves the place, he enjoys the vivacious company up at the château, he is amused by Mrs Gatz. 'This is the life . . .' he says to Pauline, as he wanders barefoot on the cool tiled floors of the sun-dazed house. 'I want to stay here for ever, don't you?' says he, reaching for her across the bed when he has tumbled in at midnight after one of those starlit evenings on the flower-hung terrace of the château.

No, Pauline would not like to stay here for ever, but it seems churlish to put a damper on Harry's exuberance. Harry is gregarious and convivial. Also, as he frequently points out, becoming at these moments serious and less exuberant, he is getting so much out of this – rubbing his ideas up against those of others, trading interests and opinions. There is the Harvard economist with whom he spars so productively and the quirky woman novelist and the brilliant twenty-five-year-old Indian philosopher. The recipients of Mrs Gatz's patronage are various and the population of the château is a shifting one. Each week there is an injection of fresh blood, while other members of the party vanish without further ado. Harry always seems to be on familiar terms with everyone, but Pauline is often at a loss, on her infrequent visits, when she is confronted with a new array of glittering performers, some of whom she eyes with misgiving.

It would of course be absurd to have such misgivings about Mrs Gatz, who is fifty plus and therefore exempt, though admittedly striking still with her coiled platinum hair, her pneumatic sun-tanned body packed into a white satin bathing costume or draped in Italian silks, and her freight of gold chains and bangles. Harry is now one of those who call Mrs Gatz Irene. He is summoned to her side, and they walk around the garden together, or sit apart by the pool, Harry leaning towards her in intimate eloquent discourse and Mrs Gatz occasionally throwing her head back to laugh uproariously.

Harry thinks Mrs Gatz is a hoot, a character – so he tells Pauline. Incredible woman, he says, grinning at some private reminiscence.

What Mrs Gatz thinks of Harry is more opaque. It is on this that Pauline reflects as she lies in bed in the early morning, hearing the insects and Harry's pecking typewriter. 'We don't see enough of you, my dear,' said Mrs Gatz yesterday, pausing on a tour of the poolside. 'But of course you have the little girl to cope with.' Her glance strays to Harry, who is sunbathing on a lilo, talking to the recently arrived Mexican sculptress, whose sleek black head bobs out of the water alongside. 'Anyway, Harry has been the life and soul of the party.' She looks again at Pauline, thoughtfully. Mrs Gatz has small black shiny eyes; the effect is that of being inspected by a bird – an impersonal scrutiny, perhaps with a view to action of some kind. 'He's quite something, your husband, isn't he? I dare say he leads you a dance.' She pauses, seems about to continue, and then does not. She takes a cigarette from the pocket of her towelling robe, lights it, inhales deeply. 'Well, good luck, my dear,' she says, and moves on.

It is of this that Pauline thinks, lying under the stripes of morning sunshine. She thinks about the attractive process of strangling Mrs Gatz, of drowning her in the turquoise swimming pool. In due course, in the fullness of time, she will think about Harry.

*

'Hi!' calls Teresa. 'Come and talk to us. We're bored.' She is in the garden with Luke. Pauline has waved from her bathroom window. Luke stares up and beams.

Pauline joins them on the grass. This is supposed to be a lawn but it is a perfunctory one because too infrequently mown. The flower borders are similarly shaggy, stands of magenta phlox elbowed by clumps of evening primrose and lupins, all of them interwoven with goosegrass and bind-weed. Over the years Pauline has attempted to curb and control the garden and has been both exasperated and awed by its tenacity. Green stuff pours from the ground in a seasonal flood, indiscriminate and unstoppable, and then declines into a sulky winter detritus of brown stems and blackened leaf mould. And Pauline recognizes that her inability to make much of a mark upon this identifies her occupancy of World's End for the dilettante affair that it is. None of the previous residents would have allowed this disorder. They were in the business of obstructing the forces of nature.

So Pauline and Teresa sprawl on the grass while Luke makes forays into the fringes of rampant growth. Teresa has been idly plaiting withered iris leaves. She has made Luke a sort of hat, which he is now gleefully destroying.

'I don't suppose you remember a place in France with a swimming pool,' says Pauline.

'No. When?'

'You were two.'

'I remember a place somewhere with a black dog that I was frightened of,' Teresa offers.

'That was later. Much later. Bristol.'

They look at one another, speculatively, each of them considering a shuffled pack of images, some of which are shared, but with skewed and incommunicable vision.

'The turquoise swimming pool was in Lot-et-Garonne,' says Pauline. 'You were more impressed with it than I was. It sprang to mind, for some reason. The weather, I dare say. We should get Luke one of these plastic paddling pools.'

'I'll ask Maurice to bring one back from London.'

'Maurice is going to London again?'

'Yes,' says Teresa. Her face has taken on a shuttered look. She does not look at Pauline. 'Just for a couple of days.'

Pauline wanders around the house. This is not the Victorian terrace house but another, larger, house, in another town. For Harry is now a professor and his academic rise has been accompanied by a housing upgrade. Pauline supposes that she should be pleased about this. She walks from room to room while Teresa is at the primary school round the corner and tries to think about furnishings and décor. In fact she thinks about Teresa, who is nervous of a small boy who allegedly pulled her hair and of the threat of mince for school dinner and of some dog in the street. And Pauline thinks of Harry.

The house is full of Harry, though Harry of course is not there. His smell is around – clinging to the scarf which hangs in the hall, spilling from the bedroom wardrobe, a miasma on the sheets of the bed. Harry himself is teaching or writing or reading or arguing or laughing with someone (who?). If Pauline goes into his study she finds the desk covered with Harry – his handwriting, letters addressed to him, sometimes his diary. She reads the letters, which are almost exclusively concerned with Harry's professional life, and learns from them the extent to which Harry does not bother to tell her what he is thinking and doing. She had not known that Harry applied for a prestigious job in the States which, as it happens, he did not get. She remembers the American woman historian from Berkeley who was around last year and whom Harry found so stimulating, and wonders. Pauline spends much time wondering, these days. Speculating. Imagining.

Occasionally she looks at Harry's diary. She would prefer

not to do this, but is impelled. The diary is an engagement diary and while some of the entries are clear enough (seminar 2.00, senate meeting 4.00) others are cryptic. Phone D. 18th. P. – 4.30. Or simply a hieroglyphic – a squiggle, a curlicue. Dental appointments? Library-book renewal dates? Consultations with MI5? Or something else entirely? It is this conjectural something else that Pauline ponders.

Confrontation is self-defeating, she has come to realize. Harry is not so much defensive or evasive as perplexed. An invisible observer of such an exchange between them would see Pauline as the flailing accuser, resting her case on inference and conjecture, while Harry is the voice of sweet reason, explaining that he is a busy man, that he knows and sees many people, some of whom are indeed women, that these accusations are not reasonable, not sensible.

And all the time she knows, she knows.

'I've had an idea,' says Pauline. 'Maurice is going to London tomorrow . . .'

'I am indeed,' says Maurice. 'Anything I can get you?'

Pauline addresses Teresa. 'Why don't you go with him and leave Luke with me? Have a break. He'd be fine if it's just for a night or so.'

'Oh . . .' Teresa is taken aback. She hesitates. She looks at Maurice. 'Well, thanks, but . . . I don't know . . .'

Maurice is considering the proposal. 'Well, that's a thought . . .' It is beautifully done. His tone is just right. He is in no way put out. He looks at Teresa. 'What do you think?'

Teresa is in a quandary. Pauline knows precisely what is going through her head. She has never yet left Luke overnight. He is entirely used to Pauline, is frequently alone with her. But each morning of his life he has woken to find Teresa there. If he cries in the night it is she who comforts him.

'Well . . .' she says.

'Go on,' Pauline urges.

Teresa havers. At last she says, 'Thanks, but I don't think I will. I mean, it's really nice of you but I think I'd rather not. When he's bigger maybe . . .'

Maurice shrugs. 'OK. If that's how you feel. Sure there's nothing I can bring you, Pauline?'

Chapter Eleven

Maurice goes to London. Pauline watches the car move away along the track and vanish into the wheat. As soon as it is out of sight she gets up from her desk, goes down the stairs and outside. Teresa's front door is open. 'Hi!' Pauline calls. She goes into Teresa's kitchen, where Teresa is standing at the sink looking out of the window with Luke trying to climb up one of her legs. She turns and Pauline sees that she has hastily rearranged her face. She smiles, after a fashion: 'Hi!'

'How about this . . .' says Pauline briskly. 'How about we teach Luke to swim today? There's a swimming pool at Hadbury now. A bit crummy, but it'll do. I wouldn't mind a plunge myself.'

'Oh . . . Well – yes. Great. Shouldn't you work, though?'

'I could do with a day off. I need to adjust. I've got unicorns on the brain and I should be thinking North Sea oil.'

'I beg your pardon?' says Teresa.

'I'll explain later. Go and find your swimming costume.'

Pauline drives – Teresa beside her, Luke stowed into the child container behind them. The landscape is simmering, the fields quivering in a heat haze, mirages of shining liquid on the road ahead. 'Idiot weather,' says Pauline. 'It'll all end in tears. Cataclysmic thunderstorms and snow in August.'

'Mmn . . .' Teresa is staring out of the window but she is not thinking about the weather. Pauline shoots a look at her.

'I'll tell you about these unicorns. Are you sitting comfortably? Then I'll begin. There was once a Lady. Her name was

Talusa. She was beautiful – that goes without saying. Beautiful and reasonably clever and virtuous up to a point. She fell in love with a Knight. The Knight was called Rohan. And the Knight fell in love right back so everything was fine in that department. The problem was that the Lady's parents didn't approve of the Knight. They thought he wasn't rich enough. This is a traditional story in some ways, you note.'

'Mum,' says Teresa, 'what is all this?'

'It's a novel. Written by a young man who lives half-way up a Welsh mountain – also a somewhat traditional figure. Anyway . . . if her parents wouldn't let her marry him she would run away with him. So her parents packed her off to a convenient friend of theirs who owned a castle in a distant place of unspeakable desolation, where he was to lock her up and keep her safe. This character was known as the Lord of the Far Land and needless to say he had designs on the Lady himself. So Talusa escaped from him, being a not unresourceful girl and powered as she was by consuming passion. And she began to search for the Knight, who was of course also searching for her.'

'How had she met the Knight in the first place?' inquires Teresa. 'Through a dating agency?'

'This is a serious story about serious matters. I'll treat that remark with the contempt it deserves. As a matter of fact Rohan met Talusa because he rescued her from a unicorn. And of course we know what *that's* all about, and I have to admit that I felt a certain resistance to the scene at first. Oh, come on . . . I thought. But it's cleverly done – in one way he's hamming it up and in another it's rather beautiful and moving and distinctly erotic. Talusa is picking flowers in this meadow and there's the unicorn, only she hasn't seen it. It's stalking her. And Rohan who is hunting comes out of the wood and sees what's going on. Luke, stop that racket – I'm telling your mother an interesting tale and she can't hear a word. Have you brought some juice for him? Right – that's better. So Talusa looks up and sees the unicorn and Rohan both at once, and it's simultaneous panic and unquenchable desire. The unicorn is thundering through the flowers towards Talusa now, horn at the ready, and Rohan raises his bow and takes aim . . .'

'And bang goes another endangered species,' says Teresa.

'This is not a politically correct story. And in any case Rohan's arrow does not kill the unicorn. The unicorn is merely wounded. It turns on Rohan, who manages to elude it and to snatch up Talusa, fling her on to his horse and gallop away with her. The unicorn is left bleeding on to the cowslips and will turn up later on in the story because it is now consumed with hatred for the Knight and is out to get him. Or the Lady, as the case may be. And indeed this becomes a recurrent theme. At one point Talusa is surrounded by an entire herd of unicorns. And on another occasion the unicorn turns up fortuitously when the Knight is busy dealing with a dragon, and the dragon's attention is diverted in the nick of time. There's a chilling pursuit by werewolves when Talusa is searching for the Knight in an impenetrable forest to which she has been directed by a sorcerer with ambivalent motives . . . Luke sounds as though he's dropped his juice.'

Teresa dives over into the back of the car; Luke is once more silenced. 'It sounds a weird novel. Is this what people read nowadays?'

'Probably not. I fear for him, this young man. Mercifully his next opus appears to be more like a fictional version of the stuff on those machines in amusement arcades – quite incomprehensible unless you're into that sort of thing but I dare say there's a market of enthusiasts and maybe he'll make his fortune. Personally I rather go for the Lady and the Knight, though of course he's got it all wrong, my young man up his mountain.'

'Got what wrong?' asks Teresa after a moment.

'Love. Unswerving irresistible romantic love to die for.'

'So who dies? The Knight, I suppose.'

'He does not. I told you this story is not politically correct. Talusa searches in vain for the Knight, overcoming insuperable difficulties and fortified by her trust and devotion. And indeed to begin with the Knight too is searching. But he displays an increasing tendency towards distraction, not to say dalliance. He finds frequent consolation with obliging wood sprites and water nymphs and suchlike riff-raff and eventually he drifts into a liaison with an extremely fetching witch.'

'Definitely incorrect,' says Teresa. 'Even children's books don't have witches these days. So what about the Lady?'

'She gets to hear about the Knight and his witch. Naturally. There's always someone on hand to make sure a person hears about that sort of thing. And her heart is broken. She is drained of all joy, all hope, all expectation. She wants only to die. This is of course where I part company with my author. He lets her kill herself. He allows her – he encourages her. She drowns herself in a lake deep in the forest and sinks to oblivion, clutching armfuls of flowers. It's the Lady of Shalott and Ophelia rolled into one. Totally unacceptable.'

'I don't know about that,' says Teresa, rather coolly.

'Huh . . . Acquiescence. Tantamount to saying to the Knight – I'm terribly terribly hurt but I'll remove myself from the scene and not bother you any further. Sanctimonious self-sacrifice.'

'There's nothing she could do about her feelings. If that's how she felt, then that's how she felt.'

'It's not feelings I'm talking about – it's actions.'

'So what should she have done, then?' demands Teresa.

'Oh, there's a rich choice. She could have done a deal with the unicorn or the werewolves or the Lord of the Far Land and had the pair of them duffed up or written off entirely.

We don't have the constrictions of the rule of law in this story, so it's each for herself. She could have relieved her feelings by setting the tabloid press on them or by sending them poison-pen letters for the next ten years. Best of all, she could have just walked away from the whole situation and set herself up with a more traditionally reliable Knight if she felt pair-bonding to be so absolutely essential. Or she could have cashed in on her recent experience and contacts to set up a lucrative Adventure Holiday tourism agency and become very rich.'

'Mum,' says Teresa, 'you've missed the Hadbury turn, you know.'

'Never mind, we'll go the long way round. Is Luke asleep?'

'Yes. Did you say all this to the author?'

'Good heavens no. Give me credit for a degree of professional tact. It's his book. I keep my opinions to myself. Well – up to a point. And it must have something if the reader's responses are thus aroused. I doubt if I'll start being opinionated about the history of the North Sea oil industry.'

The Hadbury swimming pool is on the outskirts of the town, a part of the surrounding belt which services the place and the surrounding area – industrial estates, hypermarkets, golf course, arts-and-leisure complex. The countryside cannot now survive without the facilities available to an urban population, and Hadbury supplies these.

Pauline and Teresa get into their swimming costumes in a clammy changing room and instal themselves beside the training pool, which pullulates with small children. Luke is at first silent with amazement. He stands on the battered grass of the play area and stares at this scene of manic leaping figures and of heaving blue water which is backed by continuous noise – a high-pitched clamour as though the chatter of a flock of birds were turned up to an exaggerated volume. Teresa takes him into the water. She jumps him up and down.

His amazement turns to apprehension and then to delight. His fickle universe has come up yet again with a new dimension of experience, in which air melts into water, in which dry becomes wet becomes warm becomes cold.

Pauline joins them. 'You go and have a proper swim in the big pool. I'll take him for a bit.'

Teresa goes. Pauline walks Luke around in the pool, amid the shrieks and the thrashing limbs. She trails him in his plastic ring on the sparkling, dimpled, chlorine-smelling water. She has forgotten now that turquoise pool in France and is thinking of her own mother, who did not do things like this with Teresa. Her own mother, she realizes, did not much care for children. She saw them simply as an essential accessory if you were to be a fully paid-up member of society. They were a credential, along with the mortgage and the pension. You married, you secured an income and a house, you had children – in her case, one child. And in due course your own child too gave birth, thus conferring upon you genetic respectability in the eyes of the world.

Pauline took Teresa on visits to her grandparents every six months or so. Harry did not accompany them – he was of course always too busy. Pauline's parents accepted this without comment and perhaps with relief. They did not know how to deal with Harry; his conversation baffled them and his clothes unsettled Pauline's mother. 'I thought you said he had a senior position now in his work? So what will people think if he wears jeans all the time like that?'

'They'll think he's reassuringly conventional,' said Pauline. Her mother looked at her with scepticism.

Teresa was a source of interest to her grandparents, but not an emotional focus. On each visit Pauline's mother would comment favourably (or otherwise) on the child's growth and appearance, and then leave it at that. She was without the capacity to revel in what was demonstrably a standard procedure. 'Well, she's coming along quite normally, that's the thing,' she would say. Pauline realized that her own childhood too had been without that dimension of exaltation.

At the darkest point of the Harry years she felt impelled, on one occasion, to correct her mother's complacent vision of her circumstances. Honesty had driven her to try this once or twice before, but her oblique attempts to counter her mother's construction of a marriage that mirrored her own had been brushed aside.

'Harry well?' her mother inquired.

'Harry is well, so far as I know. I don't see a great deal of him.'

Her mother ignored this invitation to a more intimate exchange, for such it was. 'He'll have a lot on his plate, now he's in this new job.'

And when Pauline stepped further yet into disclosure her mother backed off like a nervous cat.

'Harry well?'

'I wouldn't know. Harry is in America.'

Her mother looked away, sensing danger. 'It's nice that he's in demand like this.'

'Is it?' said Pauline. 'Yes and no. The trouble is that the more he is in demand with others the less my demands are taken into account.'

Her mother looked disapproving, but not of Harry. 'Men have to put their work first, that's reasonable. Harry's doing well, that's the main thing, isn't it?'

'Mother,' said Pauline, 'I'm not talking about Harry's work.'

At which point her mother glimpsed the truth, and took cover. 'I wonder what Teresa's up to in the garden – I'll just pop out and see.'

Pauline never raised the subject again, and when shortly afterwards she announced that she was leaving Harry, and for what reason, her mother's response came in the form of conventional expressions of pained regret that carried the implication that Pauline herself must be found wanting in some way. Pauline perceived that the concept of marital infidelity was not one with which her mother was familiar. She knew of it as a theme of fiction and of drama (she read library books and went occasionally to a film) but did not see it as applicable to real life and least of all to her immediate world. The notion of her own husband consorting with another woman was inconceivable. His infidelities were with the golf club, the Sunday newspapers and the test match on the radio.

Teresa returns from her swim. She sits on the grass with her wet hair sleeked back and a towel over her shoulders, watching the children in the pool. There is a pinched look on her face, a look which Pauline knows intimately, has seen time and time again since Teresa was six, nine, twelve and washed up on some malign reef of guilt, chagrin, disappointment, betrayal.

Pauline talks. She talks about the fact that Luke's hair will soon need cutting, about Hugh who called yesterday and sent fond messages to Teresa, about a news item that caught her attention over breakfast. She talks about Chaundy with whom she had a chat yesterday. The wheat, she tells Teresa, is burning up, it seems – you'd think the stuff would revel in all this sun, but no, it's frying and Chaundy is losing money by the day, unless we have rain. 'My heart does not bleed – he's a rapacious so-and-so . . .' Teresa makes perfunctory responses. 'Mmn . . .' she says. 'Did he?' 'Really? I didn't know that.' She is elsewhere, plunged in private malaise.

Something has happened. There has been some hint – something amiss, something awry.

Pauline takes a breath. Then she reaches again for the unicorns. '. . . So I'm quite sorry to be finished with this book,' she tells Teresa. 'It's a change to find yourself so involved with a story that you start arguing with it. In a way I think it's because it reminded me of a woman I once knew to whom that sort of thing happened – minus of course the unicorn or the dragon or the werewolves but the same damn business of obsessive, inescapable passion for a guy who was not similarly obsessed and who was having it off with wood sprites or the equivalent right, left and centre.'

Teresa blinks. She removes a discarded ice-cream spoon from Luke's grasp and delves in her holdall for a toy.

'It's odd – at the time I could see exactly why she went on the way she did. It seemed as though there was no alternative. Now I'd want to take her in hand.'

'What happened to her?' asks Teresa. She does not sound much interested.

'Oh, she came to her senses in the end and turned her back on it all. I've rather lost touch with her. I don't feel we'd have much in common now. You know how you grow out of people? Though . . . actually I did run into her not so long ago and she talked a bit about him, her ex, because . . . well, um, because I'd come across him at one point . . . and she said that what she felt about him now was something like what you'd feel about a housebreaker. He was someone who had walked in and hijacked a large chunk of her life and she resented that because life is life, after all.'

Teresa says nothing. Either she is still uninterested or this notion does not appeal to her.

Pauline shrugs. 'And at the time she was besotted. I know, because I was around and took note. Should we make tracks before Luke succeeds in throwing himself into the pool?'

They drive back to World's End. Luke sleeps. Pauline puts on a tape. Teresa stares out at the shimmering landscape, at the cloudless sky, at passing traffic – coaches from France and Germany, a container lorry from Poland, car transporters, tractors, battered pick-up trucks, cars towing caravans. This is the deep of summer, and this is the depths of the English countryside.

Pauline carries Luke, still sleeping, into the cottage. Teresa follows with the holdall, the towels and swimming costumes. The red eye is blinking on the answering machine. Teresa walks straight to it, presses the button. Maurice speaks: 'It's me. Just to say I'll be back in the evening on Wednesday, not morning – a couple more things have cropped up. OK? Oh – and James and Carol will be down for the weekend.'

Teresa turns. She takes Luke from Pauline. Her face is neutral, blank. Luke wakes up and starts to cry.

Pauline stands with Harry on a street corner. They have had lunch together in a restaurant – a rare treat. Harry got back from the States yesterday, fell jet-lagged into deep sleep, woke and said, 'I'll have to rush – I'm teaching at ten. Tell you what – let's meet for lunch. I'll take you to that Italian place.' And so they have lunched, with Harry on a high – elated, exuberant, affectionate. And now they are parting on this street corner because Harry has a seminar at three and must rush again.

He seems abstracted now – abstracted and incandescent all at once. And suddenly he squeezes Pauline's arm – companionable, high-spirited, slightly tipsy. 'Isn't life wonderful!' he exclaims.

She understands that he has a new woman.

Harry reaches for her in the early morning. She drifts up from sleep to find him making love to her, that familiar warm invasion, and to begin with she is responding in her sleep – naturally, comfortably. And then she opens her eyes and looks up into his and sees that she is not there. It is not to her that Harry is making love, but to someone else. She sees this and goes cold. The act has become an obscenity.

*

Pauline realizes that she is an expert, a connoisseur. She has a subject, the special subject on which she is the leading authority. She is the authority on jealousy. She knows everything that there is to be known about jealousy. She could write a treatise on jealousy, a disquisition, a learned paper with footnotes and appendices. She could give seminars on jealousy, she could run a symposium, she could devise a degree course on the evolution and manifestations of jealousy. She could instruct the uninitiated upon the way in which jealousy combines physical with mental effects. If jealousy is a disease, she would argue, then we have to determine if its origins are biological or if they are in the mind. She would publish the definitive description of the symptoms of jealousy – the perpetual churning of the guts, the nausea that surges each morning as the sufferer awakes to a fresh realization of what is happening, the hollow plunge that succeeds each new uncertainty, each new suspicion. It would appear that jealousy is sited in the stomach, she would say, but the mental symptoms displayed must also be taken into account: the obsessive concentration upon a single issue, the feverish pursuit of evidence, the awful heightened awareness. And then there are the periods of remission, when the belief arises that nothing is going on after all, that it is a mistake, that all is well – bouts of false security that serve only to intensify the disease when it comes roaring back.

'Pauline, why don't you leave Harry?' says her friend Linda. 'He'll go on doing it, you know. If it's not this Julia person it'll be someone else.'

And Pauline does not reply. Because she knows that this is what she has to do.

Maurice returns. Pauline hears the car. She is startled, because as it happens she is not at this moment in the cottage at

World's End at all but elsewhere and in another time and expecting someone quite different who will arrive – if he arrives at all – on foot or by taxi, conspicuously, filling the place at once with his presence. And there is something she is going to say, words that have rolled in her head for days, that are honed now to a fine precision, words whose hour has come.

So Pauline is briefly startled. And then she sees the car, and Maurice who unfolds from the driving seat, stumbling as he does so (that slight infirmity in one leg) and reaches into the back for the Gladstone bag. Pauline returns at once from her seething elsewhere, registers Maurice and continues in a different key to chop and slice ingredients for the casserole she is making. Pauline is not a vehement cook. She eats in the spasmodic and opportunistic way of those who live alone and she seldom spends time on the careful preparation of food, but today she has shopped in the village and decided on impulse to make this casserole, which will do for her supper and can then be put in the freezer as a hostage to fortune. Even if those two are coming for the weekend it is by rights her turn to act as Saturday-night hostess. The casserole will come in handy. She assembles the different piles – pinkish-white umbrella-shaped slices of mushroom, translucent curves of onion, scarlet sections of pepper – she hears the front door slam next door, Maurice's voice, the sound of Luke – she sweeps the vegetables into a frying pan and starts to cut a slab of meat into cubes. From time to time she looks out of the window, across the track at the wheat which is changing colour by the day. She remembers the green rash of early spring, which was succeeded by a thick pelt, but cannot now see them in her head and thinks again how odd it is that some things hang there, indestructible – Harry's face and voice on a street corner, the feel of his hand on her arm – but the ordinary processes of change are so hard to recover.

What did that hedge look like in May? Why does language hang there in the mind – a voice, a sequence of words – but she cannot now summon up the cuckoo?

She completes the preparations for the casserole and puts it in the oven. The phone rings.

'I merely wish to tell you,' says Hugh, 'that the Alma-Tadema exhibition is not to be missed. I strongly advise that you emerge however briefly from this self-imposed exile before it comes off. I forgot to mention it the other day.'

'Mmn . . . Well, I'll see. Maybe.'

Hugh expounds further upon this exhibition. Eventually he senses a certain inadequacy in her response. 'Is all well? You sound a bit . . . unsettled.'

Pauline hesitates. 'I suppose all's well. Maybe I am un-settled. I've been thinking a lot lately. I've been thinking about Harry.'

'I hope he hasn't been bothering you,' says Hugh sternly. He knows about Harry's occasional overtures.

'Oh no – I don't mean Harry these days. I mean Harry then.'

'Ah. I see.' Now Hugh is in retreat. He is not a man for emotional confidences. He has a working knowledge of Pauline's past and of Harry's role but does not care to mull over the matter, as Pauline well knows.

'Don't worry,' says Pauline. 'A tot of whisky and a dose of the telly will calm me down nicely.'

'Good-night then, my dear. And I urge you to bear the Alma-Tadema in mind. I shall pursue the matter.'

The light soaks away at last and World's End stands isol-ated in the summer night. Pauline draws her curtains, eats a helping of the casserole and zaps through the airwaves in search of distraction. She dips into Californian simulated crime, into the wildlife of the Siberian tundra, into the prob-lems of emigrant Albanians. Eventually, quite late, she switches off, tidies up the kitchen, opens the back door to empty rubbish into the bin. She stands then for a moment because it seems that everything is not quite as it should be, and indeed it is not, for a wedge of darkness beyond her suddenly moves.

'Christ, Maurice!' she says irritably. 'You scared the hell out of me.'

'Sorry.' He steps forward into the light, and deals her the Maurice smile – confiding, conspiratorial. 'I was enjoying the night. Teresa's gone to bed. Have a drink?'

'No, thanks.' Maurice has had several, Pauline sees. 'I'm going to bed too.'

'All right, then – abandon me.' He empties his glass. He stretches – sensual, cat-like. He gestures at the sky – the sizzling stars, the sickle moon. 'Look at that! Life's pretty good, isn't it, Pauline?'

She stares at him for an instant, and goes inside.

Chapter Twelve

The Museum of Rural Life is well attended on this Saturday afternoon but not crowded because the day is as usual remorselessly fine and most people have chosen to amuse themselves in the open air. It is Maurice of course who has proposed the visit to the museum, which is an item on his research itinerary, and the others have acquiesced for their own reasons. James and Carol are compliant because they are visitors and visitors should comply. Moreover, so far as James is concerned this expedition is a professional concern, in the service of Maurice's book. Teresa is there because she is driven to be where Maurice is, and Pauline, who knows this, is there herself because it is conceivable that her presence might be of some help to Teresa.

The museum is in the centre of a small county town that has escaped the commercial and industrial fate of Hadbury and now earns its keep as a display of well-groomed buildings with attendant antique shops, pubs and restaurants. Outside the museum stand the town stocks, also scrupulously maintained and with an explanatory text in gothic script. Maurice pauses to take a photograph, though his subject is not the stocks *per se* but the giggling adolescents who are trying to fit their legs through the holes. No doubt this will furnish some ironic sub-text in the book.

Pauline stalks the rooms with curled lip. She inspects the elegant arrangements of flails and scythes and sickles and shears (shapely artefacts spotlit against a white wall) and the facsimile dairy with its churns and creamers. She stares at the sepia photographs of quaintly clad folk going about their tasks – reaping, mowing, shoeing horses, milking cows. The children assembled for a Sunday School group portrait, looking out at her from the 1870s, inscrutable, pinned up there now as a museum exhibit. There is a frozen gentility about this entire assemblage. The objects displayed are detached from any function and have become décor, the explanatory text and pictures invite an attitude of scientific observation. This is how this was done; this is the process for doing that. But these are the people who lived at World's End, thinks Pauline, and it was not thus at all. These are the men and women to whose spirits she occasionally offers guilty apology. As though they should care.

The museum is tactfully instructive, mindful that visitors are here of their own volition and that if they feel unduly hectored they will head for the pub or the craft boutiques immediately instead of later. So it tempers information with appealing displays. Pauline is now in the room devoted to an explanation of agricultural change in the eighteenth and nineteenth centuries. There is a model of a village field system, before and after enclosure – an intriguing miniature layout of ploughed fields, fallow land, meadows, woodland, common land. There are framed copies of Enclosure Acts. There are panels that give accounts of rural discontent in large print and with short sentences accompanied by grainy representations of disaffected peasantry.

Pauline looks round for the others. The museum is a sequence of smallish rooms so that the party tends to become separated, perhaps because people move at different paces, perhaps for other reasons. Sometimes she can see them all, sometimes not. Right now Maurice is at the far side of this room with Carol and James, the three of them inspecting some display of metalware. Teresa has just come in, with Luke asleep in the buggy.

Pauline is aware of Teresa. She is painfully aware of what Teresa is doing. Teresa is watching Maurice. She is working desperately at apparent detachment – moving idly from one item to another – but all the time she is seeing only Maurice.

The metalwork at which they are looking is an exhibit of man-traps.

'Ouch!' says Carol.

James peers at some rusty marks on the iron teeth. 'Blood, do you think?'

'Undoubtedly,' says Maurice.

'Oh, come on . . .' says Carol. 'They'd have cleaned them up before they put them in here.'

James moves away, wanders off into the next room. Carol and Maurice remain where they are, looking now at each other rather than at the display.

'It's rust, not blood,' says Carol. She is smiling, as though they share a joke.

'Not necessarily,' says Maurice. 'There could be an argument for retaining what may or may not be blood. It increases authenticity.'

They continue to look at one another. If they are conscious that they are observed they do not care. Is this innocence or insouciance? Teresa has shot a glance across the room and Pauline knows that this is what she is thinking. Are they? Do they? Is all this in my head alone?

'Rust,' says Carol.

'Well, you may be right,' says Maurice. 'We'll never know, will we?' And they move on together into the next room, without turning, without looking round for anyone else.

Pauline walks across to examine the man-traps. She sees the jagged teeth, the simple but efficient mechanism. Teresa joins her, stands beside her staring unseeing at the traps. And it seems to Pauline that the room is filled with a silent scream. The scream of some hapless nineteenth-century labourer? Or Teresa's rigidly controlled distress?

'This is an appalling place,' says Pauline. 'Let's get out and find some coffee.'

Dinner in Pauline's kitchen. The five of them, and the disembodied presence of Luke who occasionally sighs or snuffles from the plastic dish of the baby-alarm. Drinks were taken earlier in the garden, they have worked through the smoked mackerel Pauline produced for a starter and are now on the casserole. Maurice is in fine fettle. He has orchestrated the evening, steering the conversation, killing off stale subjects and producing new ones with a flourish. He is entirely even-handed in his attention – he is casually familiar with both James and Carol, joshing James in the way that appears to be the distinguishing feature of their relationship. Now and then he treats Teresa to an aside, when a note of intimacy creeps into his voice. He makes much of Pauline, perhaps because she is technically the hostess, perhaps for some more complex reason. Now he is opening a further bottle of the wine he has contributed.

'Another?' says Teresa.

'Another.' He pats her shoulder, propitiating. 'We've earned it, haven't we, James? A working weekend.'

James holds out his glass. 'If you say so. It hardly feels like work – a couple of hours on Chapter Eight and a trundle round a museum.'

'I loved that museum,' says Carol. 'It was like the set for one of those TV adaptations of Hardy. It made you want to go and live there in a long skirt and a shawl, like Tess.'

'I can't see you settling for the lifestyle of a milkmaid,' says James. 'But you'd look the part, properly got up.'

Carol pulls a face at him. Yes, thinks Pauline – subtract the designer T-shirt in that fetching cornflower blue to set off the eyes, and the white jeans and the trainers, mess up the fifty-quid haircut, add some grime and a few calloused fingers and she fits the stereotype. That pink-and-gold buttery look. Youth, health, sex.

Maurice is grinning. 'How did it grab you, Pauline? The museum.'

'It didn't,' says Pauline. 'Voyeurism. Nostalgic tripe. There's another helping of casserole if anyone wants it.'

'Goodness!' says Carol with a little laugh. 'That's pretty dismissive.' She glances at Maurice.

Maurice is watching Pauline. He is delighted, it would seem. 'Voyeurism? Tell us more, Pauline. I didn't realize you felt so strongly.'

Pauline looks at him coolly. Carol she ignores. 'Where are the blood and sweat, I ask? Where are the children with rickets and the dead babies and the chronic illness and the untreated disease and the festering injuries and the aching bones and the cold and the wet and the grinding labour each day and every day?'

Carol grimaces. 'Surely it wasn't as dire as all that?'

James holds out his plate. 'Would it be insensitive to claim the last helping of casserole?'

'Good point,' says Maurice to Pauline. 'The museum as cosmetic exercise.'

Pauline dumps casserole on to James's plate. 'No doubt you already have a chapter on that.'

'I do, as it happens.'

The baby-alarm gives a plaintive cry.

'Uh-oh . . .' says Carol, solicitous, looking at Teresa.

There is a more positive wail. Teresa gets up and leaves the room.

'The exhibits at the Tower of London are hardly cosmetic,'

says James. 'Instruments of torture. Dungeons. The scaffold.'

'Oh, that's different. People don't identify in the same way. It's historical violence so it's over and done with. Besides, disease and discomfort don't fit in with what a Museum of Rural Life is seeking to promote. The country is better. The country is healthy. The country is arcadia.' Maurice looks at Pauline for endorsement but Pauline is now stacking plates, rather violently, and pays him no attention.

'Interesting,' says James, 'I'd never thought of it like that. The museum industry is going to hate this book. But all the better. It will generate controversial reviews and promote lots of interest.'

'Can I do anything, Pauline?' inquires Carol.

'No, thanks. There's cheese but we'll wait till Teresa comes back.'

'In that case where's your loo?' says James.

'Up.' Pauline turns to the sink and puts the plates into the basin. Behind her Maurice and Carol are talking about an industrial museum in the Potteries which Maurice has visited. Carol is saying she'd like to go. 'We'll fix something up,' says Maurice. 'I need to check it out again anyway.' Pauline goes into the larder to fetch the cheese. She unwraps it and puts it on the board and hunts for a packet of biscuits. When she returns Maurice is standing behind Carol's chair, reaching for the wine on the dresser and Pauline sees for an instant his other hand resting on the nape of Carol's neck before it slides away and Maurice is busy filling glasses.

James returns. 'Lethal stairs you've got, Pauline.'

'I know. You learn caution.'

'A glass of red, Pauline?' asks Maurice. 'Or are you staying with the white?'

'Neither.'

He is brought up short by the edge to her voice. She sees a sudden shock in his eyes, a wariness. And then it is extinguished – he is putting the wine bottle on the dresser, returning to his seat, telling James that they must all go to this museum in the Potteries at some point. And Teresa has come back into the room.

'OK?' says Pauline.

Teresa nods. 'I hope so.' She sits down. Cheese is passed around, and fruit. The room is littered with the debris of eating and drinking. An inviting scene, you might think. Convivial, relaxed. But Pauline is aware only of a spiderweb of tension, of the force-lines between this person and that, of the shuttered look in Teresa's eyes, of the way in which people glance at one another, or do not. Only James perhaps is excluded, eating a peach, that wing of black hair flopping on his forehead, talking on, agreeably blurred with wine.

It is Monday, and they have gone, Carol and James. World's End is embarked upon another working week – Maurice in his study, Pauline in hers, Teresa in attendance upon Luke. Chaundy's tractor has roared back and forth along the track upon some errand, the wheat is ripening by the hour. Pauline has chatted to the postman, received the weather forecast and learnt that there was a nasty pile-up on the main road last night. She has taken their mail in to Maurice and Teresa and seen that Teresa's mood has changed, that the shuttered look has gone. Again, something has happened – something has been said or done and now Teresa's state of mind is different. She is doubting her own conjectures. She is in remission. Pauline sees this and shivers for her. She returns to her own cottage, goes up to the study and immerses herself in the North Sea oil industry.

The phone rings. 'It's me. Chris.'

'Hi!' says Pauline. 'How's it going with the revision of that chapter?'

'Well, it isn't, I'm afraid.'

'Perhaps you should climb your mountain again. Or a different one. Get yourself unblocked.'

'I don't think that would help,' says Chris Rogers dourly.

A pause. 'Is anything wrong?' Pauline inquires.

'Yes. My wife's gone. She's left me.'

'Oh.' A further pause. 'Oh, dear,' says Pauline. Then, cautiously, 'Do you know where she's gone?'

'Yes. She's gone to her mother.'

'Ah. In that case I think one can safely say she'll be back. It won't last.'

'Do you think so?'

'I do,' says Pauline firmly. 'But it's a shot across the bows, put it that way. You'll have to do some thinking. About what the problem may be.'

'I *am*,' says Chris. 'I'm thinking like crazy. When I'm not cooking and feeding the kids and doing the washing.'

'Perhaps she doesn't like living half-way up a Welsh mountain.'

'You could have a point there.'

'Promise her Swansea,' says Pauline. 'Maybe that'll do the trick. I mean . . . things have been reasonably OK between you hitherto, have they?'

'I thought so.'

'Where does her mother live?'

'In a small village in Shropshire.'

'In that case I give her a week,' says Pauline. 'She'll be back. Have the children make piteous phone calls.'

In the late afternoon Pauline, Teresa and Luke take a walk up the track as far as Chaundy's chicken houses just over the brow of the hill. At first Maurice is going to accompany them. He needs some fresh air, he says. He is all set to come and then the phone rings. Someone from English Heritage is returning a call he made earlier. 'Go,' he says, his hand on the

mouthpiece. 'This'll take a while. Maybe I'll catch you up.'
'OK,' says Teresa. She is still in remission, Pauline sees. She
has persuaded herself that all is well, that she was mistaken,
that she misinterpreted whatever it was she saw or heard to
send a spear of ice into her guts. Of course he isn't, she has
told herself. Of course they aren't. And so she blithely sets
off up the track with Pauline, the buggy rattling over the
potholes, Luke chanting out some wordless paean of praise
to the wheat, to the grass, to the cool blue sky.

Teresa too is exulting. She talks – the unfettered spiel of a
mind at ease. She has always been like this – bounding from
gloom to animation. And her physical appearance reflects this
volatility. In a state of depression, she becomes anonymous –
she has a pale, pinched, unmemorable look. When she is
elated, she is vibrant – her eyes glisten, her skin glows, her
face becomes arresting. She is like this now, as she turns to
Pauline in conclusion of an anecdote. And Pauline sees
again Maurice's hand slide from the nape of a neck, and feels
some hideous sense of enforced complicity, of deceit, of
betrayal.

When Teresa was a child Pauline used to have dreams in
which she watched helpless as Teresa went spinning beneath
the wheels of a truck, or pitched from the open doors of
trains. Sometimes these enactments were not dreams but
waking fantasies of horror from which she had to jolt herself
free – involuntary contemplations of some awful contingency.
But none of it has come about. Pauline has kept Teresa safe
from the thundering wheels and the gaping doors, Teresa is a
grown woman sound in mind and body, and now Pauline sees
that malevolence cannot be detected or anticipated, that it can
come stalking out of the sunshine at any moment, that there
is nothing you can do and that she has had a hand in this
herself. I did this, she thinks, watching Teresa at Maurice's side
after their marriage. I didn't mean to, but I did.

And so, together but poles apart, they walk up the track in the soft light of the afternoon. Now it is Teresa who is talkative, and Pauline who falls silent – Teresa who shoots a cautious glance at one point, wondering if anything is amiss. They climb the slope of the hill, pause while Luke is released from the buggy to investigate the belt of long grass alongside the fence. They continue to the top, and dip down into the hollow where the two sheds of the chicken houses stand isolated on an island of concrete.

'Like prison buildings,' says Teresa. 'No wonder they shove them up here out of sight.'

'It's not the kind of thing where they're all in little cages. Have you seen inside? It looks as though one of Chaundy's men is here now.'

There is a car sitting at the end of the track, one of the beat-up vehicles that ply daily past World's End. And as they approach the shed the door opens and a man comes out.

Teresa waves. 'It's the one who gave Luke a ride in the tractor,' she says to Pauline. 'Hello! Can we have a look inside?'

'If you can stand the smell.'

And indeed the stench comes rolling from the open door, not an agreeable, organic, farmyard smell but something rank and so thick that it ought to be visible – a greenish miasma. 'Help!' says Teresa. And then, 'Gawd . . . look at that!' as they peer through the smell into the cavern of the shed. For the entire floor ripples away from them as Chaundy's man goes back inside, carrying a sack – a tide of baby chicks, a yellow flood that ebbs and flows, that swirls around the feed hoppers, that washes up against the walls, that disintegrates here and there into inert heaps of fluff which Chaundy's man picks up and slings into a bucket.

'What do you do with them?' asks Teresa, eyeing the bucket of corpses.

'Put them out for the foxes,' says Chaundy's man laconically. 'Come up here at night,' he goes on, 'and they're there waiting – you sees a ring of green eyes out there in the dark . . .' He demonstrates the operative system for the sheds – the lighting that dims automatically, the thermostats that control the ventilation, the mechanism whereby a continuous stream of grain is fed into the hoppers. He is proud of the technology. 'This place can run itself, all but,' he says.

'What happens if there's a power cut?' enquires Pauline.

'Ah. Then you're in a spot of bother. We got to come up here and see to things.'

In the second shed are chicks at a further stage of development, leggy and feathered, a rougher and deeper tide which nearly covers the floor and surges now around the feed hoppers. Chaundy's man recites statistics – so much grain per chick, weight gain of so much by the first six weeks, so much more thereafter.

Maurice has arrived. He has come up behind them and stands looking into the shed.

'And then what?' says Teresa to Chaundy's man.

'Then the slaughterers come. Kill and crate up in a morning. And we get the sheds ready for the next lot.'

'The contemporary farmyard,' says Maurice. 'Chicken salad for supper, is it?'

Teresa has lifted Luke up to see the chickens. 'And here am I reading him Beatrix Potter.'

'You carry right on. Otherwise how is he to learn the proper image of rural life?' Maurice lays a hand on Teresa's shoulder, and Pauline feels herself go tense.

'My husband is being snide,' says Teresa to Chaundy's man, who is standing by, a sack over his shoulder. 'I'm sorry – we're holding you up.'

'That's all right. I'll get one of the birds for the baby to have a look.'

He dumps his sack and dives into the seething mass of chicks. He comes up with a single bug-eyed, quill-covered creature that he holds out in front of Luke.

Luke stares at the bird. Expressions flee across his face – surprise, mistrust and finally rejection as he clutches Teresa's leg for reassurance.

'There you are, Luke,' says Maurice. 'Chicken tikka masala. Or coq au vin, as the case may be.' He glances at Pauline for a confirming smile, for approval of the joke, and Pauline looks away.

'Well,' says Chaundy's man. 'It's a short life and a merry one. They don't know anything about it.' He drops the chicken back into the mass and picks up his sack.

'Thanks for showing us,' says Teresa. 'We'll stop getting under your feet.'

They move away back down the track. 'There . . .' says Teresa to Luke. 'Wasn't that exciting? Sally Henny-Penny will never be the same again.'

'Nor will Tandoori chicken,' says Maurice. He looks again at Pauline. 'Your mother thinks my humour is in poor taste.'

'I wasn't thinking of you at all, Maurice, as it happens,' says Pauline.

Maurice pulls a face – the reprimanded schoolboy – and Teresa looks put out. Why is Pauline so churlishly clouding a pleasant stroll? And then Maurice sweeps it aside, this unwelcome note, this hint of a snub, and starts to talk about farming methods. Farming is the only industry to pretend that it is no such thing, he says. Farming pretends that it is a public benefit and is therefore exempt from controls or criticism. Teresa says, 'Yes, but . . .' and, 'I would have thought that . . .' and, 'But what about . . .' Luke is once more singing to the flowing wheat and Pauline walks three paces behind them noting various things. She notes that Maurice is high with well-being, that he is the cat who has tasted cream, that he brims with private satisfaction. She notes all this because she is the expert on such things and it is indeed true that she is not thinking of Maurice as the three of them go down the hill to World's End.

Pauline and Harry sit at a kitchen table, eating breakfast. Ostensibly eating breakfast. Harry drinks coffee. Pauline neither eats nor drinks. Silence hangs. Pauline stares at Harry, who does not return her gaze. Teresa erupts into the room, pig-tailed, stick-limbed: 'Mum, where are my gym shoes?'

'In the laundry-room.'

Teresa goes.

'Why?' says Pauline at last. Not – why her? Not – why anyone? Just – why?

Harry looks at her now. He does not slide an exploratory finger towards her hand. He just looks. Then he shrugs. 'These things happen, Pauline,' he says. 'There isn't anything I can do about it.'

Chapter Thirteen

Pauline is with Luke in the World's End garden. She is minding Luke while Teresa takes a break. Minding Luke consists of following him in his erratic progress about the place and intervening when he embarks upon something hazardous. Luke weaves across the lawn and falls on his knees at the edge of the orchard prairie, investigating the high waving grass. Pauline tries to see the world through his eyes – unstable as a home movie, rocking and swaying, rising up from time to time to clout you to the ground, furnished with wonders. Anything can happen out there, and does. A woman could turn into a tree, or a man into a beetle. Pigs might fly. Luke's world is fantasy made manifest, he inhabits a dimension of eternal unpredictability, in which there are no preconceptions and few expectations. And there is no past and no future, just a tumultuous present.

Luke has found something in the long grass, and is putting it into his mouth. Pauline swoops on him and removes a small stone. Luke wails in outrage. Pauline throws his ball into the grass. Luke stops crying and lumbers in pursuit.

Everything matters with desperate intensity, but nothing continues to matter. Is this a good way to live? wonders Pauline. Is this the original Eden of the senses or is it a harsh imprisonment? Is Luke freed or shackled? One thing is for sure – you would not wish to revisit the country in which he lives, knowing what you now know.

Luke is approaching a clump of nettles. Pauline picks him

up and takes him to see the big apple tree. She sits him on one of the branches, holds him secure and bounces the branch up and down. Luke shrieks with joy.

Teresa has come out of the house. She wades through the grass towards them. 'Your phone keeps ringing,' she says.

'I know,' replies Pauline. 'It will calm down, left to itself.' And as she speaks she sees in Teresa's face that the period of remission is over. Now what? she thinks. Now what?

Pauline's own mother did not read her daughter's face. Perhaps she did not care for what she saw there. More probably, the language and references were not ones she understood. Pauline's mother spent her life in desperate evasion of everything that she termed tiresome. Emotional difficulties above all were tiresome. If you structured your life with sufficient caution you could avoid these, and when Pauline's mother saw that her daughter was not doing so, indeed had apparently laid herself open to tiresomeness with every move, she turned her head away and ignored the problem – presumably lest she herself become infected.

And thus, on a day when Pauline has come because there are things that have to be said, out of expediency and out of despair, her mother puts up a determined defence.

'I'm leaving Harry,' Pauline says.

'If you mean that,' says her mother, looking out of the window, 'and I hope you don't, then I think that's very wrong of you.'

'Mother,' says Pauline, 'Harry is sleeping with another woman. And before this woman there was a different one, and before that one, another. And another.'

Pauline's mother flinches. She is on the ropes now. She glances wildly at Pauline. At last: 'There could be some misunderstanding,' she ventures.

Pauline stares at her. Her mother glances again and whatever she sees in Pauline's stare reduces her to silence.

'Well, your father and I will think it's a great pity if this happens,' she remarks eventually.

Pauline has hardly heard her. She is far away in a dark tunnel with no apparent exit. 'You know something?' she says. 'I wish he had died.'

'You don't mean that,' says her mother. 'That's a terrible thing to say. You don't mean it.'

'Oh, I do. If he were dead, I would be unhappy. Pure and simple – just unhappy. That would be quite straightforward, compared with this.'

Her mother rams herself into the corner of the sofa. There is no escape. Tiresomeness has forced its ugly way into her armoured life. She watches Pauline with alarm, and something close to dislike.

'And incidentally,' says Hugh, 'this is the third time I've called. The machine witters on about your unavailability. I thought you were a slave to your desk, down there. I thought that was the point of the exile.'

'I've been in the garden with Luke.'

'How's the dragon book?'

'In abeyance. The author has a domestic crisis. It's North Sea oil now. How's business?'

'Ticking over. I had a nice little find this week. Executors' sale. Cottage in Suffolk, somebody's aunt recently deceased, and there in her library was a clutch of Hogarth Press books, mint condition . . .'

Pauline listens to Hugh and pictures the scene – Hugh in that raincoat, with the battered briefcase, prowling in some room that smells of damp, and of old books.

'. . . The niece was cock-a-hoop. Nasty little piece of work, stood there licking her lips as the prices went up, plans a holiday in the Bahamas with her boyfriend on the proceeds – several, I should think.'

'Well,' says Pauline, 'that's books for you. The knock-on effect. My living, and yours, and someone's unearned spree in the Caribbean. Deceptive things, books.'

'How's friend Maurice getting on with his?'

'All right, so far as I know.'

Hugh's ear is more acute than one might think. 'Is anything wrong? You sound a touch . . . uptight.'

'I'm fine,' says Pauline, adjusting her tone. 'Fine, fine. Maurice writes his book. I interfere with other people's books. Teresa and Luke seize the day. The wheat field grows, all five-thousand-pounds'-worth of it.'

'You don't sound fine to me,' says Hugh. 'You confirm all my worst fears about rural life.'

Chaundy's car is approaching World's End as Pauline comes out of her front door. Neither is particularly inclined to an exchange of civilities, but decency requires this. Chaundy slows down, stops, turns his head.

'No sign of rain,' says Pauline, who knows the correct language.

'Too late for rain, anyway,' Chaundy replies, surly. It is of course the wheat that is under discussion, standing stiff and motionless all around them.

'What would rain do now?' inquires Pauline.

'Knock it down, won't it?' says Chaundy. 'One good thunder-storm and that lot'll be flattened.' He revs up, grinds the gears. 'Well, better be getting on.' The Peugeot bangs away up the track.

Pauline wraps kitchen rubbish in a sheet of the local paper and observes as she does so the chronicles of mayhem. Her chicken bones and tea bags and potato peelings sprawl across accounts of Saturday-night riots outside pubs, of adolescent joyriders incinerated in car smashes, of Dutch barns set ablaze and of primary schools vandalized. This tranquil landscape apparently heaves with unrest. There is more here than meets the eye. She pushes aside wilted lettuce leaves to read of a knifing in the centre of Hadbury in the small hours of a Sunday morning. A farmer is prosecuted for tipping effluent into a local stream. And the weather continues to break records. Agricultural shows announce unparalleled attendances. A Scandinavian tourist suffered heatstroke while on a cycling trip.

'There's a first novel,' says Pauline's former colleague. 'We'd love you to do that, if you can fit it in after the oil book. Psychological drama with a theatrical setting. How does that grab you?'

'So long as the author has a stable domestic life and doesn't live on a Welsh mountain. Sorry . . . Yes, I'll do it.'

'Great,' says the colleague. She turns to more important matters and relays some professional chat. 'By the way,' she adds, 'I saw Maurice recently. Week or two ago. Having lunch.' She names a Covent Garden restaurant. 'I thought he was holed up down there, like you.'

'He makes forays to London,' says Pauline. 'In pursuit of the Tourist Authority or whatever.'

'Well, it wasn't the Tourist Authority he was in pursuit of when I saw him. The face rang a bell. In our trade. Short blonde hair.'

Pauline is silent.

'Anyway,' says the colleague hastily, 'as I say, I saw him. He seemed fairly taken up so I didn't go and have a word. So . . . Glad you're having such a productive summer. God, I envy you. We're frying in London. I'll get that typescript off to you next week. Bye now.'

Pauline stares out at the wheat, at the rolling flank of the hill, at the crest of trees against the skyline. She thinks of her colleague without affection. And then of Maurice. And finally of Teresa. She thinks of another Teresa, a vanished Teresa, who is hunched in despair on the window-seat of the new house.

'Listen,' she says to Teresa, 'it'll be all right. In time. You see. Just give it a bit longer.'

Teresa's eyes gleam with tears. The sun falls through the window on to her pale face with those eyes of shining anguish. 'They don't like me,' she says. 'Diana said I could go about with her and today she won't talk to me even. She just walks off. I'm the only person without a friend.' She is eight, and life has bared its fangs.

'It's because you're new,' says Pauline firmly. 'Look, you've only been at the school half a term. Give it time.'

'I hate this place,' weeps Teresa. 'I hate the school and the place and I hate this house. It's never going to be all right.'

'It will, it will,' says Pauline. She wants to tell Teresa that this is nothing, on the scale of things – but of course it is, it is. Right now, for Teresa, there is no worse, she is pitched into an abyss. And Pauline aches for her, helpless.

Harry walks into the room. He notices Teresa. 'What's the matter, sweetie?' He turns to Pauline. 'Don't wait supper for me – I probably won't get back till later. D'you know where my leather jacket is? It seems to have walked.'

'I've no idea,' says Pauline. 'I dare say you left it in the university.'

'Well, I hope so.' Harry notices Teresa again. 'What's up with her?'

'She's unhappy,' says Pauline. 'Things aren't going well at school.'

Harry puts an arm round Teresa and tickles her ear. 'Cheer up, poppet. Life's a dream. "Row, row, row your boat gently down the stream. Merrily, merrily, merrily, merrily, life is but a dream." Remember?' He used to sing this to an infant Teresa, time was.

'Would that it were,' says Pauline.

Teresa wriggles away. 'I'm not a baby, am I?' She glares at him.

'Oh, dear . . .' Harry pulls a chastened face at Pauline, who looks away. 'Well . . . I must dash. Bye now – see you.'

Harry goes. It is as though a distracting gust of wind has blown through the room. Everything is still and quiet once more. Teresa heaves with an involuntary dry sob.

'Tell you what,' says Pauline. 'You can stay up and watch telly, and we'll have supper on a tray.'

Teresa heaves again. 'OK.' She wipes her nose on the back of her hand. 'Could we have beefburgers and chips?'

'It's me, I'm afraid,' says Chris Rogers. 'Is this a nuisance? Just say so and I'll bugger off.'

'Not at all.' Pauline turns down the radio and takes the phone to the sofa.

'The kids are asleep and this is the only time I have to myself.'

'She's not back yet, then?'

'No.'

'Are you . . . talking?' Pauline inquires delicately.

'We're in negotiation, as you might say. I'm getting a bit frantic, I can tell you. That's why I rang, really. Sorry to make you a sort of agony aunt.'

'Feel free,' says Pauline. 'I've always seen editorial work as a flexible brief. Is she still with her mother?'

'Yes. Frankly, if you ask me I think her mother's been sticking her oar in.'

'Her mother,' says Pauline sternly, 'has her child's interests at heart, no doubt. You can hardly blame her for that. She's concerned. Do they want to get you down off that mountain, is that it?'

'Well, that . . . yes. And other things that are less negotiable. Actually I'm getting fairly pissed off with the mountain myself. I'm talking to a guy I know in Swansea who may be able to find us somewhere cheap enough there. Can I ask you something?'

'Within reason.'

'Is my book crap?'

'No.'

'You're sure?' says Chris Rogers anxiously.

'Listen,' says Pauline, 'you paid it the compliment of writing it. Now stand by it.'

'Yes,' says Chris humbly.

'And it's not crap. It's original and provocative.'

'It's just that I've been wondering if I'm in the wrong trade.'

'Ah, well, that's as may be,' says Pauline. 'You've not exactly picked an easy ride. But that's another matter. The book is a thing apart. They tend to have a life of their own.'

'Ah, all that stuff . . .' says Chris. 'I didn't know you were into that sort of thing.'

'I'm not talking higher criticism,' says Pauline. 'I'm talking self-evident truths. Leave the book to its own devices. It's you we have to think about now. When did you last . . . negotiate?'

'At lunchtime. D'you think I should call her again this evening?'

'I should go right ahead and do just that.'

There is a day of such sledgehammer heat that no one ventures outside. And something curious happens to the wheat. It seems to hiss. Pauline keeps all her windows open, and through them comes this sound, as of some furtively restless surrounding sea.

*

'Hi!' says Maurice.

He steps into the garden, a glass of white wine in his hand. It is early evening. Teresa is putting Luke to bed. Pauline is reading on the seat at the end of the lawn. Maurice waves his glass at her, querying.

'No, thanks.'

He stands there, taking a gulp of wine, eyeing her over the top of the glass. He does not join her on the seat.

Pauline marks the page with a leaf and closes her book. She looks at Maurice, at that familiar triangular face, the slightly beaky nose, the springy hair. Once this was the face of a stranger to whom she casually talked at a party. That unexceptional exchange flicks into her mind and she experiences it again, but loaded now, everything that it holds streaming away from it – Teresa, Luke, this moment here at World's End. My doing, she thinks, all my doing. My fault. I should have stayed home with a headache that evening.

'Too hot today,' says Maurice.

Pauline agrees.

'Is it true that computers can go haywire above a certain temperature?'

Pauline says that she has not heard that this is the case.

Maurice talks about his work. He is going over Chapter Eight at the moment. Chapter Eight is concerned with the use of nostalgic imagery in advertising. Maurice has assembled an impressive range of examples. He stands there talking about petrol ads and the concept of remote and depopulated landscape, about whisky and the cult of gracious living. This is quite interesting, as it goes. Pauline listens with half an ear. And Maurice talks with an eye upon her. Both are aware of a sub-text, something new and disturbing that lurks below the surface of what Maurice is saying and to which Pauline is apparently listening. It is as though they are watching one another across a great distance – mistrustful and wary. Both are waiting to see which way the cat will jump. What are you doing? Pauline thinks. What have you done? And she sees that Maurice is thinking also: what do you know? What will you do?

From the open window of the cottage drifts the sound of Teresa talking to Luke, of Luke's wordless responses.

Pauline looks up from her breakfast coffee at the sound of a car engine. Maurice's car. She watches as it reverses out on to the track and heads for the road. It is eight-fifteen.

At nine-thirty the postman leaves the mail in the box at the gate. Teresa does not come out so Pauline takes the letters to the garden, where Luke is falling in and out of the plastic paddling pool.

'All for Maurice, in fact,' says Pauline, of the letters.

'Maurice is in London till Friday.' Teresa says this in a tone of absolute neutrality. Strenuous and painful neutrality.

'Oh, I see. I hadn't realized he was going.'

'I thought I'd said.' Teresa is offhand now, dismissive. It is a struggle, the achievement of this air of detachment. She is clenched with tension, Pauline sees.

'Maybe you did. Anyway . . .' Pauline puts the letters down on the bench.

'Thanks.'

'If you want my car for anything, take it. I'm not going anywhere.'

'Oh, right, thanks. I might go up to the village later.'

'Well, then . . . Let me know if there's anything I can do.'

Teresa stares at her.

'If you want to get rid of Luke for a bit.'

'Oh, right,' says Teresa.

Pauline goes. Teresa is unreachable, she realizes. Teresa is cut off beyond the fog of her own obsession. Nothing else matters.

*

Pauline faces Harry across a darkening room. She stands as far from him as she can get because if she came close she might not be able to say what she is about to say. The room is dark because she has sat waiting for this moment as the evening fell and has been too intent to switch on the light. And now here at last is Harry, with his coat still over his arm because he is brought up short by what she has said, by what she is saying, and has neglected to put it down.

'I don't trust you,' says Pauline. 'I don't trust you and never shall, and I cannot go on living in a state of permanent doubt. I love you, and wish to God that I didn't.'

Chapter Fourteen

It is late July, and the place has now ripened. Tall buff grasses wave along the roadsides, the hogweed heads have turned from cream to brown. And the fields of winter wheat are straw-coloured. The landscape is a patchwork of fawn and green carved up by the dark lattice of hedges. The trees are dusky brooding shapes. The hay is down, the former hayfields are dotted with shiny black plastic drums. The summer has peaked, the year is tipping over. What became of spring? How can all this have come about in a few impetuous weeks? All this has happened under her nose, Pauline sees, and yet only now is she aware of the extremity of change. This landscape is unstable. It rushes unstoppably ahead, locked into its impervious cycle.

Maurice is back. She heard his car late in the evening, but did not look out. This morning she saw him from the window – in the garden, briefly attending Luke. Holding Luke's hand as the two of them tour the lawn, throwing a ball for Luke – the father. And then Teresa comes out and Pauline turns away. She is not a voyeur. What is between them is no concern of hers. Except of course that it is.

They will be here again this weekend, it seems, those others. Carol and James. Teresa has earlier released this information with the desperate neutrality that is becoming habitual. Maurice needs James to go through Chapters Nine and Ten with him. No, they couldn't do this while Maurice was in London because Maurice was too busy checking references and seeing people. And no, Maurice can't just send James a copy because they need to go over it together.

Don't ask, Teresa's eyes say. Eyes that are blank, giving nothing away. Don't ask questions. There's nothing wrong. And there isn't anything you could do if there were.

Pauline picks up the phone and puts it down again, several times within the hour. Shall I? Shall I not?

She has turned aside, in the past. She has ignored the hints, the veiled suggestions. She has told herself that all this is chit-chat, gossip, that it is unfair to Maurice to pay attention to this sort of stuff. So what if he had a few girlfriends? she has thought. Par for the course – Maurice is forty-four, one would not expect otherwise.

The old acquaintance answers at once. 'Yes? Pauline! Good to hear you!' The old acquaintance of whom Pauline is not all that fond and who has known Maurice for many a long year, longer than Pauline, better than Pauline.

Pauline has her alibi, her pretext for calling like this, out of the blue. A complex professional inquiry which the acquaintance is only too happy to discuss at length until eventually the matter is exhausted and the conversation turns to more personal matters, as Pauline knew it would, and especially to such matters as they have in common.

'And how is Maurice?' says the acquaintance. 'Dear me – I still can't get used to thinking of Maurice as a married man.' There is a note in her voice – a faintly lubricious note which Pauline has anticipated and which she detests. Well, she has asked for this.

Maurice is fine, she replies. Busy on his book. Busy – period. She allows the faintest note of distaste to creep into her voice. She allows an inviting silence. Into which the acquaintance leaps. She talks about Maurice. She tells Maurice anecdotes, which are purportedly entertaining but most of which are to a greater or lesser extent to Maurice's discredit. They illustrate Maurice's preoccupation with his own concerns, Maurice's unswerving egotism. And as the woman talks Pauline recognizes the distant grinding of an axe. There is an edge to this. Once, time was, this woman had been close enough to Maurice for such things to matter. Pauline flinches. You asked for this, she tells herself again.

Oh yes, says the acquaintance, that's Maurice all right. Typical Maurice. But he can charm the birds off the trees, of course. Always good company, is Maurice. And maybe he's different these days, maybe marriage . . . The acquaintance here allows an inviting pause, which Pauline fills with some noncommittal sound, and the other is soon in full flow once more. He may well have changed his spots, she says – probably all he needed was the love of a good woman. She laughs. But I have to say that when I knew him well, where women were concerned Maurice was one of those for whom the grass is always greener on the other side of the fence. Know what I mean?

Pauline murmurs that she knows what is meant. And I've had enough of this, she thinks. She edges back into the conversation, starts to swing it round, to wind it up. A few minutes later she is alone once more. Disliking that confiding voice. Disliking herself.

Pauline withdraws, in so far as withdrawal is possible within the parameters of World's End. She avoids Maurice. This is not difficult, since the only common territory is the garden, and she can see if he is out there and time her own sorties accordingly. And Maurice would seem to be doing the same, since he does not appear when she sits on the seat in the early evening, or when she has joined Teresa and Luke for a while.

Teresa is trying to behave as though unconcerned. She has

sensed Pauline's disquiet, and so struggles to camouflage her own unrest. She pays determined attention to Luke, and when Pauline is around she makes brittle attempts at conversation, inconsequential stuff about the weather, the plants in the garden, Luke's doings. This valour distresses Pauline so much that she can hardly bear to be with Teresa.

Pauline sits in her study and thinks about these things. Most of all she thinks about Maurice.

'It's me,' says Chris Rogers. 'I just wanted to say I think I may have made a breakthrough.'

'Ah,' says Pauline. 'That chapter?'

'No, no. With my wife.'

'Of course,' says Pauline. 'Forgive me. She's coming back?'

'Well, let's say she's beginning to make some very promising noises. And one of the children has got a temperature, which helps. She's a bit fazed about that.'

'Yes – she would be, I imagine.'

'I've got that in hand myself,' says Chris defensively. 'I'm giving him Calpol and I'm taking him down to the surgery tomorrow.'

'Good,' says Pauline. 'All credit to you.'

'Anyway . . . With things looking up a bit I just felt I wanted to spread the good news. So with any luck I can get stuck into that chapter again before too long.'

'I shall look forward to it,' says Pauline.

Pauline glances out of her window and sees Teresa and Maurice in the garden. Within a few seconds she has turned away again but in those moments she has absorbed an entire scene, and the messages implicit within it. Luke is presumably asleep upstairs, for Teresa is reading the newspaper. Except that she is not. She is sitting there, visibly tense, holding the newspaper and occasionally looking over it at Maurice. Maurice is reading a book and taking notes, and he is doing precisely that. He is absorbed in what he is doing, at ease with himself and with the world, it would seem.

Pauline is shopping in Hadbury when James and Carol arrive. She does not usually shop on a Saturday morning so this is perhaps a deliberate move – suffice it that as she ate her breakfast and stared out at the sunny morning it had seemed suddenly urgent that she restock the fridge and freezer. And so when she returns there is that other car drawn up alongside Maurice's.

She has not been able to find any way of avoiding the communal evening meal. 'You'll come over tomorrow night, won't you?' said Teresa yesterday, in level tones. It is not possible to plead a headache twenty-four hours in advance, nor is an alternative engagement plausible at World's End. So that is an unavoidable obligation, towards which Pauline occasionally throws a queasy glance as the day progresses.

She remains within her own four walls, and tries not to think of the group next door. This is difficult. It is a natural process to look out of a window from time to time, and whenever she does she is liable to catch a glimpse of them – separately, collectively. She sees Maurice and James sitting together on the seat, mugs of coffee in hand, evidently taking a break from the rigours of editorial discussion. She sees Teresa wander alone with Luke up the track and back again. She sees Carol stretched out on a rug on the grass, wearing a pair of shorts and a halter top, slapping sun cream on her arms and legs.

She sees Maurice come out of the cottage and stand looking down at Carol. She cannot hear what is said, and Maurice's back is turned to her. Carol does not move. She simply gazes up at Maurice, smiling, her eyes masked by sunglasses. And then, within a few moments, Maurice turns and goes back inside.

In the late afternoon she sees Teresa and Luke again on the track, joined presently by James, who stands chatting to Teresa. Where is Carol? Ah ... James's voice rises up to Pauline's open window. Carol is having a bath, it seems. Maurice is rewriting a passage and has released James, so James is proposing a stroll up to the top of the hill.

Pauline cannot quite hear what Teresa says but she can see from Teresa's stance, from her movements, from the way she moves her head, that she is resisting these suggestions. And Pauline knows why. She knows what Teresa is thinking and what Teresa is feeling. She knows this in the pit of her stomach, and would rather not, but the knowledge is inescapable. It is the inexorable product of experience and of empathy.

For animals, the protection and preservation of their young is a simple imperative. Attack and if feasible kill anything that looks like harming them. An enviable system, thinks Pauline. Straightforward, uncomplicated, perfectly understood by all concerned.

'So ...' says Maurice. 'How about the rural fayre tomorrow? Steam rally, parade of vintage tractors ... How about it?'

'There's cream in the fridge, Mum,' says Teresa, serving apple tart. 'Could you get it out?'

'Actually,' says James, 'I think we'll have to get back in the morning.'

'Must we?' says Carol.

'My aunt,' says James reprovingly.

'Do you want it in a jug?' inquires Pauline.

'The carton will do,' replies Teresa.

'James has this aunt coming up from Bournemouth,' Carol explains. 'We've got to give her tea. What a bore. Couldn't we have got flu?'

'No,' says James. 'This is an aunt I like.'

Carol pulls a face at Maurice across the table, a mock spoiled-child face.

'Never mind,' says Maurice. 'We'll find another rural fayre next time. And Pauline is delighted to be let off, aren't you, Pauline?'

'If you say so,' says Pauline. 'Cream, James?'

'Gorgeous apple tart,' says Carol. 'Apples out of the garden?'

'Of course,' says Maurice. 'Dew-picked at dawn.'

'You don't pick apples in July,' says Teresa. 'Sainsbury's.'

'Whoops!' says Carol. She points a finger at Maurice. 'You did that on purpose – leading me on.'

'On the contrary,' says Maurice. 'I've no idea when you pick apples.'

'And here you are writing an enormous book on country life,' she continues, beaming. 'Shame on you!'

'My task is the deconstruction of a myth,' says Maurice. 'Not horticultural information.' He grins back at her.

'And strictly speaking,' says James, 'this book is about the tourist industry.'

'Well I know *that*,' says Carol. 'I've read lots of it, haven't I?'

Teresa gets up. She puts on the draining-board her plate of apple tart, some of it uneaten. 'How many people want coffee?'

'Not me, thanks,' says Pauline. 'I'll be off now, if you don't mind.'

'Don't do that,' says Maurice. 'James has brought a bottle of Calvados. Where are the small glasses, Teresa?'

'Thank you, but no thanks, James,' says Pauline. She heads for the door.

'In the dresser cupboard,' says Teresa. 'Good-night, Mum.'

Pauline closes her front door. She puts the kettle on, makes herself a cup of coffee, sits down, picks up the newspaper and then rises again to search for her reading glasses. She has left them next door, she now remembers.

She goes out of her cottage and heads again for Teresa's kitchen. In order to reach the front door she must pass the open window and thus she sees for a couple of seconds the lit room that she has so recently left, an inviting warm cavern in the night. Teresa is no longer there – probably she has gone upstairs to check on Luke. James is not there either, but from the garden beyond drifts the smell of the cigarette that he is considerately smoking out of doors. Teresa does not like smoking in rooms inhabited by Luke.

Maurice and Carol are seated at opposite sides of the table, in the centre of which their four hands are entwined. Pauline sees, as she walks quickly past the window, the look that blazes from Maurice to Carol, from Carol to Maurice.

Pauline walks into the room. The hands retreat as she does so. She does not look at Carol or at Maurice but crosses over to the dresser and picks up her spectacles.

'Oh,' says Carol, 'you forgot your glasses . . .'

'Correct,' says Pauline. 'I forgot my glasses.'

Maurice stands up. He keeps his face turned from Pauline, takes his glass and walks through the door that leads to the sitting-room. Carol remains where she is. She has seen what is in Pauline's face and she does not at once look away but stares for an instant – a blue stare which is a bland declaration of hostilities. This is the way it is, says Carol's stare. This is the way it's going to be. Sorry, and all that – but this is how things are.

Pauline walks out of the room. Myra Sams rears again in her head, Myra Sams and her successors.

Pauline and Teresa are in the garden, entertaining Luke. It is Monday morning. Maurice is at his desk. James and Carol are gone. Teresa has the scoured look of someone who has not slept. And Luke is apparently in a state of acute neurosis, alternating between manic activity and furious tears.

'He's tired,' says Pauline. 'Shall I take him up and see if he'll go in his cot?'

'I will,' says Teresa with an effort.

'Stay there,' says Pauline.

She takes Luke up to his room, where, after a few petulant minutes, he flakes out. From behind Maurice's door comes the tap of his keyboard. Pauline makes a couple of mugs of coffee and returns to the garden where Teresa sits staring at the tangled flowerbed. There is a distant rhythmic thumping sound – harvest has begun. Somewhere over the hill the wheat is falling to the combine.

Pauline hands Teresa a mug of coffee.

'Oh . . . thanks. Sorry – you ought to be working.'

'I'm only too happy not to,' says Pauline. 'The current manuscript is profoundly boring.'

'What happened to the unicorns?' asks Teresa dully.

'Their creator has domestic problems. His wife walked out on him.'

'Why?' says Teresa, with a glimmer of interest.

Pauline explains, and sees Teresa's interest fade. Teresa is thinking that this woman does not know when she is well off.

There is a silence – a silence in which a wordless conversation takes place, the product of years of intimacy and of intuitive interpretation of the set of a mouth, of the flavour of a glance – the undertow of all that is unspoken. Look, says Pauline – I know. Don't think I don't know because I say nothing. And Teresa tells her – I know you know, and I don't want you to say anything. If you said anything I would get up and walk away. Because I can't stand to talk about it, least of all with you.

174

'What's that noise?' says Teresa after a while.

'The combine. They're starting to harvest.'

Teresa nods.

'It always reminds me of the place near Marlborough. That was in the middle of a cornfield too.'

Teresa nods again. Each recalls the cottage rented once for a summer holiday.

'It was the summer I got my first period,' says Teresa. 'I wasn't interested in anything but brands of sanitary towel. I didn't notice the cornfield.'

'I remember you being preoccupied. I took it for the onset of adolescent gloom.'

'Was Harry there? I can't see him, somehow.'

'Intermittently,' says Pauline. It was also the summer of a Canadian Ph.D. student called Cheryl in whose progress Harry had taken an inordinate interest, but Pauline is not going to go into that. The thump-thump-thump of the combine, and Harry's phone calls saying he'll be down to join them at the weekend if he can manage it, but he may still be tied up with work.

Teresa throws her a look. Maybe she has recaptured some vague adolescent apprehension of adult mysteries. 'I had a postcard from him yesterday. He's going to be in London the second week of August.'

'Then you'll have to take Luke up to see him,' says Pauline briskly.

'I suppose so,' mutters Teresa without enthusiasm.

Inside the cottage the phone rings, and then stops almost immediately. Maurice has picked it up. Teresa stares at the grass, chewing her lip.

'It was that summer that gave me the idea I wanted somewhere of my own in the country one day,' says Pauline. She sees World's End hanging spectral over the time and the place, implicit from the moment that she first entertained this notion, walking on the downs perhaps, or cooking a meal in the rented kitchen. A vision of solitude and independence, the first determined contemplation of life after Harry. She perceives the tortuous invisible line that leads inexorably from there to here.

'Mmn . . .' Teresa is paying only token attention.

Pauline slides a look at her. She knows exactly how it is. That condition in which there can be no diversions, no departures from the central grinding concern. In which there is no past, but only this consuming present, in which all energies have to be devoted to the pursuit of possibilities and contingent events. What will he do? Will he go to London again? Is he on the phone with her right now?

The condition in which a life can be laid waste, thinks Pauline. The condition in which whole chunks of my life were devastated.

'Listen . . .' she begins – and then pauses. Teresa raises her head from contemplation of the grass.

'Yes?' says Teresa cautiously – without encouragement.

Pauline takes a breath. 'You know what I should have done?' she says at last, in a rush. 'I should have cut adrift from Harry years and years before I did. I should have said enough is enough – cut our losses and got out.'

'Oh . . .' Teresa is startled.

'Then that summer would never have been and maybe I'd never have got a penchant for country living and none of us would be here now. The thought occurred, that's all. And incidentally so far as I'm concerned Harry today is neither here nor there. Maybe I should make that clear. It'll save you being so tactful.'

'I see.' Teresa is now alert. She is also perplexed. Things are being said which are not for saying. Forbidden ground is suddenly invaded.

'It's something that happens. You should know, that's all.

What was unendurable becomes . . . well, as though it happened to someone else. Someone you feel sorry for but a bit impatient with.'

Teresa considers this. She is still thrown by these disclosures. She eyes her mother.

'That's how it goes,' says Pauline. 'But don't get me wrong. It's not that it ceases to matter – whatever there was back then – but simply that it moves off into some other dimension. An interesting process. Anyway . . . I just thought I'd mention it. And you don't need to pick your way through a minefield where Harry is concerned. There isn't one.'

'I see,' says Teresa. 'Well . . . I'm glad you told me.' She is moving this information around, trying it out for size. 'And . . . well, I'm glad anyway.' She seems about to add to this, and then does not. Something else now swarms up in the look she gives Pauline. But it's not the same, say Teresa's eyes, it's not the same at all. Don't think that. Of course it isn't.

Evening. Silence. The combine has gone home, leaving a void that now seems unnatural. The place is in suspension – an airless dusk, in which birds call and the wheat stands absolutely still.

Pauline goes out to her car in search of a mislaid notebook. She fails to find it, and when she emerges from the car and stands up there is Maurice coming out of the cottage.

He walks over to her. He does not bother with the circumlocution of greeting or weather commentary. He gives her a half-smile, which would seem to be the white flag of the messenger come in peace. 'Perhaps we should talk,' he says.

Pauline does not reply at once. She considers him. Then she says, 'What would we talk about, Maurice?'

Maurice observes her in silence. He gives the slightest of shrugs. So be it, says his look. If that's the way you want it. He turns away and walks back to the cottage.

Chapter Fifteen

At midnight the phone rings.

'Pauline?' says Hugh. His voice is disarrayed.

'Are you all right, Hugh?'

'Yes . . .' he says. 'At least . . . No. Elaine is dead.'

Pauline knows, at once, what has happened. She is silent for a moment. Then – 'Oh, Hugh . . . How?'

'Pills. I don't know where she got them from. I used to check, from time to time. This has always been on the cards – I've realized that.'

'Yes,' says Pauline. 'Yes, I suppose so.' She struggles to think what to say, what to do. 'Would you like me to come?'

'Not right now. Later, maybe. Now it's all practical things. I'm best just getting on with it.' He sounds less disarrayed now, just weary. 'The funeral's on Tuesday.'

'Oh,' says Pauline. Her thoughts are rushing in all directions. That poor bleak woman. Alone with the pills. Hugh. This funeral. Should she . . . ? Is it appropriate that she attend the funeral?

'No,' says Hugh, ahead of her, or alongside. 'Don't come to it. It's going to be her brother and his family. There was a brother, you know – not that we saw that much of him. And . . .' His voice trails away.

And no one, thinks Pauline. Elaine had no friends.

'And Margery,' says Hugh. 'She'll be there.'

No, thinks Pauline, I shouldn't go. It wouldn't do. But poor old Hugh . . . a gust of empathy sweeps through her. 'I wish I was with you,' she says.

'Well, maybe if you were thinking of coming to London later in the week, say . . . When it's all over. That would perk me up. But not if it's a nuisance.'

'Oh, Hugh,' she says. 'Of course I'll come. Wednesday?'

They talk a little more and when she puts the phone down she lies there thinking of that despairing woman, shut away in her inescapable neurosis, and of Hugh, who must be grieving for something that happened long ago rather than for this act of desperation. He has never talked of the woman he first married and whom he lost long since. The disoriented note in his voice now is that of shock and bewilderment. His task will be to acclimatize himself to a life in which he is freed of that millstone which is so familiar that it has become also perhaps a kind of tether. He will be adrift.

'. . . so I'm going up to see him on Wednesday,' she explains to Teresa. And also, incidentally, to Maurice. She would have preferred to have this conversation with Teresa alone, but Maurice came into the kitchen half-way through and she has had to accept his muttered expressions of dismay. He has met Hugh only twice and there was no particular accord between them.

'Of course,' says Teresa. She glances at Maurice.

'Wednesday . . .' says Maurice. 'Right. Well, look, I'll see if I can switch my appointment and go up on Monday so I can be back by then.'

Pauline turns to him, sharply.

'I have to see someone at English Heritage, and do a stint in the library, but I'll try to do it earlier. Teresa had better not be left here on her own and without a car.'

'No,' says Pauline. 'She had better not.'

'Exactly,' says Maurice. He avoids her eye. 'Right. I'll get hold of him – the English Heritage man.' He leaves the room.

Pauline confronts Teresa. 'Or you could go with him. Do that, instead. If he has to bounce to and fro. This summer of isolation and application seems to be breaking down.' She tries to be light, to make it sound like a careless juggling of alternatives.

'No,' says Teresa. 'I've thought about that. It would be worse.' She has abandoned pretences.

'Oh . . .' Pauline is wrenched now by Teresa's expression, by her tone. Something more has happened. Something said, something done.

'I still wouldn't know where he was or what he was doing. And Luke would cry in the car and there's all his things to take, the cot and the buggy . . . I'd have to sit there wondering where Maurice was and when he'd be back just the same. I may as well do it here as there.' She pauses, draws a breath – a little jerky gasp of stress. 'Give my love to Hugh,' she says. 'If you talk to him before you go. Tell him I'm so sorry.'

Pauline nods. She is carved up by what she sees in Teresa's eyes, by Teresa's painfully level tone, by her own familiarity with Teresa's private darkness.

Maurice arrives at Pauline's door. He has come, ostensibly, to borrow some paper. The village shop does not rise to A4 copy paper. Pauline finds him standing at the foot of the stairs with this request on his lips. She climbs the stairs, collects a wad of paper and descends once more.

'I'll pay you back,' says Maurice, with a furtive smile.

'No need.'

He does not go, but continues to stand there.

'Well . . .' says Pauline, dismissive now. Go, she thinks, before too much is said.

'I know what you've been thinking, Pauline,' says Maurice.

'In that case there's no need for me to make any comment.'

'You could perhaps be exaggerating things, you know.'

'Could I?' says Pauline, starting to smoulder. 'If that's what you feel, then that is your problem, not mine.'

Maurice spreads his hands in a gesture of deprecation. 'I can see that nothing I say is going to make any difference. But if it's any help let me tell you that James and Carol won't be coming down here for weekends any more. It isn't working out so well that way. It'll be more convenient if James and I get together in London every now and then.'

I see, thinks Pauline. Yes, more convenient in every way, no doubt. She does not speak, and Maurice continues to stand there, looking up at her because she is several steps above him on that steeply raked flight of stairs. It is dark inside, the stairwell of the cottage is unlit, and Maurice is framed in the brilliance of the out-of-doors beyond – the blue and gold and green of sky and wheat and hedge, a flare of light and colour. Pauline cannot see his face very well, and would not wish to because whichever approach he has assumed would madden her – propitiation, defiance, conspiracy.

'Just at this moment,' says Maurice slowly, 'you're probably wishing I'd never married Teresa. You shouldn't do that. Whatever there is right now that may be . . .'

Pauline cuts him off. 'Wrong, Maurice. Just at this moment I'm thinking that if I could kill you I probably would. A reaction you won't understand, but that too is your problem.'

Maurice stares up at her. 'I've always thought of you as a level-headed woman, Pauline. Don't disillusion me. Thank you for the paper.' He turns, and goes.

The landscape is now being pulverized. On the other side of the hill the invisible combine is thrashing away at the spring wheat, day after day. Tractors roar down the track past

World's End, towing trailer-loads of grain. On the roads, lines of traffic crawl in procession behind an isolated combine or tractor. The monster eyes of agricultural machinery sweep the fields with shafts of light late into the evening. This is the time of year when it is made clear that the countryside is not scenery but an industrial enterprise. The coaches carrying tour parties to Stratford must queue up behind the combine which occupies most of the road, the caravan-towing cars and the hired camper vans must sit panting behind the tractor waiting to turn right into its destined field.

Pauline meets Chaundy on the track. They halt their cars for the statutory exchange.

'Busy time for you,' says Pauline.

'Have this lot down next,' says Chaundy. They gaze at the seething wheat. 'The weather better bloody well hold another couple of weeks,' he adds.

'Is it a good harvest?' Pauline inquires.

Chaundy shrugs. 'All burnt up, isn't it?' His disgruntled tone implies that this is a deliberate act on someone's part – the government probably, or the EC, or conceivably Pauline herself has had a hand in it. He slams the Peugeot into gear once more, a fearful grinding sound which indicates that communication is at an end. He eyes Pauline, with the expression of a man who feels he may have forgotten something. It comes to him. 'Everything OK with you?' he says, perfunctorily, the car already edging forward.

'Fine,' says Pauline. 'Just fine.'

Honour is satisfied.

And such ritual dances are perfectly appropriate, thinks Pauline, as she makes her way along the shelves of the Mace Store in the village, trying to remember what it is that she has come here for. Chaundy is nothing to her, and she is even less to Chaundy. All that is required is mutual recognition and an indication of non-hostility. Dogs also do it.

Fine, you declare, whatever your state of mind, whatever your physical condition. The decencies require this, not that you come clean and mention that you are bankrupt, on bail for assault or terminally ill.

Well, as it happens, Mr Chaundy, I am in profound distress because I believe that my daughter is about to suffer her husband's serial infidelity. A man to whom, incidentally, she was introduced by myself. And my own husband was similarly inclined, so I am something of a connoisseur of the emotions aroused.

No, no . . . Fine, just fine.

Tomato purée, that was it. And fruit. And milk.

She phones Hugh, but encounters only the answering machine. He is not at the shop, either. Margery greets her with conspiratorial warmth. 'He should be back soon, Mrs Carter. I'll tell him you rang. He's . . . well, he's not really himself, between you and me. He's all at sixes and sevens. It's been a blow, this. Though one can't but feel . . .' She leaves something delicately unspoken. 'He's going to need his friends, Mrs Carter.' A further implication is there, giving Pauline pause for uneasy thought.

And in an hour or so Hugh calls back. 'Do you know any hymns?'

'Mmn . . .' says Pauline. Fight the good fight, she thinks. No, that's the one for marriage services. 'I'm not very strong in that area. Do you really need a hymn? Why don't you just have some organ music?'

'That's a good idea.' Hugh perks up. 'Bach. Organ music is always Bach, isn't it? I'll tell them to do that. But there's this address.' His voice falls again. 'Someone has to talk about Elaine. I suppose her brother might. The priest usually does, apparently. But . . .'

But in this instance what is he to say? What, indeed, is

anyone to say? Pauline remembers the bright platitudes mouthed by clerics at the funerals of her parents, dutiful, well-meaning men who had never met the people in question and were concerned merely to provide a smoothly gift-wrapped occasion. 'Don't,' she says. 'Tell them you don't want that either. Read something, instead. Read a poem. Did Elaine like poetry, ever?'

There is a silence. She feels Hugh rummaging in some unthinkable past, when Elaine was a whole woman. 'Actually,' he says, 'we once went on holiday in France, and I remember walking on the beach one evening and she was reciting Keats. Something she'd learnt by heart at school. "Season of mists and mellow fruitfulness".'

'There you are, then,' says Pauline. 'Read that.'

'I could, couldn't I?' Hugh sounds encouraged. 'And you'll come on Wednesday?' he goes on.

'Of course.'

The days seem now to inch one into another. There is Saturday. There is Sunday. On Sunday evening the sky clouded over and the air thickened. Rumours of rain. But now it is Monday and the sun is out again, as ever.

This is the day on which Maurice will go to London, to return on Wednesday before Pauline herself leaves. Pauline had intended to stay clear of him until after his departure, but at breakfast time she is forced to visit when she finds that the postman has included with the mail that he has pushed through her door an envelope addressed to Maurice, which may or may not be of importance but decency requires that she hand it over before he leaves.

When Pauline enters the room she knows that they have had a row. They are silent now, but the air is loaded. It carries still the freight of whatever has been said and felt in here. The remains of breakfast are on the table, and Luke is clutching a piece of toast and making Luke-noises which seem to float free of the turbulence, the shock waves of anger and accusation and defiance. Teresa is ramrod stiff, her mouth a knot of distress. Maurice is tense, his face set in ill-temper.

Pauline hands him the letter. 'This got put through my door by mistake.'

Maurice adjusts his expression, but not much. 'Thank you, Pauline.' He sees Teresa shoot a glance at the letter. 'This is from a woman at the National Trust, supplying some figures for which I have asked. Do please read it if you would like to.'

Teresa freezes, and turns away.

Pauline goes. Shortly afterwards, from the tranquillity of her cottage, where the air is uncharged and the radio is quietly telling a short story, she hears Maurice's car start up and then recede along the track.

Three hours later Teresa is composed, or nearly so. She comes over to ask if she might take Pauline's car to go to the village shop. Luke is asleep. Could Pauline check up on him from time to time? Pauline replies that she will take some work over to Teresa's sitting-room.

And thus she is going over a page of the North Sea oil manuscript when the phone rings.

'Hello?' says a male voice. Harry's voice, as it happens.

'Hello,' says Pauline.

'Teresa?' says Harry tentatively.

'No. It's me – Pauline.'

'Oh. Hello.' This hello is different – it is a deft combination of greeting and a cautious testing of the waters. I should like to talk to you, it says – but will you talk to me? 'I was just calling to fix up something with Teresa in London the week after next, when I'm over.'

'And Luke.'

'Right,' says Harry hastily. 'And Luke. How is Luke?'

'Luke is just fine. Teresa's out at the moment. Do you want to call her later?'

'Sure,' says Harry. 'In an hour or so?'

'She'll be back by then. I'll tell her.'

'And how are *you*?' says Harry.

'Fine. Just fine. Well, I'll tell Teresa . . .'

'I suppose . . . I wondered if maybe you'd be around too, the week after next. Maybe we could have a meal? It would be great to see you.'

'I'm afraid I shan't be in London just then. I'm working down here the whole summer.'

'Oh. No chance at all?'

'No chance at all,' says Pauline firmly.

When he has rung off she examines her own response to that voice. She probes and prods for a reaction. The blood running a little quicker? The heart beating a touch faster? No, she decides – nothing at all. What there is, though, is the slightest twinge of compunction. She has caught the disappointment in Harry's voice and it has induced this flicker of guilt that she cannot – will not – oblige him. Dear God! she thinks. That it should come to this!

On Tuesday there is a hot dry wind. The wheat ripples – surges of light and dark that dissolve into one another. Flurries of dust scud along the track. From time to time Pauline meets up with Teresa and Luke in the garden. Luke is irritable – he has a rash and is out of sorts. He is demanding and consuming. Pauline watches Teresa's patient attention to him, and sees that she is acting mechanically. Part of her is elsewhere – in attendance upon Maurice. She is watching him somewhere in London – seeing him, seeing her. Or perhaps she is replaying what has been said between Maurice and herself.

In the evening Pauline goes for a walk up to the top of the hill. When she looks back down at World's End she sees it suddenly for what it is – a small grey building crouched in the valley, tucked against the backdrop of the field, isolated and intensely local. She thinks of its previous inhabitants, for whom the horizon stretched little further than the crest of this hill, the rim of the field and the curved sweep in front of her – trees, more fields, and the white flashes of car windscreens that mark the hidden road.

When she gets back to her study the answering machine is bleeping. Hugh has had second thoughts about the meeting place arranged for tomorrow evening and suggests an alternative – would she mind calling for him at the shop. Chris Rogers says, 'Hi! Something to report. I'll try you again.'

'It's me,' he says, later. 'Have you got a moment?'

'Of course.'

'It's just that she's coming back. My wife. Tomorrow.'

'Congratulations,' says Pauline. 'How's your little boy?'

'Oh, he's fine. Whatever it was got better.'

'Ah. So it's not just maternal concern that's bringing her back.'

'No,' says Chris Rogers. 'I've been doing some very intensive manipulation of various contacts and I've got us a house in downtown Swansea, at a rent I reckon we can just about manage.'

'Well, good,' says Pauline. 'Excellent. So it's the prospect of the bright lights, then?'

'Actually, she says she's been missing us.'

'Of course.'

'And I think being with her mother . . .'

'That too. Didn't I tell you?'

'You did,' says Chris. 'You've been very supportive. Over and beyond the call of duty. I hope your authors aren't all such pains in the neck.'

'Mostly they only talk to me about semi-colons and the acceptability of the hanging participle. And they don't write books about unicorns and werewolves.'

'Ah, that,' says Chris. 'I was just coming to that – to say that now I'll be able to get down to the rewriting of that chapter.'

'Delighted to hear it.'

'So I'll be in touch. Sorry to have interrupted your evening, but I felt sort of celebratory.' He is struck suddenly by a thought. 'All this time I have no idea if you . . . I mean what your own arrangements . . .'

'I live alone,' says Pauline. 'My period of marital crisis is long done with. Water under the bridge.'

'Oh,' Chris sounds embarrassed. Chastened, maybe. 'I'm sorry. I thought perhaps . . .'

'So I'll look forward to hearing from you in due course, with the revised werewolves,' says Pauline. 'And in the meantime take my advice and make much of your wife.'

'Don't wait for Maurice to get back,' says Teresa. 'Go whenever you want to.' It is Wednesday morning and she has come to Pauline's door early, with Luke astride her hip.

'Well . . .' Pauline is hesitant. 'When do you think he'll be back?'

'Lunchtime, he said. I'll be all right.'

Teresa's face is pinched, her eyes dark-circled. Pauline reads there the sleepless night, the ugly scurrying thoughts.

Luke beams suddenly in belated greeting. 'Da,' he says to Pauline – untroubled, ecstatic.

'I've just made coffee,' says Pauline. 'Come on – it'll perk you up.'

Teresa walks into the kitchen. She stands there, chewing her lip. 'I suppose you know,' she says.

Pauline nods.

'Before I did, probably.'

'Look,' says Pauline, 'this isn't necessarily . . .'

Teresa sits down. 'I will have that coffee, please.'

Pauline pours coffee into flowered mugs. Sunshine drenches the room. Luke is squatting peaceably on the floor, closely examining a bit of fluff. Somewhere, the combine is already at work.

'All last night,' says Teresa, 'I was thinking, maybe he's in bed with her right now. I imagined to myself how they'd have worked it – she'd have told James she had to go and visit a relation or something. I rang at eleven and he wasn't there, not that I really expected him to be. He'd said he was going to have dinner with a guy I don't know. So I supposed he was really with her. I thought about ringing James, with some excuse or other, to see if she was at home.' Teresa sees Pauline shrink. 'No, I didn't do it. I just thought about it, for hours. I've no idea if James knows. I suppose he will eventually.'

Luke has discovered Pauline's spectacles. She removes them and distracts him with an apple.

'I never imagined anything like this could happen,' says Teresa.

'No one does.'

'It's like being kicked in the stomach.'

'Look,' says Pauline. She begins again: 'It may well be that . . .'

'Oh, it's true all right. I picked up the other phone once and he was talking to her. I knew then, when I heard how their voices sounded. I've seen the way they look at each other. They aren't going to be coming here any more, incidentally – her and James. Maurice says.'

'No. I see. You've . . . talked to Maurice, then? What else does he say?'

Teresa's mouth tightens. She stares over Pauline's shoulder and out of the window. 'Maurice doesn't say much. He implies that I am paranoic and possessive. He doesn't say they are and he doesn't say they aren't. He shrugs and steps aside. He gets angry. I am made to feel . . . unreasonable.' She stares at Pauline. 'How is this possible?'

'I don't know,' says Pauline. But she does.

'Maurice says things like, "I wonder why you're reacting like this." He says, "I thought you liked James and Carol." He looks at me as though I had been listening at keyholes or reading other people's letters. He walks out of the room. And then later it is as though nothing had happened. He talks about other things, as though nothing were wrong. He is . . . affectionate.'

'I see,' says Pauline. Yes, that's how it goes.

'I don't know where I am. I begin to think it's all in my head. And then I hear something, or see something, and I know it isn't.'

Luke has bumped himself on the table. He starts to whimper. Pauline picks him up and consoles. This saves her from having to say anything. And she has nothing to say, in any case.

Teresa stares at Luke, but she does not seem to be seeing him. 'I feel as though I had been dropped into a black pit. I had no idea you could feel like this. Right at this moment I wish . . .' She looks away, cuts herself off. Her mouth tightens again.

Right now you wish you'd never met Maurice, never married him. You would even wish Luke back into non-existence, to be released from this. 'So do I,' says Pauline. 'I wish that too. All except for . . .' She gets up, holding Luke, and dumps him on Teresa's lap. 'We'll stop talking about it – this is doing no good to anyone. Drink some more coffee.'

There they sit, in the World's End kitchen – together, apart, and elsewhere. Teresa is in London, stalking Maurice, and she is in last week and the week before that and the one before that – interpreting a glance, replaying a conversation. Pauline too is tapping in to other times, other places. Only Luke is here and now, lurching about the room to investigate the fringe on the rug, a feather, a matchstick, a sunbeam.

Chapter Sixteen

Follett Rare Books is closed when Pauline arrives at six-thirty. Hugh will be in the office at the back: she is to ring the bell. She pauses to glance at the window – a display of first edition children's books with Arthur Rackham and Dulac illustrations and another of early-nineteenth-century topographical literature – and sees that in fact Margery is there, who looks up and comes at once to the door.

'He got caught by a client, Mrs Carter, so I stayed on to let you in. It looks as though he can't get rid of him.'

'Perhaps we should rescue him by pretending I'm another client.'

Margery seems doubtful. No, thinks Pauline. I don't look the part – no raincoat, no shabby briefcase. 'Plenty of time. Was yesterday . . . all right?'

'It was nicely done, as these things go.' The discreet reservation in Margery's tone conveys a whole scenario. Pauline sees the tiny congregation in a crematorium chapel, the fervent display of flowers. She hears the emollient language of the ritual.

Margery sighs. 'Anyway, it's over now. He'll be relieved.' It is not clear if she is referring to the funeral or to something more general. She is a woman in her early fifties, small and dapper, always clad in a neat but self-effacing suit or dress. It occurs to Pauline that she has no idea of Margery's personal circumstances. Is she widowed or separated? Neither? She is patently attached to Hugh, but with the devotion, it has always seemed, of one who is a natural amanuensis. She runs the business when Hugh is out of the country, is always at his elbow with deft reminders. Hugh has depended on her for years. And what has she felt for him, all this time? Pauline looks at Margery with a new awareness.

'He's held up well,' says Margery in a lowered voice, with a glance at the door to Hugh's office. 'I'm afraid it may hit him harder in the next week or two. He's going to need support.'

'Yes,' says Pauline. 'I'm glad he's got you here, Margery. I know you've been a terrific help.'

Margery gives a small shrug, which seems to imply that this is not worth mentioning, or that it is what she is paid to be in any case. 'He deserves a break, poor man. I'd like to think he might have a happier time.'

'So would I.'

'Quite.' Margery has sat down at her desk and pulls out a chair for Pauline. Her glance is both cautious and a touch severe. Don't mess with me, it seems to say. Pauline's new awareness is further sharpened. 'I know you're one of his closest friends, Mrs Carter, so we both want the same thing for him, I'm sure.' She breaks off as Hugh's door opens and Hugh emerges with a Japanese man, whom he escorts into the street with an apologetic nod at Pauline.

'Well, I'll be off now,' says Margery. She collects her coat and bag. 'I'll leave him in your hands, Mrs Carter.' She pauses at the door, where Hugh has disengaged himself from the Japanese, and has a brief subdued exchange with him before she lets herself out and clicks away down the street. She is a woman who always wears high heels.

'Sorry about that,' says Hugh. 'Nice people to do business with, Japanese, but you both have to spend so much time being polite that it all takes twice as long. Margery said she'd look after you.'

'She has. Did he buy anything?'

'Oh, this and that,' says Hugh vaguely. 'They're all into botanical stuff at the moment and I'm not up in that. Shall we go? I'm desperate for a drink. I thought we'd eat Italian, if that's all right with you.'

In the restaurant he disposes of a Campari in a few gulps. 'I'm going to have another, I'm afraid. I'm not usually like this, am I? Do you think I'm going to turn into an old soak?'

'I shouldn't think so. You've had a rough week, that's all.'

'Too right.' He looks suddenly weary, wipes a hand across his face. 'Well, it's over now . . .' He is silent for a moment. 'Anyway, this is a treat. Thank you for coming.'

'Tell me something,' says Pauline. 'Has Margery ever been married?'

'Good heavens, no. She lives in Richmond with another woman.'

Of course, thinks Pauline. How obtuse of me. She says, 'I'd been imagining Margery cherishing a secret passion for you over the years, and coming out with it now.'

'Last thing she'd do, frankly. Her friend's Swiss. Yvette. Makes the most incredible cakes. Margery sometimes brings me one.'

The waitress takes their orders. 'This'll be my first proper meal since . . . well, since it happened,' says Hugh. 'I haven't felt like eating. I haven't been to the house much. I've been dossing down in my office but I suppose I can't really go on doing that.'

'Sell it.'

'The office?' says Hugh, startled.

'No, no – the house. You don't have to live there any more. Buy a flat in town. It's what you'd always have preferred.'

'Yes. Yes, I could, couldn't I?' Hugh ponders this. He seems ambushed by this new freedom of choice. 'Yes . . . well . . . I suppose I shall.'

'When you're ready. You don't need to rush into anything.'

'No.' He frowns, staring down at the bread he is dismembering. 'Do you know . . . we'd been married for twenty-seven years. I didn't quite realize that, till I had to sort out her papers. I always gave her flowers on the anniversaries, but I never counted them. For obvious reasons, I suppose.'

'Hugh . . . When did it all begin? Elaine's illness?'

He looks at her over the top of his glasses. She has entered forbidden territory and for a moment it seems as though he will deflect the question – swerve off into a discussion of the restaurant or an account of some book-buying excursion. Then he gives up.

'Right away, almost. I thought I'd done it, in some way. She was fine, and then within a year or so she was turning into someone else. Couldn't talk to anyone. Didn't want to leave the house. She'd never been a bouncing extrovert, exactly, but it was obvious something had gone appallingly wrong. I took her to see people, of course. Specialists.'

'What did they say?'

'Oh, everything. Agoraphobia, it was, at one point. Parental abuse. Something nasty in the woodshed when she was six. Sexual dysfunction.'

'Was it?'

'Sex? Well, she wasn't much interested, put it that way. But I'm not excessively demanding in that area myself.' Hugh avoids Pauline's eye. 'An adequate sufficiency, that's all I ever asked. All the same, I thought at first it must be my fault.'

'It wasn't your fault,' says Pauline. 'It would have happened whatever – I'm sure of that.'

'Yes, I think that now. In a way, I know what it was. Simply . . . she thought nothing of herself. She thought she had absolutely nothing to offer – that she was dull, plain, unintelligent, incompetent. Other people became a threat. The only thing to do was to hide. Low self-esteem, isn't that what they call it?'

'Yes, I think so.'

'And so eventually it drove her . . . well, she stopped being what you might call normal in any sense. I find that the worst thing of all – that a woman can be demolished just by her own opinion of herself.'

Pauline nods. 'The opposite happens, too. People who create themselves.' She thinks of those soaring complacencies that can power a whole career, the confidence that constructs its own image.

Food has arrived. Hugh starts to talk of the funeral. 'You were right about the organ music. A hymn would have been pathetic. It was all pretty dire, as it was. There's that moment when the coffin starts to slide away, and I thought . . . but really Elaine went long ago, to all intents and purposes. For years she's hardly spoken to me, you know.'

'It's over now,' says Pauline gently. 'Everything can be different.'

'Yes. I've been trying to think about that.'

'Eat your saltimbocca. Isn't that what it is?'

Hugh picks up his knife and fork. 'Mmn. Jolly good, too. Now tell me what you've been doing.'

'Nothing,' says Pauline. 'Working. Watching this field of wheat.'

'Come back to London.'

'No. Not yet, anyway.'

He catches something in her tone. 'I don't understand what's keeping you down there like this.'

'The weather,' Pauline suggests. 'This is the best summer for fifty years, we're being told.'

'Nonsense.' He looks at her narrowly. 'There's something else, I can tell.' He stops eating, arrested by a sudden insight. 'Oh God . . . I should have thought of it before. Have you . . . is there a man?'

196

Pauline laughs. 'I should be so lucky . . . Of course there's not a man, Hugh.'

He sighs. 'Well, I'm afraid I'm glad to hear it. I would have felt even more disorientated than I already am.'

Back in her flat, much later, she cannot sleep. She lies listening to the city night – the shrill pulse of a car-alarm down the road, the howl of a police siren. Voices, footsteps, a slammed door. Anonymous and neutral.

Pauline thinks of World's End, perched in the silent darkness of its valley. She conjures it up in the mind – the smell of it, the feel of it. But there is nothing neutral there. It is full of voices and faces. Most of all, there is Teresa's kitchen at breakfast earlier this week, vibrant with ill-feeling.

'Hi!' says Teresa. 'How was Hugh?' She has come out on to the track as Pauline's car pulls up, and peers through a shroud of mystery, pretending casual pleasure at seeing her mother. 'How was he?' she says again, as though unaware that she is repeating herself.

'Hugh seems to be surfacing. We had a nice evening.'

'Well, good.'

From the open window of Maurice's study comes the rasp of his printer. Scrape, scrape – back and forth. Shall I tell you what to do? thinks Pauline. Burn his book. It wonderfully concentrates the mind. But Teresa will do no such thing, she will not even burn a tentative page or two. She is not the book-burning type. It is she who will burn.

Pauline goes inside to attend to the mail and the answering machine. There is a card from the friends who proposed the Venice trip in September. The North Sea oil author has left a message with some queries. It is time for lunch, so she makes herself a salad and reads the paper for a while before going up to her study. She starts to go through the points raised by the North Sea oil author, but cannot concentrate. She sits at her desk, staring at the typescript in front of her.

I could go away, she thinks. I could turn my back on it all, since there is nothing I can do. I could go to London and work there and ring up my friends and have them in for supper and go to the pictures and jolly Hugh along. In September, apparently, I am in any case to go to Venice.

But she knows that she will stay. It must be seen out now, this summer, come what may.

July has slid over into August. And the place is burnt up. The verges are bleached now – buff plumes of grass and the brown candelabra of hogweed. The blue lakes of flax have drained away. Instead there are the poppies – scarlet threads on a field of ripe wheat, or a brilliant flush along the roadside. And much of the wheat is down – there are sweeps of golden stubble dotted with bales of straw.

At World's End, the days creep by. Maurice comes and goes a lot. He appears in constant need of newspapers, cans of beer, bottles of wine, paperclips . . . the car disappears down the track in a cloud of dust and returns half an hour later, an hour later, from the village or from Hadbury or wherever he has been. He is restless, that is clear enough. He patrols the garden in the evenings, tipping back glasses of red wine. Several times he disappears for longer – two hours, an afternoon. He is checking out some local tourist sites, says Teresa. A jaunt, then, justified in the name of research. But Teresa has not joined him on these trips. 'Luke would get all hot and whingey,' she explains, pre-empting Pauline's comment. 'Anyway, I've already been there.'

It is quiet these days, at World's End. The only voice continuously heard is Luke's. Through the open windows of the cottage Pauline hears Luke. She hears Teresa talking to Luke.

She does not hear Teresa talking to Maurice, or Maurice talking to Teresa. At night the television quacks away, or a promenade concert spills into the warm darkness.

Pauline does not want to think about what is being said or what is not being said next door. Particularly, she does not want to think about what is not being said, because she is obliged to infer this every time she sees Teresa and looks closely at her face – when Teresa is wandering in the garden with Luke, or holding him as he tries to climb the fence beside the track. Teresa's face is changing, by the day. It is losing its volatility. There are no longer those sudden illuminations – those flights from sobriety, from preoccupation into an instant vibrancy. The sun no longer comes out, in Teresa's face. Especially, there is no longer that glow each time that she sees Maurice – when he walks into a room, when he turns towards her.

'Me, I'm afraid,' says Chris Rogers.

'Ah. Everything OK, I hope? Your wife . . . ?'

'She's back, yes. Thank God. Things are pretty good in that department. The thing is . . . I still haven't been able to get down to that chapter.'

'Oh dear,' says Pauline.

'What happened is that Tom was very ill. Our three-year-old. Just suddenly, like that – wham! Bright as a button one day, getting in everyone's hair, the usual . . . and then twenty-four hours later it was all telephones and ambulances and doctors running along hospital corridors and him unconscious all hung about with tubes. Christ! I never want to go through anything like that again.'

'Is he all right?'

'Yes. He's going to be fine, they say. Sue's at the hospital now, but they're going to let him home next week. It was some devastating form of pneumonia. Anyway . . . it's over now. Jesus! I didn't know you could feel like that. It's like being thrown into a black pit.'

Pauline is silenced. 'Yes,' she says at last. 'I can imagine. I've never had that experience – but I can imagine.'

'I've never asked. Did you have children?'

'Yes. One.'

'Right, then you can. Imagine, that is. I mean, up till now as far as I'm concerned being a parent has been a matter of initial euphoria and amazement and then sleepless incarceration with miniature megalomaniacs whose sole purpose is to do themselves an injury. You're either spinning with anxiety or homicidal. You'd also kill for them if you had to. I mean, for Christ's sake, you cease to be human. I look at wildlife programmes and think, yes, that's right, that's me, nothing but a vehicle for the genetic drive. Right?'

'Right,' says Pauline. 'My sentiments entirely.'

'And then this happens and you realize that you'd seen nothing. You were a screaming innocent, before. Whew! But it comes to an end, I'm told, eventually.'

'What does?'

'Well, they grow up. Yours must have done. Son? Daughter?'

'Daughter. End – did you say?'

'Well, not end, I suppose,' says Chris. 'But I mean they acquire some sense of self-preservation and they let you go to sleep at night.'

'Oh – is that what they do?'

A pause. Chris sounds guarded. 'I've got it wrong, have I?'

'Slightly wrong, I'm afraid. What in fact happens is that instead of getting there in the nick of time before they fall out of the window or pull the kettle over on themselves you have to stand on one side and watch it happen. Or wait for it to happen. Or wonder if it's going to happen.'

'Oh,' says Chris. 'My plan was to say – right, you're on your own now. Take care, I'm going into emotional retirement.'

'You can say that. Unfortunately you don't feel that. Would that you did. Still – this isn't quite what you're wanting to hear at the moment.'

'I take your point – it's a life sentence. In that case I'd better tie up this book while there's a brief respite. I just thought I should explain the delay.'

'Let me have the chapter when you can,' says Pauline. 'And I'm really glad Tom's all right.'

Maurice goes to London again. Pauline does not know this until late in the afternoon when she becomes aware that the car which left early that morning has never returned. She finds Teresa and Luke in the garden. Luke is throwing his wooden bricks into the flower bed and Teresa is patiently retrieving them.

'Maurice is away?' says Pauline baldly.

'There was this lecture he wanted to go to in London. And some papers he needed.' Teresa's tone is flat. She looks at Pauline, straight. 'That's what he said anyway. He'll be back tomorrow.'

Pauline feels that icy fist in her guts. As must Teresa. She can find nothing to say, so she gets down on the grass and starts to build a tower for Luke out of his blocks. She builds the tower and Luke knocks it over and then she builds it again and Luke knocks it over once more. Teresa sits on the bench and watches, silent. Luke is ecstatic.

Pauline dreams. She dreams of Harry.

Harry walks in through the kitchen door at World's End. 'Well, hello!' he says. 'And how are *you*?' He is not a day older. He is just as he was when last Pauline saw him, many years ago now. He is simply Harry.

'Go away,' says Pauline irritably. 'I don't want you here.'

Harry shakes his head reprovingly. 'Not so loud. Teresa will hear.'

'I intend that Teresa should hear.'

Now Harry is censorious. 'Then you're a bad mother, Pauline.'

'Look who's talking!' snaps Pauline.

Harry shakes his head. 'I always adored Teresa.'

'When you had a spare moment.'

'Pauline,' says Harry. 'I had *work* to do.'

'We've all got work to do.'

'Sweetie, I didn't come here to argue.'

'I didn't ask you to come here,' says Pauline. 'I want you to go.'

And now Harry starts to cry. He stands there with rivers of tears running down his face. This is a dream, and in dreams belief is suspended, so it does not occur to Pauline that such behaviour is inconceivable and quite out of character. Never does Harry cry – never, never. Nor is she surprised by the presence of Teresa, aged about six, who has arrived now in the World's End kitchen and stares at her weeping father.

'Don't take any notice of him,' says Pauline to Teresa, but Teresa goes on staring.

And now, because this is a dream, the World's End kitchen has melted away into the terraced house of long ago. Pauline does not question this either, but she does question the fact that Harry – who is no longer weeping – is now accompanied by a posse of women, some of whom she recognizes and some of whom she does not. Myra Sams, Mrs Gatz, others.

'Don't think I'm making them lunch,' says Pauline, 'because I'm not. There arc dozens of them.'

'Pauline, you've always had this tendency to exaggerate,' says Harry. The women, who lurk behind him, grey, shadowy un-persons like souls in purgatory, say and do nothing. They simply are.

'Get rid of them,' says Pauline. 'Now.'

'I can't,' says Harry. 'They've happened, that's all. There's nothing I can do about it. You know that.'

Chapter Seventeen

The combines are creeping nearer to World's End. The thump-thump has reached the top of the hill. Soon it will be the turn of the World's End field. The twenty-acre. This apparently is what the field is called. Pauline established that from Chaundy, once. 'What do you call this field?' she asked. 'It's the twenty-acre,' Chaundy replied shortly, staring at her as though she had uttered an imbecility. 'I thought fields had individual names,' said Pauline. 'Things like Perkin's Piece and Wood Assarts and Long Lea.' 'I wouldn't know about that,' said Chaundy. 'This is the twenty-acre, as far as I am concerned.' Pauline remembered that her information came from a television programme and supposed that these must be the last repositories of such arcane lore.

The twenty-acre will shortly fall to the combine; the tractors roar along the track, bearing away the grain from the ten-acre over the hill, or the fifteen-acre, or the twenty-five. It is not a good harvest, by all accounts. The local paper carries a photograph of a farmer with accusatory expression demonstrating a shrivelled head of wheat. Even the national news, hitting an August deficit of political scandals or international disaster, mentions the fact, coupled with items on hose-pipe bans and parched reservoirs. The nation is in any case on holiday now, and not interested in industrial economy.

At World's End, the harvest is a question of scenery and background noise. World's End has its own preoccupation.

Pauline and Maurice avoid one another, on the whole. That

is, Pauline sometimes finds herself in the garden with Teresa and Maurice, or in Teresa's kitchen when Maurice is there, but she tries to avoid being alone with him. She has nothing further to say to Maurice, now or quite possibly at any point, though this is a prospect hard to contemplate. Maurice is scrupulously polite to Pauline in Teresa's presence and does not appear to be keeping out of her way, but just to be pursuing his own daily course. If this brings him into Pauline's orbit, so be it. He makes a remark – some anodyne, inconsequential remark – or simply gives her that quirky smile. Look, he seems to be saying, this bout of ill will is on your side only. Let's behave like reasonable people.

And thus the days unfurl. Tight, tense days. Blue and gold days in which the sun pours down.

Pauline notes that Maurice's car has departed on one of those forays to Hadbury or wherever, so she goes next door to visit. She entertains Luke while Teresa washes her hair, upstairs. The phone rings. 'Could you get it, Mum?' calls Teresa.

'Hello?'

'Teresa?' says the voice of James Saltash, doubtfully.

'No, it's Pauline.'

'I thought it might be. Hi . . .' James hesitates. 'Is Maurice there?'

'He's out just now, in fact. Shall I ask Teresa to tell him to call you back?'

'No need,' says James. A little chill, his voice – a little taut. But the stiffness is not for her, Pauline senses. 'Just . . . if someone could say to him that the indexer who did his last book isn't going to be available so we're making inquiries about someone else. I only need to hear from him if he isn't happy about that.'

'Right,' says Pauline.

'Everything OK with you? It's sweltering here – you're

lucky to be out of it.' They chat for a minute before Pauline puts down the phone.

So he knows. Or if he doesn't know then he has got a whiff of it, a whiff pungent enough to have derailed him. Poor guy. Though of course so far as he is concerned, if he did but know it, this is a merciful dispensation which will probably in the fullness of time detach him from that girl, if he has any sense of self-preservation, and make him available for someone more his weight. But right now he is unhinged, which is apparent simply from his voice – from the way in which he utters Maurice's name, from a reserve that is not natural to him. Remarkable thing, the human voice, thinks Pauline. Amazingly expressive, willy-nilly. No wonder the acting profession can do what it does. She reflects upon the versatility of speech. It helps, these days, to turn the mind to these interesting abstract matters.

'A career on the stage, maybe?' she says to Luke. 'Say Daddy. No – don't. Say Mummy. Mum-mum-mum . . .'

Luke gazes at her. He beams. He smacks his lips together. 'Mmmmm . . .' he says. Perhaps.

The combine has arrived. It crawls back and forth all day. A yellow thrashing monster that consumes the wheat. A day, two days, then it is gone. The straw is baled and the field is a new, stripped landscape, a rolling golden expanse of stubble brushed this way and that by wheel tracks. All over it stand the drums of baled straw, packed and perfect spirals. By day they look like giant cotton reels, but at night they change. They become strange monolithic presences, a sculptural army gathered upon the slope of the hill, staring down at World's End with blank faces.

Pauline has forgotten that Harry will have arrived in London by now. She is taken aback when Teresa says that she will be off early the next morning. Her bemusement is apparent. 'London,' says Teresa. 'Harry. Remember?'

'Of course.'

'We'll take Luke to the zoo or somewhere.'

Pauline cannot quite envisage Harry at the zoo, now or ever. 'Well, that should be fun,' she says. 'For Luke, anyway.'

'Maurice isn't coming. There's no point, really. It's only for me to show Luke to Harry. Plus, Maurice isn't keen on car journeys with Luke.' Teresa gives a dry little laugh. Pauline is shaken by this laugh – which is more a snort, a stifled explosion. It is an indication of how far Teresa has travelled in the last few weeks. Once it would have been impossible for her to imply criticism of Maurice, to suggest inadequacy. Pauline glimpses for an instant the person whom Teresa may become, in the climate of Maurice – bitter, shrewish, trapped.

'Maybe I should drive you up,' Pauline suggests.

'I'll be fine.' Teresa is edgy now. She does not want solicitude. She wants to get this duty done, that is all. Pauline feels again a glimmer of compunction for Harry, who is reduced to an obligation. Thus are the mighty fallen.

'And I'll get back by lunchtime on Friday,' says Teresa.

Hugh phones. 'Listen,' he says, 'have you got a moment?'

'Well, of course I have,' says Pauline. 'You don't have pressing engagements down here at half-past ten at night.'

'I've been sitting in the office for the last couple of hours all on my own drinking a bottle of Hungarian red, otherwise I'd probably never have got up a sufficient head of steam to say this. Would you . . . conceivably . . . think of marrying me?'

'Oh . . .' Pauline is thrown, entirely. 'Oh, Hugh, are you sure you . . . look, I think we should both think very carefully about this. I mean . . . well, just – let's both of us think about it.'

They both know, at once, that she is saying no.

'Just a thought,' says Hugh. 'Possibly a misplaced one.

Anyway, turn the idea over.' He starts to talk about a book auction he has been to, and an eccentric Danish client, and an exhibition that Pauline must not miss. He is amiable, in good spirits, a trifle blurred by wine. Pauline knows that he will never raise the question of marriage again, unless invited to do so. And her own spontaneous resistance makes her cringe. But I'm right, she thinks, I know I am. It wouldn't do, not now. Not ever.

Teresa goes to London. Pauline comes out to say goodbye but does not linger. From her window she sees Teresa stow Luke into his car-seat. She sees Maurice carry a bag out for Teresa. Then Teresa drives off and Maurice does not wave or watch the departing car but goes straight back into the cottage. Where he will presumably be bound to stay until her return. No restless excursion for you today, thinks Pauline. Have to sit down and buckle to. Nothing but the fax and the phone. Unless you choose to come begging for the use of my car.

It is hotter still. Pauline finds her study stifling, even with the window wide open. She drifts about the cottage half the morning, fixing herself cold drinks. Hugh is in her head – his voice on the phone last night, his words. Has she offended him? Can they return to the status quo? Surely, she thinks, surely what they have is sturdy enough to withstand a precarious moment. She considers calling him, and decides against it. Best to let this pass, let it subside – allow Hugh to attribute his rush of blood to the Hungarian red, and bury the episode.

She thinks of Teresa and Luke on the motorway, with a twinge of anxiety, and would like to check their arrival. A further phone call that it would be wiser not to make.

At lunchtime she takes a drink into the garden and sits for a while in the shade of the apple tree. Maurice does not emerge and indeed she barely thinks of him. It is very quiet now at World's End – without Luke's shrieks and babbling, without the clatter of the combine. Just birds, and the occasional distant roar of an aircraft.

Pauline achieves some work during the afternoon. The sun is off her study now, so it is cooler, and indeed when at five or so she decides to stop, and looks out of the window, it seems that the sun has disappeared altogether. The sky is dull – not so much clouded as curiously opaque. The air is thick and heavy, and from somewhere far away there comes a long shuddering sound. The radio talked this morning of scattered thunderstorms. But scattering elsewhere, evidently, thinks Pauline. She goes down, makes a cup of tea and sits reading as she drinks it. Then she climbs the stairs to have a bath. She lies in the water for a long time, half dozing. And when eventually she gets out the small room is almost dark and she has to switch on the light. Looking out, she sees that a grey mass has tipped up from behind the hill. The sky growls again, nearer.

For the next couple of hours the storm circles the valley. Once it retreats altogether, the sky clears and there is thin sunshine. The birds sing tumultuously. Pauline cooks herself some supper and eats it while watching the long shadows cast by the straw bales, dark fingers pointing across the stubble. And then the shadows melt away, the sky darkens once more – darkens so that it seems dusk has fallen, but it is only seven o'clock on a summer evening. It is very still and the birdsong is now quite maniacal, ringing out in the silence. The air has thickened again – it becomes so dense that there is a feeling of pressure, as though everything were being compacted. A flare of sheet lightning, more thunder. This, thinks Pauline, is going to be the father and mother of all storms. She goes round the house closing windows, because she has met up with this before at

World's End and knows what is to come. The valley seems in some way to trap storms. They sit on top of it and generate a great deal of water, all of it trying to find vulnerable points of entry. She puts some wads of newspaper under the back door.

The sky splits, right overhead. Brilliant white light and then a massive clap of thunder which rolls away into a silence in which Pauline hears the first rain smash against the window. She stands watching, interested in this elemental process. Within minutes the rain is so heavy that she can barely pick out the shapes of the straw bales in the field and presently they are wiped out entirely behind a thick grey screen of rain, which turns soon to hail, a curtain of obliterating white. Sheet lightning, fork lightning, cracks of thunder. The kitchen light flickers.

Pauline goes to the dresser and takes out the candlesticks and candles. This is the next stage, familiar also. Rural electricity supplies, she has learnt, are pathetically susceptible to bad weather.

The wads of newspaper against the back door are soaked. She replaces them and goes round the cottage mopping window sills. There is so much noise now that she cannot hear her own footsteps. She returns to the kitchen at the moment when the lights flicker again and then go out. She lights candles, puts one on the table and another on the dresser. The room becomes a cavern of light and darkness – softer, older. Pauline sits down in the basket chair by the dresser and admires the effect. The green eye on the fridge is extinguished, and the glimmering green and red digital figures on the cooker and the microwave. The place is brown and sepia now, like an old oil painting, with gold pools of light around the candles. The window becomes a square of vivid white as lightning flares. Hail is bouncing up from the sill. Thunder cracks again. Pauline is unperturbed. Others have sat out storms in this room, she thinks, looking at much the same things.

A cup of coffee might be nice. She starts to get up and then remembers that this is not possible. Something else occurs. She picks up the phone. Dead. Of course – that too. Another familiar thunderstorm ritual.

She has a glass of wine instead of the coffee and settles down with it beside the candle. She peers at the newspaper, watches the unearthly glare of the lightning, waits for the next peal of thunder. She tours the room again, mopping, and takes a suspicious look at her bedroom ceiling, known to be a frail spot. So far, so good. And now the lightning is a little less intense, the thunder is more remote. The rain is not thrashing down so hard. The storm is on the way out. But there is small hope that the electricity will be restored before morning – she knows this from experience.

By half-past nine the rain has stopped and the thunder is miles away. Pauline opens the front door to look out briefly at the sodden landscape, almost dark by now. Then she tidies the kitchen, groping rather in the dusky light, and climbs the stairs again for another inspection of the bedroom ceiling, carrying one of the candlesticks.

From the bedroom she hears the sound of a car on the track. It goes past with glaring lights and she is puzzled for a moment until she remembers the chicken houses. Of course – emergency measures necessary in the event of a power failure.

She is in the bathroom, checking out another ceiling which has also been known to let in rain, when she hears a sound downstairs. Someone has come into the cottage through the unlocked front door. For a moment her stomach lurches – and then she thinks of Maurice, almost forgotten until now. And indeed when she comes out on to the landing there he is, already half-way up the stairs.

'You could have knocked,' says Pauline. 'I thought you were some marauder.'

Maurice stumbles and puts out a hand to steady himself. When he speaks Pauline realizes that he is rather drunk. 'Someone's just gone past in a car. What d'you think they're up to?'

'Nothing. They have to do something about the chicken houses when the electricity goes off.'

'Why hasn't it come on again?'

'It usually doesn't, for hours. Have you got candles?' she adds perfunctorily. She knows that Teresa has a supply but conceivably Maurice does not know where they are.

Maurice waves a hand dismissively. He has joined her on the landing now and stands with his back to the stairs, while she is at the door of the bathroom. 'Come over and have a drink. I'm in the middle of a very good bottle of claret.'

'I'm going to bed,' says Pauline. 'And you'd do well to check out your upstairs ceilings. This roof can leak.'

'Pauline,' says Maurice, 'why are you giving me the cold shoulder?'

They stand facing each other on the landing. Behind Maurice is the black drop of the narrow staircase. Only his face is lit by her candle – bony, shadowed, grinning.

'You know why,' she says.

'Oh, come on,' says Maurice. 'You're a grown woman. These things happen – you must know that.'

She stares at him.

'Freezing me out won't help. There's nothing I can do about it. Or you. I'm sorry, but there it is.'

Later, much later, when she tries to recover each moment, she knows that she moved towards him, powered by anger. She has never felt such rage – it came roaring up from somewhere deep within. The whole scene is distorted by its ferocity. She moves. She may have spoken, she may have raised her hand. Maurice lurches. He is unsteadied – perhaps by the drink, perhaps by something else. He puts his weight on his weak leg and then takes a step back to regain his balance.

He pitches head first backwards down the precipitate stairs, into the small hallway at the bottom. Again, later, much later, Pauline will always think that she heard the crack when his neck broke as he hit the door.

Many people will have much to say about Maurice's death, in the days and weeks to come. They say these things to Pauline in quiet confidential voices – her friends, Teresa's friends. To Teresa they speak differently. They are brisk and practical, they want her to visit, to bring Luke, to come with them to this and to that. They want to fill her days. But to Pauline they talk in those hushed voices. They murmur that it could have been even worse, couldn't it . . . I mean, they say, he might *not* have died. He might have survived. But after a fall like that . . . The implications hang unspoken. Maurice paralysed, brain-damaged. Teresa shackled at thirty to a vegetable on a bed. It's an appalling tragedy, God knows, they say – but you can imagine an even worse situation.

Yes, says Pauline, you can.

As it is, they say, when – *when* – she gets over it she can make a new life.

Yes, says Pauline. Yes, she can.

And of course Luke hardly had time to know him. I mean, he won't *remember*.

No, says Pauline. No, he won't.

But it's hideous, they say. Unbelievable. Out of the blue, like that. Maurice, of all people.

Hugh says, 'Sell that place.'

'Probably,' says Pauline.

'And for God's sake come back to London now the inquest's over. Pack up and come back.'

'Yes,' she says. 'Yes, I think I will.' And only then does she tell him about this summer at World's End.

Chaundy's man says, 'That bugger.' He says it standing in the entrance to the cottage, looking at the staircase, after the ambulance has been and gone and he has stayed on because he doesn't think that Pauline is in a fit state to be left alone just yet, after what has happened, and after she has driven up the hill to get help from whoever was up there at the chicken houses. 'That bugger,' he says – and Pauline thinks for a confused moment that he is referring to Maurice, but it is of course the staircase he is talking about. 'My auntie come a cropper on that once,' he goes on, 'but not as bad as this.' And it transpires that relatives of his lived here, time was. 'Damp old place,' says Chaundy's man. 'My auntie was glad to get shot of it and move to the village. Different now, of course,' he adds hastily.

Harry says, 'I'm only calling to say . . . if there's anything I can do, anything at all. I've told Teresa I hope perhaps she'll think of coming out to LA for a bit. Later. To have a break.'

'That might be a good idea,' says Pauline. 'Later.'

'What a God-awful thing to happen,' says Harry. 'It stops you in your tracks. I mean, you think . . .' Pauline understands Harry to be saying that Maurice's death has thrust him into contemplation of his own mortality. 'I wish I'd had a chance to know him better,' he goes on. 'We only met the once. How do you think Teresa is now? I talked to her last week and I thought she seemed . . . well, fairly calm, considering. Is she all right, do you think?'

'I don't know,' says Pauline. 'I hope so.'

Harry pauses. 'If you felt like coming out to LA with her . . . later. I'd like that a lot.'

'I rather doubt if I could manage it,' says Pauline. 'But thank you for the thought.'

James Saltash says little. He stands with Pauline in

Maurice's study at World's End to which he has come in order to go through Maurice's manuscript and his notes and take away what is essential.

'We can publish,' he says. 'He'd got far enough with the revisions for me to see how to sew it up. And then there'll be some money for Teresa.' He picks up pieces of paper and puts them down again. The wedge of black hair flops on to his forehead. He still seems puppyish, but now like a puppy that has had a bad experience and is wary. He does not look much at Pauline. 'Would you give my love to Teresa?'

'Yes, of course.'

'By the way, I should maybe say . . . Carol and I have split up.'

'Ah,' says Pauline. 'Right. I see.'

And James Saltash is evidently too locked into private malaise to notice a neutrality that might be thought a little unsympathetic. He continues to pick up handfuls of paper and put them down again. 'Anyway,' he says. 'I'll get on with this. Don't bother about me. I'm sure you're busy.' He does not speak of Maurice. Maurice is subsumed into his own book. He has become a professional commitment.

Teresa says least of all. When she emerges from the grey silence of shock she takes on a different kind of reticence. She talks about everything and anything except Maurice. Her friends are concerned about this. Don't you think this is bad for her? they say to Pauline. Shouldn't she be . . . well, *remembering*? Shouldn't she talk it out? Do you think she's suppressing it all?

To Pauline Teresa says, 'I don't know what happened and I don't want to know.' They stare at one another. The words hang there for an instant. Later, and thereafter, it is as though they had never been spoken.

READ MORE IN PENGUIN

In every corner of the world, on every subject under the sun, Penguin represents quality and variety – the very best in publishing today.

For complete information about books available from Penguin – including Puffins, Penguin Classics and Arkana – and how to order them, write to us at the appropriate address below. Please note that for copyright reasons the selection of books varies from country to country.

In the United Kingdom: Please write to *Dept. EP, Penguin Books Ltd, Bath Road, Harmondsworth, West Drayton, Middlesex UB7 ODA*

In the United States: Please write to *Consumer Sales, Penguin USA, P.O. Box 999, Dept. 17109, Bergenfield, New Jersey 07621-0120*. VISA and MasterCard holders call 1-800-253-6476 to order Penguin titles

In Canada: Please write to *Penguin Books Canada Ltd, 10 Alcorn Avenue, Suite 300, Toronto, Ontario M4V 3B2*

In Australia: Please write to *Penguin Books Australia Ltd, P.O. Box 257, Ringwood, Victoria 3134*

In New Zealand: Please write to *Penguin Books (NZ) Ltd, Private Bag 102902, North Shore Mail Centre, Auckland 10*

In India: Please write to *Penguin Books India Pvt Ltd, 706 Eros Apartments, 56 Nehru Place, New Delhi 110 019*

In the Netherlands: Please write to *Penguin Books Netherlands bv, Postbus 3507, NL-1001 AH Amsterdam*

In Germany: Please write to *Penguin Books Deutschland GmbH, Metzlerstrasse 26, 60594 Frankfurt am Main*

In Spain: Please write to *Penguin Books S. A., Bravo Murillo 19, 1° B, 28015 Madrid*

In Italy: Please write to *Penguin Italia s.r.l., Via Felice Casati 20, I–20124 Milano*

In France: Please write to *Penguin France S. A., 17 rue Lejeune, F–31000 Toulouse*

In Japan: Please write to *Penguin Books Japan, Ishikiribashi Building, 2–5–4, Suido, Bunkyo-ku, Tokyo 112*

In South Africa: Please write to *Longman Penguin Southern Africa (Pty) Ltd, Private Bag X08, Bertsham 2013*

BY THE SAME AUTHOR

Moon Tiger
Winner of the 1987 Booker Prize

Claudia Hampton – beautiful, famous, independent – is dying. Meanwhile, she tells her nurses, 'I'm writing a history of the world.' As memories crowd in, Claudia re-creates the richly patterned mosaic of her life and times, from childhood just after the First World War to the present day. But, as Claudia the successful and popular historian knows, her story is enmeshed with the stories of others, and they too must speak: Gordon, her brother and adored adversary; Jasper, charming, untrustworthy lover and father of Lisa, her cool, conventional daughter, and – at the centre of Claudia's life – Tom, her one great love, both found and lost in wartime Egypt.

'A very clever book: it is evocative, thought-provoking and hangs curiously on the edges of the mind long after it is finished' – *Literary Review*

The Road to Lichfield

Incisive, funny, sad, *The Road to Lichfield* forces apart the twin processes of dying and loving and brilliantly traces the potent effect of the past on the present.

'A beautifully observed story of illicit love and modern marriage' – *Sunday Express*

Treasures of Time

Hugh Paxton, important archaeologist and influential man, discovers that the trouble with digging around in the past is that it disturbs the present as well. Beautifully written and acutely observed, *Treasures of Time* explores the relationship between the lives we live and the lives we think we live.

BY THE SAME AUTHOR

According to Mark

A respected literary biographer, Mark Lamming is working on the life of Gilbert Strong – a writer about whom he thinks he knows everything. A happily married man, dedicated to a life of letters, he nevertheless manages to fall in love with Strong's granddaughter. As the summer of Mark's obsession steams along, he begins to understand that nothing is ever exactly what it seems – certainly not Gilbert Strong. And certainly not himself.

'Vivid, acute . . . funny and always readable' – *Financial Times*

Judgement Day

Clare Paling, settled in a drowsy village, is confronted with an unpardonable death before she realizes that the world is a very uncertain place . . .

'I find Penelope Lively almost excessively gifted . . . the most enjoyable novel I have read for a very long time' – *The Times*

Next to Nature, Art

In the sanctuary of Framleigh Hall, the aspiring artists find that their dreams of creative bliss fade and everyday life becomes remarkably intrusive . . .

'Delightful . . . complex and exquisite. Penelope Lively's prose is beautiful and spare and she is a master of understatement' – *Daily Telegraph*

Passing On

'It begins with a funeral, which is always promising. The funeral is mother's, and she is not mourned . . . Around her grave are her children, Helen and Edward Glover, 52 and 49 respectively, mild and shabby, both of them unmarried . . . What will they do now that mother has gone? How will their lives change? That is what *Passing On* is about' – *The Times*

BY THE SAME AUTHOR

Cleopatra's Sister

Very little is known about the past of Callimbia, although Cleopatra's more beautiful sister Berenice is said to have entertained Antony there and, had he stayed, history could have turned out very differently. Howard Beamish, a palaeontologist whose only passion is for fossils, knows little of this obscure country. Lucy Faulkner, a journalist with a righteous indignation about British injustices, is a little better informed. They both have their own reasons for travelling to Nairobi, but neither expects to be set down in Callimbia's capital, Marsopolis, embroiled in the revolution that will change their lives.

'A fluent, funny, ultimately moving romance in which lovers share centre stage with Lively's persuasive meditations on history and fate . . . a book of great charm with a real intellectual resonance at its core' – *The New York Times Book Review*

Oleander, Jacaranda

'In this evocative book, Penelope Lively travels back five decades into the self-absorbed mind of her childhood. Full of colour and warmth, it is as much about the process of recall as about the past itself' – *Mail on Sunday*

'A wise, colourful and touching tale . . . It offers potent glimpses of British colonial life fifty years ago: the snake charmer in the garden; nine-year-old Penelope spying on de Gaulle at Government House . . . her deep affection for her nanny' – *The Times*

also published:

Going Back
City of the Mind
Perfect Happiness
Pack of Cards: Stories 1978–1986